S

S

Over 100
Great Novels
of
Erotic Domination

If you like one you will probably like the rest

New Titles Every Month

All titles in print are now available from:
www.onlinebookshop.com

Electronic editions of all titles can be found at:
www.adultbookshops.com

If you want to be on our confidential mailing list for our Readers' Club
Magazine (with extracts from past and forthcoming titles) write to:

SILVER MOON READER SERVICES

The Shadowline Building
6 Wembley Street
Gainsborough
DN21 2AJ
United Kingdom
or
sales@babash.com

or telephone
01427 816710
(UK office hours only)

NEW AUTHORS WELCOME

Please send submissions to
Silver Moon Books Ltd.
PO Box 5663
Nottingham
NG3 6PJ
or
editor@babash.com

First published 2004 Silver Moon Books
ISBN 1-903687-50-0
© 2004 Giselle Lorimer

Enslaving Anna

By

Giselle Lorimer

CHAPTER 1

It was her first proper job, and Marcus Sinclair could see that Anna was eager to please. A taste of real office life, sandwiched into her secretarial course. He also knew that she would be thinking herself lucky, her application having been accepted by one of the biggest and most respected companies in the city: Sinclair Precision Components, a long established and hugely successful business, nowadays specialising in supplying parts for middle eastern oil refineries.

Her new employer surveyed his latest acquisition appreciatively. She was one of the most beautiful girls he had seen in a long while. A sweet little English Rose, and no mistake. Tiny, not much more than five foot. Big brown doe-eyes and hair even darker, soft bloom of creamy young skin, slim hips, narrow waist. And huge tits. Demurely swathed in a crisp white cotton shirt, but that didn't stop him imagining how good they'd look with his cock rubbing between them……

Marcus Sinclair penned a quick note to his elder brother and partner, slipped it in an envelope, handed it to Anna.

'Take this to Charles Sinclair for me would you?" he commanded, gracing the minion with a quick smile.

Anna thought he looked nice, with his twinkling blue eyes and handsome, tanned face. His brown hair was cropped short, but even so it had a slight curl to it, that seemed to give him a rakish air. He looked like he worked out regularly, and she found him very attractive, no matter that he was twice her age.

"Of course, Sir," she said, smiling happily back at him. As she turned he noticed that her ass was good too… …high and tight, round without being fat… …nice.

Yes, his cock would enjoy breaking this one in.

Charles read his brother's message and almost laughed aloud.

"Get an eyeful of the tits on this. Which hole would you like to start with?" he read, "I think I'd prefer mouth myself."

He smiled kindly at the young girl in front of him.

"Could you please adjust that blind for me?" he asked her. 'Too much sunlight getting in, it's getting stuffy in here."

Then, as she turned and reached for the cord he looked her up and down. The tits were truly magnificent, but the rest was just as good. He knew just by looking at her that the little ass would be virgin, and that was something he really enjoyed. He didn't much care if it was his cock or the shaft of one of his brothers that would be invading her most private space, it was hearing her whimper and moan in mixed pain and pleasure as she had to take a man to the hilt that really did it for him.

"Mmmm, delish," he penned. "I think we'll leave such fine tuning for later, let's just decide which of us will play sugarpie this time. You?"

And so it was that Marcus Sinclair was assigned the job of romancing young Anna.

Anna surveyed herself in the mirror with growing dissatisfaction. A heap of cheap charity shop clothes lay discarded on the bed; she couldn't decide what to wear. Marcus would be collecting her in an hour for their third date together and she wanted to look her best. For their first evening, a trip to the theatre, she'd worn her purple silk dress. For the second, a daytime visit to the sculpture park, she'd worn her honey coloured moleskin suit, with the zip front jacket and bootleg trousers. Tonight he was taking her to an expensive French restaurant, and she had absolutely nothing suitable to wear. The silk dress would have been perfect, but she couldn't wear it again, not so soon. So the pile on the bed grew ever larger.

Eventually she settled on a lustrous cream vest top and tight black jeans. A bit too casual, but there was no helping it, they'd have to do. She didn't have much money left out of her grant, after paying the rent on her tiny and dilapidated bedsit and buying food. And the meters swallowed cash as if they were bottomless pits.

She set to work on her face. Anna was one of those females who are blithely unaware of how attractive they are to men. It wasn't so much that she was pretty, although she was. It was something more subtle and elusive… …something in the way her cheek had a particularly soft curve, the long brown hair, worn smartly high on her head for her office work, now spilling down her back almost to her waist, had a gentle lustre… …her body and face were simply very feminine, in a way that was almost old-fashioned. Maybe above all it was those huge brown eyes that made her look so defenceless; at any rate she didn't look modern and independent, she looked like she needed a man to take charge. She brought out the protective instincts in many men, and was often treated with an almost fatherly regard by males little older than herself. She was vaguely aware of this, but as yet had no idea that the very same attributes, from her round breasts to her full, plush mouth excited in some men a desire to see her bound and crying, with their come all over her sweet face.

Anna thought Marcus was wonderful. He was so unlike the boys she'd been out with. That's how she thought of them now: boys. They seemed so fumbling and inept when compared to the suave maturity of Marcus. Not that he'd even kissed her, yet. He was treating her with the utmost respect, even opening the car door for her, something she was so unused to that she blushed, alluringly if she did but know it, every time. He'd frequently put a guiding hand on her upper arm as they had looked at the sculptures, and she found herself getting wet panties just from the touch of him, the clean, male smell, his broad back so close to her. He was so much bigger and stronger than she was, she thought deliciously; he towered above her, over a foot taller. She found herself imagining him with his shirt off, looking down at her as she lay on the grass in a field full of meadow flowers. And then he would kiss her, ever so gently......

Anna was still a virgin, despite the eager attentions of her previous boyfriends. She was saving herself for the right man, and she was beginning to think Marcus might be the one.

She carefully painted her face: a little dark pencil and brown shadow to emphasize her eyes, a dusky pink lipgloss. Then she was ready, and there was still half an hour before he was due to arrive.

She lay back on her shabby couch and shut her eyes, dreaming about Marcus. She trailed her hand down the side of her body, just brushing her breast ever so slightly through the silky top, imagining it was Marcus's hand arousing her. Then again, but this time brought her hand forwards to cup her full roundness, her thumb repeatedly glancing over her nipple. Sliding her fingers beneath her jeans, down into her lace panties, she found she was already slippery, just from thinking about him. She started to gently stroke her clit, and after a few minutes stopped to pull off her jeans and knickers, already damp from her sex juices, spreading her thighs wide and hiking one heel high onto the back of the couch so as she could fuck herself hard with her left hand whilst her right rubbed furiously at her burning clit.

It wasn't enough; she needed to be naked. Carefully she folded her clothes on a chair, then lay back again. She got her right leg as high as she could, so that she was so spread it was slightly uncomfortable; for some reason she liked it like that. Her left foot trailed down to the floor. Her breasts were perfect smooth mounds, the nipples dark pink and hard and erect; she pinched them and gasped a little at the sharp stab of pain. Then she plunged her left index finger into her still virgin pussy and began fucking herself again, lifting her hips rhythmically as passion consumed her, all the while roughly strumming on her hungry clit.

Harder and harder she fucked herself, presenting a truly

8

delightful picture to unemployed labourer Carl Johnson, who occupied the neighbouring bedsit. Of course, Anna had no idea he had drilled a spyhole through the thin wall, and was sitting there, as he did nearly every night, his swollen penis hard in his massive hand, wanking off into a pair of her knickers. He'd stolen them from her used laundry bag on an occasion when he'd contrived that their visits to the local Laundromat should coincide. Now he sat there, occasionally pressing the scrap of white, embroidered cotton to his face and drinking in the rich smell of her, whilst his eyes revelled in the image of her legs spread wide, hips bucking, breasts heaving, thighs glistening with sweat, and with the fuck juices that were pouring from her pink flesh.

She had brought his attentions on herself: night after night he'd suffered the sounds of her climaxing, as he lay lonely in his bed, it had been most inconsiderate of her and his reaction only to be expected. And he was sure it was Providence that had granted him such a ringside seat at her evening passions, the couch so close to the wall that, had the plasterboard not been there, he could easily have reached out a hand and grasped the slender ankle that was pressing against the couch back. He was looking straight into her cunt as she finger fucked herself, and he could almost smell her sweet musk through the hole. It was reminiscent of the peepshow whores, who'd parade their bodies for a few pounds, but much, much better. The world was full of whores, he thought disgustedly, and wondered if he could find some way to get this particular whore impaled on his shaft, instead of just on the other side of the wall.

Anna's pussy gripped her one finger tightly as she came in a glorious orgasm, carefully stifling her cries of ecstasy to whimpers so as not to be overheard by the other tenants.

She lay back, exhausted, licking her fingers. The door buzzer sounded.

Marcus waited in the porch. It was pouring with rain, and he had an umbrella ready for young Anna. Where was the

9

silly bint? Not like her to be tardy. He was about to ring again, when he heard the scrape of the latch. Anna came out. Her face was flushed, and she looked almost guilty. He gave her his biggest smile, his eyes quickly taking in the cheap top, and the way her nipples jutted against the thin fabric in the sudden chill of the night. Her neck was blotchy he noticed, and as he bent to peck a kiss on her hair his nostrils were assailed by a sweet, musky odour. He chuckled to himself as he realised the little slut had been masturbating. She was a hot one, alright. He suppressed the urge to slip his hand inside her jeans right there and then and feel her fresh wetness: softly softly catchee monkey. He was more than prepared to bide his time. He didn't want just another girl to fuck, that was easy, anytime he went clubbing he could pick one up. No, the pleasure for him was in turning an innocent girl into a moaning, helpless, degraded, sex slave, every hole full of cock, a toy for male pleasure. This was a joint enterprise, and a profitable one, too.

He took Anna's arm and steered her towards his waiting BMW. Anna settled back against the soft leather seats; she loved the smell of this car. She realised with embarrassment that it wasn't only the rich leather she could smell; mingled with it was the delicious scent of her own juices, sweetly pungent in the increasing warmth of the car. She hoped Marcus wasn't aware of them, but something about the crease of amusement at the corner of his mouth as he drove made her fear otherwise.

The restaurant was a little way out of town, in a sprawling Victorian house. As she had anticipated, Anna felt underdressed for the occasion. There were other women in vest tops and jeans, but theirs were Armani, not from a stall at Leeds market. Perhaps sensing her discomfiture Marcus handed her a small package, elegantly gift wrapped.

"For you," he said simply, smiling again in the way that made her heart flutter.

Anna fumbled to unwrap the box. Inside was a pair of

exquisite diamond earrings. She gasped in pleasure, and Marcus said,

"Why don't you try them on?"

Then, when they were dangling from her lobes he added,

"You look very lovely tonight. I was wondering......" he paused.

"Yes?"

"My brothers and I are having a weekend party, at our house in the Dales. It's next weekend. I was wondering if you would come?"

Anna was maybe a little too young to accept with nonchalance.

"Oh yes! I'd love to!" she beamed at him, to be met with another brilliant smile.

She felt a sudden swirl of confusion. Something about that smile reminded her strangely of stage magicians, who smile as they bedazzle you, so that you don't notice what they are really doing until they open the casket and you see the beautiful assistant has vanished.

The rest of the evening passed pleasantly. He told her a little about his company and the complexities of business dealings with the Arab world. She told him how glad she was to be out of the home for children in care, and living on her own.

"I know it's shabby," she said, of her little bedsit, "but it's just wonderful to me, after all those years with no privacy."

"I quite understand," he said gently. "So you are all alone in the world?"

"Yes," she replied, her eyes flicking down for a moment with sadness. "I have no contact with my Mum, and I've never even met my father."

He reached across the table, and laid a hand on her wrist, squeezing slightly. She supposed he meant the gesture to be reassuring, but she found his touch deeply arousing, and flushed as she felt her pussy suddenly rush with wetness for him. A quick flash of the memory of her finger pounding into her as she lay on the couch, and then she was wondering what it would feel like to have this man inside her. Would it hurt? Just one finger seemed to fill her up, and a man's shaft would surely be much larger than her slim fingers. She looked into his eyes, confused by the strength of her desire, and saw how serious his face was. He squeezed tighter, then so tight she would have cried out as he was hurting her, just a little. But before she could do so his grip released.

"Come on," he said. "Let's go."

There was a look on his face she didn't understand, but his tone was commanding, slightly imperious even. Meekly she followed him out into the cold night, and clambered into the warmth of the car. They sped through the darkness in silence, and when they reached her street it seemed too soon. He showed her up the path to the porch, and then he kissed her.

Anna felt as if she'd been waiting years for this kiss, and her own response was so intense she moaned, lightly, under her breath. Nor was it the soft kiss of which she'd daydreamed; his mouth was hard and demanding against hers, his tongue probing, insistent. She clung to him in desperate arousal, whimpering with pleasure as his hand softly brushed down over her breast, then quickly pressed to her groin. She knew her jeans were soaked through with her juices, and as he ran his fingers back and forth, pressing the damp fabric up into her crack she was already close to coming. But abruptly he pulled away. Again there was that odd look on his face. Satisfaction maybe. Something else besides. Involuntarily she shivered. But now he was smiling.

"Not now," he said. 'The time isn't right. You aren't ready yet."

Anna blushed at his confidence that she'd been about to

succumb to his advances. She knew he was right.

"See you on Monday. And here……" he shoved a fat wad of notes at her. "Get yourself a pretty dress for the party on the Friday evening. Something long. Something lacy maybe."

She started to protest, but he pushed the money back to her.

"No, really, take it. It's a tiny amount for me, and it'll be a pleasure to see you in something classy."

Before we rip it off you, he finished to himself.

And with that he was gone.

The next week passed in a busy blur. Anna worked happily at the office, making tea and filing, gaily taking messages back and forth between the three Sinclair brothers, Jonathan having returned from his business trip to the United Arab Emirates. He was the eldest of the trio, in his early fifties. A still handsome man, despite being bald. Like his younger brothers he spent his spare moments working out in the gym and his taut six-pack belied his age. Anna had seen him there several times when having a lunch hour swim. The three were all tall, each of them over six foot. Muscular men who worked and played hard. The thought crossed her mind that if she hadn't been dating Marcus she would have been equally happy with either of the other brothers. They were all very much cut from the same cloth, so to speak…… presumably chips off the old block. Their father had started the business, but as far as she knew had long since retired; he must be in his seventies by now.

Jonathan noticed Anna in her swimsuit, too. A crisp, white tankini, it revealed more than she realised when wet from the pool. The dark shadow of her pubic hair was clear to see, and her hard nipples even more apparent. Anna had no idea that amongst the business notes the men exchanged she was also carrying messages such as: "She'll squeal when I ram eight inches of meat up her ass."

And: "The boys are going to enjoy this one, she's such a hot slut. I can't wait to see her mouth full of cock for the first time."

And: "I think she will like being whipped a little. So we'll just have to make sure that we whip her a lot."

The brothers' exchanges had been growing progressively more outspoken. It was now a great joke between them, how Anna dutifully carried the messages detailing the abuse she would shortly be suffering at their hands as they reduced her to a sex toy. They would use her to satisfy their darkest desires for domination and power, and then sell her on to make a healthy profit. Her own feelings and desires were, of course, entirely immaterial. You only had to look at her to see she was created for the sole purpose of male pleasure. But it was more than convenient that her innocent lust would make her so very easy to manipulate. Their vast experience had taught them that a slut like this would beg any man to fuck her, if she was handled correctly... ...and they knew exactly how to handle new girls.

Friday soon arrived. Marcus arranged to collect Anna at six. At half past five she stood before the mirror, turning this way and that, admiring her reflection. For once she was happy with her appearance. She was wearing a dress of white lace. The neck was a wide, boat style, her creamy shoulders naked. The bodice had an integral bra, which pushed her heavy breasts up into two round pillows, almost presenting them to the viewer. It was stretchy lace, and it followed her figure, as tight as a body stocking, showing her curves beautifully. It also jutted a little where it pulled tight over her pubic mound, but Anna was sure no one would notice that. The skirt was slashed to mid-thigh on one side, revealing a daring amount of leg as she walked. Underneath it she was wearing white lace panties and suspender belt, and white silk stockings. She'd had her legs waxed, and trimmed her pubic hair into a tidy triangle. Her finger and toenails were painted with a delicate, pearly, plummy polish. And she'd rubbed her thighs and belly and buttocks and breasts with a delicious scented massage bar, that left her skin with a subtle opalescence. She thought she might lose her virginity tonight, and so she had prepared her body with an almost ritualistic attention to detail. Marcus's gift of money had been so generous that after buying the dress she'd had plenty left over for the other things she needed. And after all, it was all for his benefit, she thought with an impish grin.

She'd painted her face carefully, in the same manner she always did, but with more shadow around the eyes, which stared back at her now, huge and dark and strangely melancholy. Her lips were a deep plummy pink. And she'd paid special attention to her long hair, piling it in an elegantly tousled heap high on her head, and curling the falling tendrils into ringlets.

She was ready ahead of time, and thinking about Marcus she wanted to lie back on the couch and pleasure herself once more. But, to the great disappointment of Carl, who was even now sitting pressed up against the partitioning wall, rubbing his erection, having very much enjoyed the sight of her anointing her body in preparation for its first fucking, she decided that it wasn't a good idea. Not after last time. And anyway, she'd be all the hotter tonight if she deprived herself of the pleasure of ecstatic release now.

Her weekend bag was packed and ready. She'd been unsure what to take for a weekend in the country… …should she bring hiking boots, she'd asked Marcus, but he'd been rather vague in response, just muttering something about seeing what the others wanted to do.

As it turned out, he arrived a few minutes early. Anna was glad to escape her dull room and climb into the warm nest of Marcus's BMW. He gave her a quick peck on the cheek, told her she looked 'simply ravishing' and then they sped off into the night. It was a long drive. The roads became progressively narrower and more twisting as they wove their way deep into the Yorkshire countryside. She asked him if they were near, and he said they were still some distance off. He didn't seem to want to talk, so she settled back into her seat and let her eyelids droop... ...soon she was fast asleep in the safe, leathery snug.

When she awoke it was to the sound of gravel grinding beneath the car wheels as he parked in a large driveway. Outside her window loomed the huge bulk of the house. She'd imagined he was taking her to a comfortable old farmhouse, but this was more like a mansion, reaching up into the dark. For some reason it seemed a little grim to her, but as she stepped out of the door which Marcus had so graciously opened for her, she could hear the reassuring sound of jolly male laughter, and saw that the windows of one of the rooms on the first floor were blazing with light.

He took her arm, and guided her up the marble steps. She almost expected a butler to greet them, but Marcus simply unlatched the door, and smilingly gestured to her to enter.

The hallway was empty. It was sumptuously decorated, with a beautiful Persian rug, and huge Chinese or Japanese vases. Marcus led her up the great curving staircase, to a massive oak door, and then he stopped, turned, and looked down at her. His face was suddenly utterly different. It was cold, appraising... ...and Anna shivered as he reached and adjusted a coil of her hair. The noise of the men's laughter beyond the door seemed now very loud; she took an involuntary step back.

Marcus looked her straight in the eyes.

"In you go, whore."

And then he opened the door.

CHAPTER 2

Marcus held her tightly by the upper arm, his fingers digging into her soft flesh, and pushed her ahead of him into the room. The men's voices were booming all around her; Anna felt disorientated, almost dizzy. She had thought he'd called her 'whore' but surely that could not be, she must have misheard.

The conversation around her was dying to murmurs, and all the people in the room were turning to stare at her. They were all men. Over a dozen of them, businessmen, anonymous in their dark suits. She peered at them through air hazy and heavy with cigar smoke. Fat gold rings glinted on hands wrapped around elegant crystal tumblers. She recognised Charles and Jonathan. In the centre, an older man, grizzled but unbent.

Something was wrong. They weren't flicking friendly glances at her and then looking away, the way one does when new guests arrive at a party. They were swivelling towards her, openly ogling her body. In amazement she saw some of them were beginning to rub their crotches. A voice rang out close behind her. It was Marcus:

"Gentlemen, may I present the weekend's entertainment. A nice, fresh, virgin whore."

As he spoke he pulled both her arms roughly behind her back, and pinned them there with his left arm. Anna struggled but it was no use whatsoever, he was a full foot taller than she, and almost twice her weight. He brought his free hand round to the front of her and squeezed her right breast, hard. And then the left. Even harder.

Anna was moaning and wriggling, and yet at the same time dimly aware that her panties were already wet from the sudden rush of her love juices. Reaching up to her hair, Marcus buried his fingers in it, stroking the silky tresses and rubbing her scalp with his hard fingertips. Carefully he unfastened the clips that were holding it in place, and it spilled softly down over her shoulders, down her back.

He slipped his hand into the low-cut neck of her dress, rubbing against her naked tits, brushing lightly, almost tenderly, over her nipples. Handling her with deliberate showmanship. With a sudden yank he wrenched the lacy material down, tearing her dress open so her full, ripe breasts tumbled out, for all the men to see.

"No," said Anna. "No, no, oh please, no......"

But he wasn't listening, had no intention of stopping. And anyway, somehow her voice lacked conviction, even to her own ears. Some of the audience tittered. He grasped her right nipple between his thumb and forefinger and pinched it, brutally hard. Anna yelped at the pain, but her yelp tailed into a moan as she felt her pussy grow ever wetter. A man was handling her against her will, deliberately hurting her in front of more than a dozen others for their amusement and she was aroused! What sort of a woman was she?

As if in answer to her unspoken question Marcus muttered in her ear,

"You little slut."

He was tugging at her dress again, and now Charles stepped forward to assist him. With one crude rip he tore her once lovely dress fully open, then another man handed him a knife. Anna whimpered in sheer terror, but Charles simply used the knife to cut the torn remnants of her dress completely away from her, so now she was standing there, her magnificent tits on full display for the pleasure of the assembled company, her only covering delicate lace panties, stockings and a suspender belt.

Marcus immediately slipped his hand down her panties, and laughingly brought out a glistening finger, holding it up for all to see.

"I knew it!" he said. "The slut is already wet for us."

The men laughed, enjoying her humiliation. They'd had girls who were easily aroused by rough treatment before, but this one was so wet, so easily, it really did take the biscuit.

"Born to be a whore," one of them said. She realised it was Jonathan.

Marcus's hand was back in her panties, rubbing now against her already swollen clit. Anna tried not to become aroused but it was hopeless. She held back as long as she could, but then she started to moan. Marcus kept right on rubbing, and as her body started to build towards orgasm she felt deeply ashamed to find herself pressing forward to receive his touch. But abruptly he stopped. She groaned her dissatisfaction as his hand pulled away from her hungry pussy.

The men all laughed.

"What a slut!"

"Yes, she's a whore alright."

"Bitch in heat."

Charles stepped forward with the knife again. With a practised movement he slit the lace panties at the hips. They would have fallen to the floor, but Marcus held them up, to show everyone that they were soaked. More laughter.

Then she was frog-marched forward, to the old man at the centre of the group.

"Here father, what do you think?" said Jonathan, and she realised she was meeting Sir Jonathan Sinclair senior, the founder of the prosperous company, for the first time. He must have been in his late seventies. He smiled, not at her but at his sons, and reached forward with both his wrinkly old hands to cup her fresh young breasts. He weighed each one, their milky whiteness contrasting sharply with his liver-spotted old skin, stroking his thumbs again and again over her nipples. Again and again. They had been erect before, now they jutted out like stubby pink pencils, ever harder. Betraying her. She moaned again, partly in arousal, partly in despair at the hopelessness of her situation. Even her own body was conspiring against her.

"You could hang a wet donkey jacket off those," one of

the men remarked, to loud guffaws.

Suddenly old Sir Jonathan pinched both her nipples, so hard she screamed in pain. She dipped her head to bite his hand, but before her teeth had made proper purchase she was yanked back. Marcus had wrapped his right hand in her long mane of hair, and used it to cruelly pull back her head. Her one form of defence was thwarted, her breasts presented unprotected to the old man.

"Bite me would you?" he said, clearly angry, then returned to his stroking of her presented nipples. He stroked until they were fully erect, and she was moaning loudly, wondering if she would orgasm from the attention her breasts alone were receiving. He bent his white head and began to flick one nipple gently with his tongue. She groaned in helpless pleasure, started to arch towards him in her desire. And then he bit her nipple. Not that hard, really. Not enough to make blood flow, or only the merest smudge. But as she was so aroused the pain was acute, she screamed and cried and tried to escape, as he mercilessly bit the second one. And yet somehow, to her horror, it made her even wetter.

He straightened, and pinched her sore nipples between his thumbs and forefingers again. She was sobbing unrestrainedly now. He squeezed harder and harder. Then he said:

"You bit me. That is not allowed. You are here to be used, in whatever manner we consider fit, you will accept whatever treatment we mete out with humble gratitude. Now, say, 'sorry Master'."

Perhaps Anna would have found the strength to refuse him, but as he pinched her nipples once more, even harder than before, she could only hurry to sob out her apology.

"Sorry Master," she whimpered, to be met with one more cruel pinch and rich laughter from all around her.

Sir Jonathan Sinclair was unfastening his trousers. Out sprang his cock, hugely erect, the tip glistening with pre-come. Marcus forced her to her knees, and the old man proceeded to rub his swollen member all over her face, his juices leaving a glistening snail trail as he tracked over her cheeks, eyelids, and mouth. She could smell him, a sour, animal smell, unlike any other. Then he dipped lower and rubbed his oozing glans over her breasts and particularly her nipples, drawing circles of moisture all over her pretty pink buds. Marcus had relaxed his grip on her hair a little, so that she would have a really good view of the old man's cock taking pleasure in her creamy tits. The cock headed back up, towards her mouth. Sir Jonathan pressed his shaft against her lips. Anna kept her mouth shut tight, so the penis could find no point of entry, slipping easily inside her full lips, but blocked by her little white teeth. Then someone, she knew not who, reached round from behind her to hold either side of her head with his two big hands.

"Open up!" barked Sir Jonathan, and slapped her hard, full across the face. In shock, Anna did so, just for a moment, and the hands holding her head pinched her cheeks into the sides of her mouth. It was thus impossible for Anna to close it again; to do so would have meant biting her inner cheeks.

The cock began pressing forward into her mouth. She had never realised how big a cock would feel in her mouth; it seemed enormous, suffocating. Out of the corner of her eye she caught a glint of metal; it was Charles, with the knife again. He brought it up close by her cock-stuffed face and said to someone close behind her:

"I think you can release her mouth. Father will find it easier to fuck her deeply without your hands there, and she will not dare to bite again. Will you?"

This last directed at her, and emphasized by the knife resting cold against her cheek. She shook her head in compliance, as well as one can shake one's head, when one's mouth is full of cock and a knife is upon one's face. They chuckled, and the hands holding either side of her head let go. Just for a moment she was more comfortable, but then

Sir Jonathan Sinclair himself got hold of her head, and began fucking her face. It had been bad before, but this was far worse. The cock was plunging to the back of her mouth, down into her throat, leaving Anna terrified she would choke. She was nearly gagging with each thrust, and whenever he was deep in her, her face was up against his pubic hair, which smelt so strong and strange. It was terrible, and yet, to her deepening shame, she knew that on one level she was enjoying even this. Her clit was throbbing with desire.

Something was happening behind her. As the old man thrust into her mouth, her arms were being strapped together behind her back. Wrist bound to wrist, with straps that dug in. Then a rough tug as her arms were strapped together above the elbow. And now her breasts were properly presented to her masters, jutting forward, displayed to perfection. Yet she was only dimly aware of all this, as she was concentrating all her energies on enduring the glorious assault on her mouth and throat.

Now hands grasped her ankles, pulling them apart. It brought her head lower, but this was no problem for the man using her mouth, he settled into a luxuriantly upholstered chair. And once eased down into it, resumed his steady rhythm.

Her ankles were wide apart now, and straps were being fastened around them. She tried to bring her feet together but could not, and, terrified, realised they had shackled her to a spreading bar. For a moment they all let go of her, saving only Sir Jonathan, humping away deep in her throat without pause. They were enjoying the delightful picture she presented, breasts swinging, arms bound, legs spread, mouth receiving cock.

Then she felt hands on her pussy. Expert hands, spreading her labia and rubbing her clit in little circles, in exactly the same manner she herself always used to bring herself to orgasm. There was nothing whatsoever she could do to halt or even slow the inevitable: within moments she was shaking with the blast of an enormous climax. At just the same moment old Sir Jonathan orgasmed. The invading cock spasmed and jetted, suddenly filling her mouth with a thick slimy mass of semen. In her innocence she had never imagined how copious a man's come would be, and she hurried to swallow the load, not daring to spit for fear of angering the men who surrounded her.

"Now clean me up, slut," said the old man.

There was no fight left in her, not after the humiliation of orgasming in response to their rough treatment. They knew what she was, now. She knew what she was.

So she dipped her head to his matted pubes, and began licking and licking with her soft pink tongue, savouring this strange, new, salt taste. She carefully licked all over his now shrunken penis, which, to her horror, began to twitch and swell once more.

By the time she had cleaned him to his full satisfaction his member was erect and hard once more. And fresh juices of her own were trickling down her pussy.

She felt her arms being unfastened. Her heart leapt; they were going to release her! But her relief was short-lived: silently they rebound her wrists together in front of her, and then pulled her upright. Her arms were yanked up above her head, and fastened by her bonds to a metal chain dangling from the ceiling. She was standing with her stockinged feet flat on the floor, legs still spread by the metal bar, arms taut at full stretch above her. But the bar between her legs was adjustable. A man she didn't know was lengthening it. He was big and ugly, with huge rough hands. His beer belly slopped down over his belt. He'd unzipped his flies and a massive cock was hanging out of his trousers. Wider and wider her legs were stretched, until her feet were four foot apart. And so now she was on tiptoes.

The betraying juices were trickling down her thighs, and

the ugly man reached a hand into her pussy lips and rubbed her with the flat of his palm. She moaned at the delicious sensation, but he pulled his hand away, and started unfastening his belt. She saw that some of the other men were following suit, and still others had whips and switches. She hadn't noticed before, but all around the walls of the hall were shelves and racks of whips and straps. And other things, too. She shuddered as she caught sight of a huge black dildo. It must just be for decoration she thought; it could hardly be used on a woman, it was nearly as wide as her arm.

And then her first whipping began. The men took turns to lash her, one giving her half a dozen or so strokes, then another, then another. That way they didn't tire. Hopelessly she tried to dodge the rain of blows, arching and curling this way and that. But she could not escape, even for a moment. Her feet had such a pathetic grip on the floor, touching it as she was only with her toes, that she swung helplessly back and forth under the onslaught of the abuse.

The cruel lashes fell first across her fleshy parts, her rump. But the men were not to be satisfied with that, and whipped her thighs, and then her tits. Soon her skin was crisscrossed with fine pink lines. She was crying freely by this time of course, but the pain was doing nothing to quell the strange passion that had awoken in her, and her burning cunt was aching for a man's touch.

The whipping went on and on. She was growing faint. No longer arching away from the blows, no strength left to resist. Sir Jonathan raised a hand, and the whips and belts were still.

He came right up to her. He was a tall man, she a petite girl, and with her legs strapped so wide he towered above her.

"Who am I?" he asked her.

"Sir Jonathan Sinclair," she stuttered, not understanding.

He slapped her, a single stinging blow across her face.

"No!" he said. "Not to you I'm not. That is the name by which my equals address me." With a wave of his hand that encompassed all the men in the room, he made it very clear who he meant by his equals.

"You are not my equal. You have less status even than my dog. You are on a level with......" he looked around the room, "......that chair over there," gesturing towards the chair that had supported him whilst he had used her mouth.

"You are a slave. You exist only to be used by men, to give men pleasure. That is your role, now and henceforth. There is no escaping your destiny. You are simply a sex slave, and will be used as such by anyone I wish to enjoy my property. Now," he reached out a hand, lifted her chin so he could look straight into her eyes, "who am I?"

She understood now. After all, he'd already told her once. And his last words had made it abundantly clear, even to the dazed girl.

"My Master," she stuttered.

"Yes. I am your Master. My sons, for whom you have been working, are also your Masters. You are the property of the Sinclair corporation, in which my sons and I are all equal partners. But more, all these men who are my guests," he gestured again to the assembled company, "they are all your Masters, too. As your owner I have the right to give you or sell you to whomsoever I please. And you will never forget that."

"Yes Master," she replied, knowing in her heart it was true, had, in a way, always been true. She had just not understood before, how much she craved this debasement.

He smiled at her. And reached between her legs to rub and fondle her dripping pussy. Anna groaned in pleasure, pushed towards his hand, and there was a little interval of peace, whilst the old man kindly rubbed his new slave's little clit, slipping one finger carefully into her still virgin hole.

Then he took his hand away, wiped her juices off his

fingers onto her hair, and turned to his friends and colleagues.

"Gentlemen, shall we go and eat?"

The men left the room in companionable groups. Chatting and laughing in very much the same manner they had been before Anna was presented to them.

The new slave was left alone, hanging there; naked, splayed, accessible and bruised, with nothing to do but await the return of the men who owned her.

CHAPTER 3

Anna didn't know how long she hung there. From somewhere a little way off she could hear the rise and fall of male voices, clearly in high good humour, laughing loudly in a way that suggested, even at this distance, that the jokes were of a bawdy nature. Her wrists hurt where the black leather straps were digging into them, and her thighs ached from being stretched so open. To distract herself from the discomfort she looked around the room. She had been too preoccupied with thrusting cock and probing fingers to take more than the most cursory notice of her surroundings before.

She saw she was hanging in a magnificent Tudor hallway. Twisting her head to look behind her she could see a beautiful dark oak minstrel gallery along the end wall, whilst facing her stood a great stone fireplace. The walls were dark; oak panelling that must have been four hundred years old. Arranged on the walls were the many racks of whips and straps she had noticed already. There were lengths of rope, dildos of varying sizes, and many items for which she could not begin to guess a purpose. She shivered in delicious fear as she realised what had happened to her so far this evening was surely only the beginning. This night was the first of her new life, her life as a sex slave, and she was sure her body was going to be receiving an awful lot of attention. Whether she liked it, or not. That phrase sent exquisite tingles down to her still plump clit. She wanted to touch herself, needed to come again, but in her bondage could not even rub her thighs together to release herself from frustration.

There was a broad oak table near the fireplace, where the fire of sweet scented pine logs was still blazing furiously. She looked into the scarlet and orange flames, and thought it was the most beautiful thing she had ever seen. It cast a welcome heat over her helpless nudity, over her full breasts and taut belly and spread thighs. Her buttocks and back were feeling the chill of the night air.

She was tired, and despite her discomfort began to doze, so when a quiet voice said,"Hello Anna." She thought at first it was just part of the confusion of uneasy dreams that had been spinning in her mind. But then she felt a soft, cool hand on her cheek, and opened her eyes to see a girl standing in front of her.

She was beautiful and about the same age as Anna. She had curly, ash-blonde hair that spiralled in lovely tresses down to her waist. She was very slim, almost painfully so, with big blue china doll eyes and very delicate features, and a pair of the prettiest little breasts that Anna had ever seen. Each one would provide one of the Masters with no more than a handful of soft flesh to torment, but their shape was sublime; perfect little orbs with nipples tip-tilting heavenwards. And as Anna looked at the nipples, relishing how pink and perky they were, she realised that they were very much like her own, despite the fact that the breasts were so very different.

The way the girl was dressed gave Anna a particularly good view of her nipples: she had on a neat little outfit made from transparent rubber, the colour of pink sugar icing. It was a little sports bra style top, and tiny hotpants, all trimmed with shiny black rubber. If it had been made of lycra it wouldn't have looked out of place in any aerobics class, or as a swimsuit...... if it hadn't been for the holes. There were perfect round holes revealing the girl's sweet nipples to anyone who cared to look. Again the holes were edged with the black rubber. And a much larger hole provided unfettered access to the cunt and asshole.

The slave, for slave she surely was, had almost no pubic hair. There was only a narrow rectangle of soft blonde curls, which could in no way hide, and in fact seemed to point down towards, the naked crack. The velvety mons and surrounding skin had presumably been waxed, to give the

Masters an unimpeded view of the property.

Round her neck was a smooth collar of dull metal, that seemed to have no fastening, but rather be made all of a piece. Dangling from it was a silver disc, just as a dog might wear. Anna guessed it was a name-tag.

The angelic girl spoke again:

"Hallo Anna. I'm Clara. Well, that used to be my name. Now it's Pusskins. I've come to get you down."

As she spoke she reached forward and gently stroked Anna's breast, not to arouse, but more the way one might steady a nervy animal. Then she bent down, and freed Anna's ankles. She carefully stacked the spreader bar back on the appropriate rack, as Anna slowly pulled her feet in together. Her legs were stiff and sore from the spreading.

Clara returned, and reached up to unfasten Anna's wrists. As she stood on her tip-toes to reach the bonds, her little tits rubbed softly against Anna's, their nipples making delectable contact. Anna was still in a state of high arousal after her earlier treatment, and she could feel herself moistening again in response. Suddenly she was free, and she staggered forward a step; she hadn't realised how much the chain had been supporting her. Clara held her as she stumbled, and the two women were looking directly into each others eyes. Anna blushed; she was sure her face would betray her arousal. But Clara just smiled.

"Come on," she said, and taking Anna's hand in hers, led her out of the room, by another, far smaller door.

Behind the door was a narrow stone spiral staircase, the steps worn by the passage of many feet over hundreds of years. It was cold here, away from the blazing fire, and whether it was the chill or the realisation of her predicament it was hard to say, but Anna started to shiver so hard her teeth were soon chattering. Clara looked at her in concern.

"Not much further, then we can get you warmed up."

They reached a tiny door. Beyond it was a cosy suite of

rooms: firstly a little antechamber, with whitewashed walls and a luxuriant dark red oriental rug on the floor. Then a bedroom, again richly carpeted, dominated by a four-poster bed. A fire, newly piled with logs, burned steadily beyond the foot of the bed. There were several old oak chests along one wall, a huge mirror hanging on another and a solitary chair, again of dark Tudor oak. The bed was covered in an ornate velvet coverlet, patchwork with embroidered sections, worked with a fine, gold thread. And, leading off the bedroom, through one door there was what looked like an office, through another door a bathroom with a jacuzzi, already full of steaming, scented water.

"Let me help you undress," said Clara, and then they both giggled, because Anna was so close to naked already. Except for a few bedraggled remnants. Clara unfastened the torn suspender belt and threw it carelessly away, whilst Anna peeled off her once pretty stockings, now all rent with holes and ladders. She glanced wistfully towards the bin, wherein lay the tattered remains of her finery, remembering the pretty dress that Marcus had torn from her with such obvious pleasure. Clara followed her gaze.

"It doesn't matter," she said. "You couldn't have worn those here anyway. Not suitable. That's what free women wear. If you wear anything at all you'll wear a slutsuit, like me."

She proudly arched her little back, displaying her clothing and the way it hid nothing of her most intimate parts.

"See?" she said. "You and I, we're not free women any longer. You'll never wear clothes like that again. You're a slave, to be used. That means your pussy and anus and tits must be accessible to our Masters at all times. No covering up. Partly so that it's simple for the Masters to take you, whenever and however they please. But it's more than that. It's to remind you what you are for, so you don't forget, even for a moment. You exist for male pleasure, and for no other reason."

Anna climbed into the bath, and leant back, settling into the hot depths. The welts on her buttocks caused by the whipping smarted in the perfumed water, but maybe the men had been holding back when they lashed her breasts and thighs, because although they did bear some stinging red lines, her skin was not raw all over as she had feared.

Clara poured a jugful of cool water over her hair, and began to wash it. Her fingers massaged Anna's scalp with a firm, but gentle, touch. Anna lay back deeper into the water, her face a small island in a foamy sea, her hair billowing around her in dark clouds through which Clara wove her fingers to rinse away the shampoo. Then Anna sat up, and as the water cascaded from her thick hair Clara took a big block of soap and started to soap her tender breasts. In the hot water her nipples had softened, relaxed to little nubs in the smooth pink discs of her aureolae, but as Clara soaped they tightened once more. She sighed, and opened her eyes to find Clara gazing at her with a broad happy smile on her face. The bath was very big for one person, thought Anna. As if reading her mind, Clara asked:

"Shall I get in with you?"

Anna smiled back at her, and Clara started to peel off her pink rubber. Standing there, naked except for her slave collar, she looked very vulnerable.

"How long have you been here?" Anna asked.

"Nearly sixth months," came the reply, as the lovely girl stepped in to join her, and started again to soap her full breasts.

"You have such beautiful breasts," Clara said, and sighed.

"You too!"

"But yours are so big… …mine are too small I think, but my Master won't get me modified. He says he likes me like this."

"Well… …I suppose what he likes is the most important thing," Anna said, doubtfully.

Clara laughed, "Actually, what he likes is the only thing

31

that matters at all. Do you think they're pretty then?" glancing downwards at her pert titties.

"Oh yes," Anna replied, and bending her head began to lick one of Clara's nipples.

"Stop!" Clara cried in alarm.

Anna blushed. "Oh... ...I'm sorry," she said, "I thought......"

Clara was looking anxiously towards the door. Satisfied that they were still quite alone and unobserved, she relaxed.

"It isn't that I don't want you to. It's that I'm property, and so are you. We're allowed to soap each other, but not to make love. Not to pleasure each other. You have to understand, we're *property*. We can do nothing that has any other goal than pleasing our Masters. Maybe our Master will come in, maybe he will command you to lick me. If that happens you will, of course, obey. But we must never act to please ourselves. We exist only for the pleasure of the men who use us. Remember that! This bath is pleasant for you, but it's simply to prepare you for further use, to make you more enjoyable for the men. You're property."

They got out of the bath and began to dry themselves and each other. Again Clara took Anna's hand and led her into the bedroom. She knelt down by the largest of the oaken chests, and opened it. Anna flopped down on the bed.

"Is this my bed?" she asked, lazily sprawling over the velvet coverlet.

"NO!" Clara replied, horrified. "Get off at once!" looking with alarm towards the door.

Anna hurriedly got down.

"But......"

"How many times do you need telling?" Clara was sounding exasperated. "*You're property*! You don't get a bed to sleep in. This isn't a game, you know. You're not in the middle of a naughty fantasy weekend, back to the office as usual on Monday. This is for real. You are a slave. You have no rights. You're enjoying it... ...they are experts at knowing which girls are born submissives, like you and I. But mark my words, if you were to change your mind, explain that you really didn't want to be here and ask to go home, they'd laugh in your face. And then whip you till you begged for mercy. This is for real. You're no longer free; you're a slave, to be fucked and beaten as the mood takes them. If you don't wake up to that, and start behaving accordingly they'll be beating you far beyond the point at which you find pleasure in it. Do you understand?"

Anna could only nod, mute, shocked by Clara's words. She really did have no choice in the matter, and that fact was both deeply frightening and arousing.

"This is my collar," Clara continued more gently, lightly touching the dull metal around her neck with her little hand, then lifting an iron shackle that Anna hadn't noticed hanging from the foot of the bed, attached to it by a long chain. "I sleep tethered to the bed. If my Master wants to use me I may be allowed into his bed. Quite often though he is sated by the time he returns to his room, and then I must sleep on the floor. And other times he brings another slave to pleasure him, and if he does not want use of me as well, then I must sleep on the floor. Other times he gives me to a visitor or one of his brothers, for their use for the night. Sometimes he brings one of his free women here. Then often they both use me. The free women are very cruel to us. It amuses them. If he brings a free woman to his bed, then again, after being used I must sleep on the floor. If they let me sleep at all." And she shuddered.

"So this is your Master's chamber? But which of the men......"

She didn't finish. The door was flung open, and Marcus stood there. Anna experienced a sudden flush of jealousy. So Clara was Marcus's slave. A position she coveted. And what had Clara been saying about 'her Master's free women'? She had so much wanted to be Marcus's woman. It was very clear now that his romantic attentions had been a total sham, just a device to trick her into coming freely to this place where she would be forced to relinquish all control, all dignity, all right to refusal. She flushed with shame remembering what old Sir Jonathan had said. She was just property, like a chair, or a car... ...a toy to be enjoyed.

Marcus's eyes were hungrily drinking in the pleasant sight of the two beautiful, naked, young slaves, but he was frowning.

"You should be ready by now! Hurry!" he barked.

"Yes Master," Clara immediately replied, dropping to her knees and kissing his booted feet.

Then she returned to the great oak trunk, and began sifting through garments. Tissue paper rustled. Quickly she found what she was looking for.

"Is this the one you wish her to wear, Master?" She held up a shiny black rubber catsuit.

"Yes. As I told you. And don't forget the corset."

More rummaging and rustling. Out came a short, black leather corset, stiffly boned and without any section to support or in any way cover the tits.

Marcus sat back comfortably in the one chair, and watched whilst Clara helped Anna dress in the catsuit. It was only when it was on her that Anna realised how well it fulfilled the requirements of suitable clothing for property. Her arms and legs, even her hands and feet, were totally encased in black shiny rubber. Her body was likewise covered. Except for three holes. Like Clara's hotpants, the catsuit had a large fuck-hole, rendering her virgin pussy and anus completely accessible. But whereas Clara's top just had holes for her nipples, this slut suit had holes that were just big enough for Anna's breasts to be tugged through. Either the catsuit had been designed for someone with less ample breasts, or, more likely, the holes were deliberately on the small side, as her poor breasts were squeezed tightly by the constricting rubber.

"Mmm. It's a perfect fit," said Marcus, "I guessed your measurements as you did those little tasks for me around my office. Appraising new meat is one of my skills."

Anna flushed. She was still trying to reconcile all her previous experiences and daydreams about this man with the brutal reality she was now tasting.

Next came the corset.

"Tight, Pusskins," the Master barked. He was leaning back, enjoying the spectacle. He'd unzipped his trousers and was idly stroking his large cock. Anna found it hard to tear her eyes away from it, gazing goggle-eyed like a rabbit caught in headlights.

Clara gestured for Anna to hold the high crossbar of the four poster. As she gripped it, teetering on tip-toes, Clara pulled the corset around her, and began to lace it. To Anna's disbelief she actually put her foot against Anna's back in order to pull the laces more tightly. Anna squealed in discomfort as the corset hugged deeper around her waist.

"Shut it, slut," came Marcus's instant response. She could tell from his voice that he was laughing at her.

When it was done Clara turned her round. Marcus surveyed her, obviously pleased with the effect.

"Face," he said. "You," gesturing to Anna, "sit there."

He pointed at the chest. Clara fetched some makeup, and began to paint Anna's face. Anna sat there dutifully, with no idea what she looked like. Out of the corner of her eye she could see Marcus's hand slowly sliding up and down his engorged cock.

Finally it was done. Marcus stood up, and came up close to her. He stroked her breasts and nipples, standing back and twisting each nipple none too gently, his arms outstretched, the better to observe her. Then he turned her around, felt her bottom, slipped his hand between her legs to sample her wetness, his cock brushing against her smooth buttocks.

"Tut tut tut, you little whore. I've known some sluts in

my time, but 'bitch in permanent heat' is indubitably the phrase that comes to mind for a slut like you."

He pulled her arms together behind her, gestured to Clara and, as she handed him some leather straps, strapped Anna at the wrists. Then again above the elbows. Clara passed her some high, black stilettos. With difficulty she wriggled her feet into them. Marcus yanked her up. He fastened a black leather collar around her neck, clipping it with a padlock. It was stiff and uncomfortable, and so high that she could no longer tilt her head to survey her own body.

"Come and see yourself in this nice, big, mirror," he said, pulling her over in front of it.

Anna gasped. It was like looking at someone else. With her arms pulled back, breasts poking through the over-tight rubber and her waist reduced to a mere eighteen inches by the corset, she looked like nothing so much as a blow-up sex doll. Like this, her full breasts looked massive. Her eyes were emphasized by black eyeliner, and long false lashes made them look even huger......... a bambi-face. Her lips were shiny slut-red. The collar made it abundantly clear what she was. She was a whore; but an owned whore.

"Look at your udders," said Marcus, jiggling them in his hands. "You don't have pretty titties like Pusskins do you, you have *udders*, don't you, slut?"

Stung into silence, Anna did not reply, but an urgent glance from Clara reminded her how she should respond. Too late however: Marcus pinched her nipples viciously hard. She yelped in pain.

"Well?!"

"Yes, Master."

"What sort of tits do you have?"

"Udders, Master."

"And what are they for?"

He squeezed and pulled at them as he spoke. Anna looked away from the mirror; the sight of her degradation was too much to bear, but with a swift yank on her lovely hair she was brought back into obedience.

"For your pleasure, Master." Anna whimpered out.

"And?"

"The pleasure of my other Masters and whosoever you should choose to give me to, Master."

"Good girl."

He stopped his torment and started stroking her, rubbing the nipples in delicious circles so that Anna started to moan. His cock was hot and hard against her ass crack.

"Pusskins, some pegs I think."

"But Master……"

"Silence! How dare you question my command!"

And he slapped Clara hard across the buttocks. Clara accepted the well-earned rebuke without so much as a squeak, and fetched him a box of clothes pegs. Still standing behind Anna, still directing her to look at the vision of sexual humiliation she now presented, he casually reached from behind her and without hesitation clipped a clothes peg on one of her nipples.

Anna cried out in pain, then gasped as her other nipple was pegged.

Reaching round from behind her with both his hands now, Marcus tugged gently on the pegs. Anna moaned in helpless arousal. Marcus alternated delicate movements, such as flicking the pegs, with rough tugs, so Anna was carried helpless on a roller coaster of pleasure and pain, until the two sensations seemed to blur into one.

His naked cock, hard and erect, was now rubbing against her virgin asshole, and he dipped a finger in her cunt juices and started to push it against her anal opening. Anna tensed her muscles in fear and refusal, but she was helpless against the slim invader. Little by little, thoroughly lubricated by her own body, which seemed to welcome each and every sexual attention, her muscles relaxed into acceptance, and the finger slid inside her, until in shame she felt the palm of

Marcus's hand flat against her buttocks. He pushed rhythmically, whilst Anna groaned in pleasure.

"My, but you're a tight one. You'll be crying when you have to take a cock to the hilt for the first time. But don't worry, that won't put us off. In fact, all the better."

Anna moaned in disappointment as the finger was pulled out of her. He turned her around, and looked her up and down once more.

"*Now* you're ready," he said, and Anna knew he was referring to that night, not so long ago and yet recalled as if from another age, when they had stood in her porchway and she had been about to give her virginity to him, and he had told her she wasn't ready.

He clipped a chain lead to her collar. It was exactly like those used for dogs, ending in a wide loop of woven leather for the owner to hold, to maintain total control in total comfort.

"Hmmm... ...I must get you a name tag. But first......" he got hold of her lead and gave it a quick yank, so she stumbled, but did not fall, "......first, I must decide on a name. Let me see... ...I could call you 'Three Wet Holes', or 'Gagging for cock' maybe... ...but those are just too long-winded, however appropriate. I'll have to think about it. Right now, you have a gangbang to attend."

With that he set off, back down the spiral stairs and into the hall, Anna trotting behind him as best she could.

Chapter 4

The hall was full of men once more, standing around laughing and sipping after-dinner drinks. Anna suddenly realised how hungry she was; it was now late, maybe eleven or twelve, and she'd had nothing to eat since a couple of crackers and an apple at midday. Except for a gulletful of the old man's semen, she remembered with a shudder.

There were about fifteen men in the room, and as Marcus brought her to a halt, her lead yanked high so she was twisting her neck up towards it, and teetering on the high heels, they all turned to look at her.

"Well look at those tits!"

"Udders!"

"Is she really still a virgin?"

Marcus said, "Well, let's all take a look, shall we?"

And with that Anna was bodily lifted onto the great oak table in front of the fire. She was dragged to the end of it, so as her buttocks rested just at the edge, and two men grabbed her legs, pulling them open. She could feel the heat of the fire on her naked pudenda. She was getting frightened; there were so many men, and she feared they would be rough. And even now, she still wanted to lose her virginity to Marcus.

Marcus spread her labia, and the men peered at her fuck-hole, agreeing that she was undoubtedly virgin.

"But not for much longer!" one of them said, and they all laughed.

In the centre of the floor was a giant futon, again covered in rich velvet. She was bodily lifted to it and flung down, landing on her back in an uncomfortable sprawl, her strapped arms pressing into her back. Marcus, Charles and Jonathan stepped forward. They had stripped, and the firelight glinted on their strong, hard bodies, the fine lines of their muscles. Such big men, each one well over six foot and with a body builder's physique. Any one of them would have had no problem overpowering a tall, heavily-built woman, never mind one as tiny and delicate as Anna. Even supposing she hadn't been bound. Even supposing he had been alone. All three had hugely erect cocks, the tips already glistening. Sir Jonathan Sinclair was settled comfortably in his chair, very close. A ringside seat for the coming performance.

She imagined that Charles and Jonathan would hold her open, whilst Marcus sampled the delights of her fresh pussy for the first time, but the men had other plans. She was pulled onto her knees, and pushed forward onto the mattress. With her arms strapped helpless behind her she could not support herself, and so was stuck in the ignominious position of arse raised, face half buried in mattress. Charles was behind her. He reached into her pussy, and, chuckling, showed the gathered men the glistening wetness on his fingers, before smearing it over her asshole. Only then did Anna realise what was about to happen, and why all three brothers were with her on the mattress. She struggled and squirmed, but could do nothing as the tip of Charles' rock hard cock started to press against her tight shut anus. To aid their brother Marcus and Jonathan each took hold of one of her thighs, then with their other hands tugged at her buttocks to spread them. Little by little Charles stuffed himself into her most private space. She knew it'd hurt worse if she tried to fight it, and concentrated on relaxing as the pressure gradually stretched her open, but still it hurt as he pushed into her. Finally the tip of his cock was fully inside her. He felt huge. He paused for a moment, and in her innocence she thought the worst was over, but of course, all he had done so far was to penetrate her defending muscles. The length of him was still outside her; the real fucking was about to begin.

He thrust forward, steadily. Anna squealed in pain. As he drew back the pain receded, but again he thrust, penetrating just a little bit deeper this time, and again she squealed.

Again. And again. He wasn't rough, but he was firm. Anna did not know it, but he was being careful not to damage her; she was, after all, valuable property. Nevertheless, she was going to take every inch of him, there was no doubt about that. With each thrust he went a little deeper into her, until finally he was buried up to the hilt. The pain was ebbing away, but Anna couldn't help herself from crying. She had not expected it to hurt that much.

Someone started to lift her head, and she felt the scratch of pubes against her face. It was Marcus, and she didn't have to be told what to do this time. Dutifully she opened her mouth, and lovingly licked and sucked his erect member. But Marcus was a chip off the old block for sure, and he didn't want just the soft caresses of her tongue. Holding her head firmly he started to thrust deep into her throat. She did her best to relax as both men hammered into her. The pain was subsiding, and in it's place a dark, whorish arousal was steadily growing. The men were thrusting in rhythm now, both deep inside her at the same time. She felt so full, and it was delicious. Other men were reaching to caress her breasts and stroke her thighs. She knew she had never been so completely the centre of attention before. The men standing around were enjoying the picture she made; such a beauty, trussed and displayed, being taken by two men at once.

The men using her started to change position, Charles sliding under her, pulling her back so she was sitting, impaled, on his lap, a quivering butterfly stuck helpless on a pin. Then Marcus coming forward, and Charles leaning back… …so that she ended lying on her back on top of Charles who was pumping away deep in her asshole, Marcus kneeling over her, one knee either side of her slim shoulders, fucking her face. Her head was sandwiched between the two men, she could see nothing but Marcus's pubes, as he kept steadily thrusting into her face. Her tits were completely exposed now, to all eyes except her own of course, and she could feel that men were reaching forward, some caressing and pinching her nipples, others rubbing their cocks on her soft white mounds. Then finally the moment which she had known would come. She felt her feet lifted and spread wide, then even wider, so that she was uncomfortably spread and tried to pull back, but, of course, to no avail. The thick hot warmth of a huge cock against her open pussy. The cock rubbed around her crack, teased her clit deliciously, then pressed up against her virgin pussy hole, testing...... then with a sudden fierce movement it thrust inside her, taking her virginity in a single stroke. There was a slight sting as her hymen tore, and then a glorious fullness; she was now completely stuffed with cock. Three cocks deep inside one young girl, who only a day before had never seen an erect penis, let alone touched one. What a delightful sight she presented to her owners. And oh, how she was loving it! She no longer cared how her passion shamed her; she lifted her hips to meet the cock in her cunt, which alternated in perfect time with that in her ass. The pain had long since subsided; it still hurt, but only in a way that added to her arousal. She felt her body helplessly building to climax and came, in a great wash of orgasm that swept her up and carried her someplace far far away, just as Charles filled her ass with his semen. She lay there at peace, knowing from his thrusts that Marcus would soon climax too, and not wanting it to end. But no sooner had Charles slipped out of her than she was lifted so that another man could take his place, and again her asshole was being filled with hard cock, though now it only hurt a little. Then Marcus came, pulling back so that the semen filled her mouth with its sour glutinous mass. Like the good slave she was she swallowed it down, and started to lick him clean, whilst the men thrust away in her ass and her pussy. But soon he pulled away from her greedy tongue and another cock was in her face, huge and jutting proud, a black cock this time. So she opened up and the face fucking started again. She was getting close to orgasm again from the fullness in her cunt and the knowledge that she really was now just a slave to be used, and she came as Jonathan did, for it was he who was availing himself of the pleasures of her tight pussy hole. And again, no sooner had he withdrawn from her than another man was pushing into her still sore puss.

How long her ravishment continued in this way, Anna was never able to say. Again and again, as a man finished using one of her holes another would take his place. Other men were wanking on her breasts and hair; she gratefully received her Masters' come as if they were conferring a benediction, anointing her with holy water. She was dripping with come, slippery with it. It leaked out of her ass and her pussy. Sometimes, when for a moment her mouth was empty of cock, a man would scoop up a gobbet of spunk from her sodden thighs, and feed it to her. She hungrily lapped it up; she was a whore now, and no mistake.

And so it went on, deep into the night.

And when it was finished they had all had her more than once, and she had never been empty in more than one hole at a time.

When they were finally sated they trussed her in a brutal hogtie; her ankles bound together, then pulled up behind her back to be bound to her wrists. Thus presented and exposed she was lain on the great oaken table, the heavy leather collar still fastened around her neck and linked by a heavy chain to the table leg.

A few of the men were erect again at the sight of the virgin they had turned into an owned whore displayed in such a humiliating state; nipples and pussy lips pink and swollen from use, messy with the semen of over a dozen men, so they stood around her, and wanked off onto her face.

They were about to leave, to sleep in their comfortable beds, when someone remarked, "I think we should equip her with a little treat to remember us by." They were getting something down from one of the wall racks. She whimpered as they showed it to her; smiling cruelly down at the helpless girl: the huge black dildo that she'd thought too large for actual use. It was Marcus who forced it into her cunt, as she moaned in pain and arousal yet again. He strapped it into place.

And so she was left to sleep as best she could, trussed and come-covered and burning with desire from the invader in her pussy. She wanted to stroke her clit, was desperate to come, but she could not. She could do nothing at all. No more than a car can drive itself could this girl act on her own volition. They had made a toy of her, and like any other toy, she was immobile without the guiding hand of an owner.

CHAPTER 5

Anna dozed off and on throughout the short night. She was uncomfortable but she was also exhausted. Sometime in the early hours the fire burnt itself out, and she awoke to the sound of the dawn chorus, the birds singing as though their little hearts would burst.

Not long after, Clara appeared. She said nothing, but gave Anna's arm a quick stroke and started to unstrap her. When she was finally free she tried to sit up, but needed Clara's help. She was so stiff that as she clambered down from the table she stumbled, and would have fallen, had it not been for Clara's arms around her. Clara helped her to her feet and supported her, back up the stairs to Marcus's chamber.

Their Lord and Master was asleep in bed. The coverlet had half slipped back, revealing his tanned skin and honed musculature. Anna thought how fine he looked, the dark body hair on his belly exposed, the top few curls of his pubes just visible.

"Luckily he's a deep sleeper," whispered Clara, leading Anna through to the bathroom. Again the bath was already run. The scented water smelt like heaven to Anna's aching body. Clara helped her out of her soiled garments, and into the bath, explaining that the collar would be left in place; she would never be freely naked, always she would wear this symbol of her servitude. Then she climbed in with her, and the two young girls soaked in the sweet water, soaping each other carefully, Clara remarking with mingled pleasure and concern over the many bruises and lash marks marring Anna's white skin, and how well it suited her to be collared. Suddenly the door opened. Their Master stood there, his cock already jutting from his silk dressing gown. Anna was desperately hungry. Gathering her courage she asked, "Master, please might I have something to eat?"

Marcus looked at her, a smile twitching at the corners of his handsome mouth. "Of course," he said, "you haven't been fed yet this morning." Anna hadn't noticed Clara's warning look. She was about to point out to Marcus that she hadn't eaten since lunchtime of the previous day, but before she could do so he was standing by the bath, his cock poking her face.

"Well, go on then, eat."

He was openly laughing at her now.

Anna was dismayed at her mistake, but opened her mouth and took his cock inside. This time he wanted the attentions of her tongue and lips. Anna played and sucked and licked his fat organ, thinking that maybe if she did a good enough job he would give her some proper food. Whilst she did so he stroked and squeezed her full breasts, which were slippery and prettily pink from the hot water. He came quickly in her mouth, and Anna nearly gagged at the huge load of come. She was so hungry she was feeling a bit queasy already without suddenly having a mouthful of sour, slimy semen.

"Are you still hungry, or have you had enough?" he asked. Anna was about to say that of course she was still hungry, when she saw the twinkle in his eye.

"Because if you want more, I'm sure one of the servants would be happy to oblige."

"No thank you Master," she made herself say, trying to ignore the rumblings in her belly.

"Good. I'm pleased with you both. Here."

And reaching into his dressing gown pocket he handed each of them a chocolate. The girls hungrily gobbled down the treats.

"Now, you may play," he said as they finished.

Clara smiled, without a word bent her head to Anna's breast, and started to suck and flick at the nipple. Anna moaned in delighted arousal, then flushed in shame. It was mortifying to be doing this in front of Marcus. When the men had taken her it had not been her choice, although she could not help but enjoy it she would never have wanted to

46

be used like that, so freely and by so many, if lust had not overtaken her. But this was different. She passionately wanted to make love to Clara, and to have it turned into nothing more than a spectacle for a man's enjoyment was humiliating. But still, she had no choice in the matter. Her nipples tightened under Clara's delicate attentions. Soon the women were enfolding each other in a slippery embrace, hands on nipples, mouths locked, tongues probing. Clara's lips were as soft and pink as a flower. Her tongue drove deeply into Anna's mouth. Then she stood, and rested her tiny bottom on the edge of the bath, spreading her denuded pussy lips to reveal her swollen clit.

"Lick me." Her tone was almost commanding. Anna nuzzled into the girl's pussy, breathing in the sweet musky aroma of her female parts. She stuck her tongue out and gave Clara's clitoris an experimental lick, to be rewarded by a husky moan. Encouraged she started to work all over the exposed perineum, licking and sucking, diving her tongue into the hot little hole. Clara's moans were turning into high pitched shrieks. She grabbed Anna's head and as she climaxed pressed her dripping pussy into her face, rubbing against her hard in frenetic ecstasy. At the same time Marcus spent his load directly onto them, splattering Anna's face and Clara's puss with his come. Like a tomcat marking his territory, Anna thought.

The girls washed each other off. Anna was burning with unsatisfied desire. Marcus frowned, looking at Anna's lush triangle of pubic hair.

"Pusskins, I want her bare," he said. Clara followed the direction of his gaze.

"You would like me to shave her, Master?"

"No. Hot wax."

Clara shivered, but her eyes were sparkling.

"Of course, Master."

"Please Master, no!" Anna had very sensitive skin; it'd been an ordeal for her to suffer the waxing of her legs, but the thought of her pubes being ripped out from her delicate mons and labia was terrifying. But Marcus just smiled, as he gave her face a quick slap of admonishment. The girls got out of the bath and towelled each other. Anna wouldn't look at Clara's face; she felt betrayed. Of course she knew that Clara had to obey her Master, but Anna could tell the other girl was going to enjoy inflicting such torment, and after their lovemaking that felt unforgivable.

Marcus was in a hurry. He roughly pushed her through to the bedroom, lifted her bodily and threw her down on the bed, securing her wrists to the upper bed posts. Clara was preparing the wax. Marcus knelt down above her head, a knee either side of her face. His spent cock rested on her forehead, dripping a little remaining spunk onto her cheek. It stirred again as he reached forward to grasp her ankles, pulling them up to rest on his knees. Anna's pussy was now naked and displayed, held immobile. Clara had the wax ready. She poured a little onto Anna's thick curls, then as it set ripped it away, full of Anna's offending hair. Anna shrieked in pain. Again Clara applied the wax, and again yanked it away. The process was repeated, Marcus helpfully moving her legs this way or that to allow Clara total access as she gradually worked her way over the defenceless labia. His cock was hard once more; he loved seeing submissive women learning their place in life, he loved every whimper. He would probably have loved it just as much if Anna had been totally unwilling, but it was blissfully guilt-free to torment a submissive, especially one as hot as Anna. He could see her clit was glistening with her juices once again; she just couldn't help getting aroused by being helplessly abused, and that was what made it such good fun for the men. He wondered, idly, if she could be whipped to orgasm, and guessed that she could... ...with the right training. And she was certainly in the correct place to receive that training; it would give him a tremendous amount of pleasure, meting it out. Tremendous pleasure. And that, of course, was the whole point. He sighed in satisfaction as Anna screamed, giving full voice to her agony as Clara happily tore yet more hair from her lips. He noticed Clara was taking her time, using rather small quantities of wax, stretching out the process to maximise the pain. That was good. He'd been a little disquieted by the camaraderie that had been so obviously building between the two girls; after this, Anna would know that whilst Clara was undoubtedly a slave, yet there was a pecking order amongst slaves, and she herself was at a very lowly point in the hierarchy. Clara might have to accept whippings from her Masters, but as far as Anna was concerned, she'd be meting punishment out. There would be no comforting arms where Anna could experience arousal without also accepting torment, he would make sure of that.

Clara had nearly finished now. Anna's labia were revealed in all their glory, smooth as silk, (he reached to stroke), and red from the depilation. Tiny pin pricks of blood dotted the newly exposed flesh; she hadn't been lying when she'd said her skin was sensitive. That must have really hurt, he thought happily. His cock was achingly erect, and he motioned for Clara to hurry. It was the work of a moment to strap Anna's ankles to her wrists, then he came round to the foot of the bed, took off his robe and plunged his cock straight into the beautifully denuded pussy with brutal haste. Anna moaned her pleasure. Her muscles were gripping him tightly; she really was a delightful fuck. He got hold of her nipples and pulled, stretching her breasts. Anna whimpered in mixed pain and arousal. He came quickly, her total nudity was so enticing, and anyway he wanted to deny her the release of orgasm; she would need regular reminders that her pleasure was unimportant.

Anna was left tied to the bed whilst Marcus washed and dressed. Clara dressed too, in another slutsuit of Marcus's choosing. This one was black transparent rubber, with a hole at the pussy and zips under the tits for unfettered access.

It had the coyly amusing addition of a pussycat tail in black fur, attached to the ass just above the hole. It dangled down, stroking against Pusskins' naked labia whenever she bent forward. On her head she wore cute little pussycat ears. The Master fastened a lead to her collar and they went for breakfast, Pusskins keeping close to heel, like the trained animal she was.

Anna was hungry and frustrated. But she was also still exhausted from her first night of slavery. The bed was soft and warm, still fragrant from her Master's presence. Despite her uncomfortable position she fell into a deep, dreamless sleep.

It was hours before she awoke. She felt refreshed, though hunger still gnawed at her belly. She had a sleep-sodden memory of a voice calling, and now it came again. Harsh, and just outside her room.

"Hurry up will you! We've still Lord Marcus's suite to do, and quick about it."

With that, the door was flung open and a big, beefy middle-aged woman entered, followed by a scurrying little chamber maid.

"Now what do we have here?"

The older woman approached the foot of the bed, glaring at Anna in disapproval and making no attempt to hide her disgust.

"Looks like a new slut. The Master will have left it here to be punished. You'd better go and clean the bathroom whilst I see to this."

She was already rolling up the sleeves of her uniform. The maid hastened past to the bathroom, her eyes wide in horror in her plain, pinched face. Before she went through she sneaked another look at Anna, and licked her dry lips. The horror was mingled with more than a little excitement.

The big woman was selecting a whip from the stand.

"Here Jones,' she said to the girl, "see this whip? When

it's your job to punish the whores the Masters use, be sure to go for this type. It hurts like billy-oh, but doesn't leave much mark. So you can really put your back into it, because it's the redness they go by, see? The Masters like a slut to look thoroughly whipped. With this one it takes maybe fifty strokes."

With a sadistic smile she started to lay into Anna, who yelped and wriggled as the blows rained down, but could do nothing to escape them. The brutal old matron was an expert, each lash landing at the precise spot she intended. She whipped Anna's thighs and arse, but explained to the girl who was learning her craft that to whip her tender labia was a prerogative reserved for the Masters. By the time she had finished Anna was panting and dripping with sweat. The whipping had made her strangely aroused, and she was now so frustrated that if she'd been able to move she'd have wrenched the whip from the hands of the hag, and thrust it into her burning cunt as an improvised dildo. But no such release was at hand. The two women finished cleaning the chamber then departed, the elder loudly remarking to the pink-faced Jones that all the sluts were stupid whores, beneath contempt, else why would they end up tied on a bed with their arse in the air? The women left, laughingly confident of their own superiority.

They had not been gone long when the Master and Pusskins returned, bringing with them the scent of fresh air and grass. They'd been out walking in the grounds. The Master laughed when he saw Anna's vulnerable body, glowing red and marked by many fine welts from the whip. He traced a welt with his finger, and Anna shivered in pain.

"I hadn't intended that you be whipped," he said, "I just forgot you. It is such a lovely day that after breakfast I took Pusskins out for a little trot. But no matter, I'm quite sure the beating will have done you good. Pusskins, get her ready to be the table slut for luncheon."

Luncheon. Anna was so hungry that even the words,

breakfast, luncheon, were enough to make her salivate. She licked her lips. Pusskins had unfastened her and had gone to run her a fresh bath. Anna knelt on the floor rubbing her wrists and ankles which were pink and sore from her bondage. Luncheon. She licked her lips again and swallowed.

"Are you hungry, slut?"

"Yes Master," she said, very timid.

He came and sat on the edge of the bed near her, reached in his pocket, took out a chocolate.

"Closer."

She shuffled forwards, between his open legs.

"Unzip me."

She did as commanded, his cock immediately nosing out, brushing her face. He was slowly unwrapping the chocolate, close by her nose, close by his cock. He brushed it across her lips. Anna was almost drooling, swallowing repeatedly. She was so hungry.

He laughed, and popped the chocolate into his own mouth, chewing with satisfaction. Anna could have wept with hunger and frustration.

"Get to work," he said with casual malice, pushing his cock against her lips. Anna was so hungry she felt cross and mutinous. Her lips remained stubbornly shut. Marcus's eyes blazed with fury.

Without a word he stood, pulling her to her feet by her wrists which he quickly secured to a strap that hung from the bed frame above her head. Anna was on tiptoes, arms pulled taut above her head. The Master unfastened his belt, slipped it from his waist, and raised his arm. She heard the rush of air and then the blow landed upon her naked rump and she screamed with full voice. Again he lashed her. And again. He was far stronger than the woman who'd delivered her earlier punishment, and he was not holding back. Indeed, he was beating her with every ounce of his strength. Any pride she had once had deserted her now.

"I'm sorry Master. I'm sorry Master," she whimpered in between strokes. He delivered a final uppercut, full on her burning pussy. She screamed again, the tears running down her face, and realised to her shame and confusion that she was close to orgasm from his onslaught.

He reached up, unfastened her, and she fell to the floor, crying and defeated.

He knew she had wanted him to hit her again. He roughly pushed her to her knees, settled himself back on the bed.

"Now. Get to work." Obediently, still shaking with tears, she lapped and sucked with her pink tongue at his cock, which was even harder than before. He did so enjoy beating slaves. She was taking him into her mouth, sucking him in, licking with her tongue, squeezing with her lips. She had certainly learnt fast. To think that she'd been a virgin only a day before. But she had a true intuition of how to please a man; a born whore. His pleasure was immense. She worked away at him, already knowing how to hold him at a burning high point without release for the longest possible time. When finally he came he slipped out of her, to splatter his come over her pretty tear-streaked face. She had earned an orgasm, he decided, but he was comfortable where he was. So he pulled her legs up either side of him, giving him a good view of her pussy with her little arse resting in his lap, her body lolling disregarded, her head by his feet. He inspected her hole. It was red from use and looked sore, but not overly so. Her clit was hugely swollen; he could tell the poor creature was desperate for orgasm. He took hold of it and squeezed. The slaves body shuddered and she moaned. With expert fingers he rubbed in circles keeping a steady speed. She climaxed in a few strokes, and as she did so he shoved three fingers into her tight little hole, thrusting roughly and repeatedly. He knew she'd like that. Then he let her fall to the ground. She scrabbled onto all fours, kissing his feet and thanking him.

He gently kicked her off with the toe of his boot, and told her to go and wash.

This time the bath was a speedy affair. Anna was washed and dried by Pusskins, then led back into the bedroom to be prepared. Special attention was paid to her hair, which was curled into a mass of ringlets then piled high on her head, to hang down here and there in whorish disarray. Her face was painted. Again the huge eyes, again the glossy red slut-mouth. Pusskins delved into the trunk and brought out a leather corset. It was cut to sweep low over the belly and hips, almost a dress, with lacing up both back and front. It had sturdy shoulder straps leaving triangular breast holes. Anna was laced into it, lying flat on the floor this time, Pusskins pulling the laces even tighter than before by standing on her hapless sister-slut. The whore was pulled to her feet, and the Master surveyed his slave. She looked particularly delectable like this, her white defenceless breasts hanging luminously naked between the corset straps, her newly-bared pudenda clearly visible behind the lacing, gleaming with the scented oil he'd told Pusskins to apply. Her waist was tiny. They would keep lacing her into ever tighter corsets, until eventually a man would be able to encircle her with his two hands, a simple act that nevertheless provided a lot of pleasure for a master with its implications of domination and ownership.

The corset garters were attached to fine black rubber stockings, her dainty feet encased in leather thigh boots that laced up at the back. The heels were so high she could barely walk, but then she wasn't going to be spending her time walking.

Marcus roughly pulled her arms behind her back; he enjoyed pulling the straps cruelly tight, again at the wrists and above the elbows. It was a very fine position; extremely dis-empowering whilst at the same time presenting a slave's breasts to best advantage. The slut's huge udders jutted forward, accessible to any man who wanted to squeeze or torment them. Marcus reached round from behind her, caressing gently so that she sighed as arousal began to build once more. He slipped a hand between her legs to assess her excitement; the juices were already copious. Stroking her breasts again he suddenly pinched her nipples brutally hard. She whimpered in pain and shock. Using rather too much pain like that was an ideal way of halting a slave on the brink of orgasm, reminding her very forcibly of her lowly position and the total irrelevance of her feelings, leaving her hot and ready for male usage, eager to please in the hope of being granted the release of climax.

He fastened the lead to her collar and led her and Pusskins out of the room together.

Chapter 6

Anna had to concentrate hard on not stumbling. The Master led them slowly enough down the stairs; after all, property with a broken ankle would be out of service for many weeks, but as soon as he reached the great hall he walked at a brisk pace, his two slaves trotting to keep up as best they could. Pusskins did so gracefully; she'd had many months to become used to the five inch heels she was wearing. Besides, her arms were free, which helped maintain balance. Anna had no such privilege.

The Master led them through the hall, across the landing and into a corridor. Anna could hear the sounds of men enjoying themselves, the hum of conversation. Loud laughter. She shuddered to remember how, in her innocence, she'd found those selfsame noises reassuring when she had first arrived last night. They were led into the dining room.

The men were taking their places at a long table. It was covered with a fine white damask tablecloth, and set with silver and crystal. A chandelier sparkled, beautiful in the flickering light from the fire. There were high, mullioned windows, through which Anna could see only sky. They didn't seem particularly interested in her this time; their minds probably more on their forthcoming meal. Pusskins' lead was taken by a servant, a young man dressed smartly in a white shirt and black trousers, somewhat reminiscent of an Italian waiter. He led her away to the end of the room, where Anna could see a trough, surrounded by half a dozen slave girls, all bending their heads and pushing forward as best they could for their share of the slops. Many had their arms strapped like Anna's, though, it seemed to her, less tightly, and these girls were at a disadvantage compared with the ones like Pusskins whose arms were free. Free to push, free to scoop the food into their mouths like dainty cats using their paws.

Marcus removed her lead, and attached her instead to a

long chain which was fastened to one leg of the dinner table.

"Today you are to be the luncheon slut," he said. "You will be chained beneath the table for the duration of the meal. You will work your way around the seated gentlemen, sucking each Master off, and swallowing every drop of their semen gratefully. You may not use your hands to stimulate them," here he chuckled, as it was abundantly clear that Anna's bound hands would be of no use to her anyway, even if it had been allowed.

'The touch of your hands is beneath us, unless expressly permitted. You will stimulate your Masters using only your mouth and udders, which you may rub against our cocks. If you fail to please any Master you will be taken out and flogged," with a jerk of his head he indicated a strange, curved stand, fashioned from dark wood and dull metal, like an inverted U, which stood, bristling with bondage straps and somehow menacing, a few yards from the table. "And let me warn you, the beatings you have so far received will be as nothing compared to the flogging you will merit if you fail to please."

He laughed.

"Enjoy your lunch, slut. I'm sure you'll have plenty to eat."

And with that he pushed her down to her knees, and kicked her lightly, so that she shuffled off, moving on her knees as best she could, to the darkness under the table.

It was hot under there, in the forest of legs. There was a curious smell, a mix of fine leather, from the businessmen's elegant Italian shoes, succulent food, as the lavish meal was even now being set in front of the diners, and cock. The fine worsted or Egyptian cotton trousers were all unzipped ready for the slut to pay her respects. Erections bristled all around her, each one needing the attention of her plush mouth. Anna wriggled over to the first penis, jutting hugely in front of her, and began to lick. The cock twitched appreciatively as she worked steadily over its length. Then, twisting her head to avoid banging herself against the table, she took it into her mouth. Sucking and licking she soon brought the man to orgasm. His spunk was fouler tasting than usual, but she swallowed it fearfully, remembering the whipping stand. All the time she could hear the Master she was pleasuring chatting relaxedly about his holiday plans, as though she was doing nothing more significant than polishing his shoes.

The next cock was even larger. She had trouble getting her face high enough to take it into her mouth, but no sooner than she had done so than two hands grasped her head in a vice-like grip, and she was being face-fucked. She trembled with the effort of relaxing as the huge member slammed again and again deep into her throat. Finally he came, so deep in her throat that she swallowed without even tasting him.

The scent of male arousal, the sight of the huge naked cocks, the knowledge of her servitude, and above all, the sensation of having no choice as her mouth was stretched and stuffed by cock made Anna burn with unsatisfied desire. She wanted to play with her swollen clit, but could not, trussed as she was. She thought of pressing her dripping pudenda against a table leg or shoe, to rub herself to orgasm much as an animal rubs against a fence or tree to relieve an itch, but the corset was artfully cut just a little too long, laced so very tightly over her thighs that no such action was possible. She would have needed something cock-shaped, dildo shaped, to straddle… …and there was no such object within reach. So she gleaned what pleasure she could by rubbing her aching breasts and hard nipples against every penis she serviced, moaning with pleasure as her nipples glanced over a slippery glans, burrowing her nose into richly scented pubic hair as she swallowed a man to his root.

She continued round the table. Some men just wanted her licking and sucking, others required the depths of her throat for their pleasure. She was still desperately hungry, but as she sucked she was uncomfortably aware that the edge to her hunger was being dissipated by the huge amounts of semen she was swallowing. She felt utterly degraded, to think that she was being fed on men's come. But as the next man orgasmed he pulled out of her, splattering her face and tits. It was quite deliberate. She heard a loud protestation that the slut had failed to swallow, then she was being dragged out by her feet, her breasts scratched as they rubbed against shoes and floor. Her messy face betrayed the truth of the accusation. She started to protest, to explain what had happened, but was met by a slap for her impudence. She looked to see which of the men had been so unfair. It was Sir Jonathan. She could tell from the laughter and general merriment that this was a game he regularly played.

A servant pulled her roughly to the whipping stand. Her arms were unstrapped, but only so that the leather corset could be removed as it would clearly afford her far too much protection from the blows she would be receiving. Soon she stood there stripped, quite naked except for the rubber stockings and heels. Her arms were re-strapped behind her, and for a moment the men simply enjoyed her nakedness, getting the servants to pull her by her hair this way and that, so as they could feast their eyes upon every aspect of their property. She was shivering with shock and fear.

Then she was bent over the flogging stand, her ankles were strapped wide apart, her neck pulled down and her collar clipped to the other side by a short chain, so as she was bent almost double.

Her full breasts were squashed hard up against the cold metal of the stand, but at a word from Sir Jonathan a lever was turned, opening two holes to their fullest extent. As her breasts slipped into the holes they were roughly tugged completely through by another servant. The lever was turned again, the holes shrinking again, until they felt like two hands gripping her tits. And yet further was the lever turned, so now the cold metal had Anna's breasts in a vice-like grip. The mechanism was locked into place, so that there could be no easing of her bondage should she pull against it. She was to be held securely in place by her own breasts whilst they took pleasure in tormenting her.

Her strapped arms afforded her no protection. A hand, or hands, casually reached to feel her pussy, fingers slipping into both her cunt and asshole. She moaned in arousal, and pushed against the fingers that knew so well that she was now a toy for pleasure.

Something was strapped onto her head, some sort of bit. It tasted of leather and metal, and covered both her upper and lower teeth, holding her mouth open. She didn't understand the purpose of it until a chair was pulled in front of the stand. It was perfectly designed to fit up against the stand, and be at just the right height, so that when old Sir Jonathan seated himself, her mouth nestled in his pubic hair. She guessed then that her mouth would be used by her Master whilst she was flogged, and the bit was to allow full access and prevent her biting. Of course, no slave would intentionally bite one of her owners or their guests, but if the pain of a flogging was very great, biting down would be a natural and uncontrollable reaction.

Her cheek rested upon Sir Jonathan's damp and flaccid cock. He got hold of her breasts and stroked them almost gently. Already they were engorged from the bondage, and very sensitive. She moaned softly, in desire and despair. He stopped the stroking and held her left breast still and plumped, as one of the servants reached under to access it. She yelped in pain, as a clip was attached to the engorged nipple. Then her other breast was similarly clipped. But worse was to come. The servants brought short chains, from which were suspended little metal baskets. These were attached to the clips. The weight of the chains pulled down on her breasts, increasing the torment. The function of the baskets was to hold weights. Placing these was the prerogative of Sir Jonathan Sinclair, who proceeded to pile small stones into the baskets. One at a time he added them, each one increasing the pull on her abused flesh. Anna's nipples stretched and ached, but there was to be no release, no respite. When her breasts were stretched to his full satisfaction the old man leant back with a happy smile. Anna knew that the torment had made her even wetter, even hungrier for cock, and she was deeply ashamed.

Then the flogging started. She would have begged for mercy as they beat her, but with the bit in her mouth she couldn't use words, only cry like an inarticulate animal. She bucked in pain, but was held in place, not so much by the neck chain, which had some play in it, but by her tethered, weighted breasts, which hurt excruciatingly as she reared in a futile attempt to escape the lash. The cock against her cheek quickly twitched into life, was stuffed into her helplessly open mouth. Sir Jonathan was enjoying seeing her beaten. A beautiful girl, totally in his power, being cruelly treated for his pleasure. He sighed contentedly and thrust hard into her mouth. Anna whimpered as he grabbed her breasts and held them tightly, using them almost like handles as he fucked her face. Full of cock, her nostrils assailed by the scent of maleness, lashed again and again over her buttocks and defenceless pudenda, her breasts tormented, Anna realised she was going to come. The orgasm was huge, roaring on and on like furious waves breaking on a rocky shore. She screamed her ecstasy, as loud as was possible given the over-full state of her little mouth, and hardly noticed the satisfied laughter which was returned. They had won, and no mistake. Her slut's soul had betrayed her to a life of sexual slavery, and if she didn't know it before, she knew it now. She had orgasmed, not from any attentions paid to her pussy or clit, but simply from the joyous humiliation of being beaten and cruelly used.

She slumped against the stand, exhausted. Several of the

men had finished their meal and they came over to fuck her, entranced by her total defeat. They were deliberately rough, driving hard into her puss or ass; they liked it best that way, and besides, they wanted to see her come again from rough treatment. She just couldn't help but respond, arching her buttocks up to meet the cocks.

Sir Jonathan continued to use her mouth as his guests fucked the slave's other holes. He chuckled when someone remarked how fortuitous it was that females came equipped with three holes for men to enjoy, clear evidence that the almighty had intended them to be used by several shafts at once. Then he came, his spasming cock filling her mouth with a thick wad of semen. She swallowed it down, trying not to gag. It was so unpleasantly thick, and she was so hungry for real food. She was vaguely aware of Sir Jonathan offering his chair to one of the guests.

The position she was in did not allow cocks to simultaneously access both her vagina and anus, so after a moment's discussion a butt plug was selected and began to be pushed into her tight asshole. It was far thicker than a penis, and she wept fresh tears as she stretched to accommodate it. They were saying she was a little too tight for Sir Jonathan, and that leaving the butt plug in place for a few days would loosen her nicely. The thought of this cruel invader in her rear for so long was truly intolerable, and she tried to fight to prevent its penetration. But her puny struggles were greeted with much merriment and easily overcome. Once it was inside her Anna was awash with waves of pleasure, as the men pressed rhythmically on the end of the plug whilst they fucked her cunt. Soon she came again, her moans muffled by yet another cock that was filling her mouth.

Eventually they tired of using her, and retired to another room for cigars and coffee. She had thought that she would be released, or at least left in peace for a while. But no, now it was the turn of the servants. There were strict rules governing servants' usage of slaves in the Sinclair Manor, the principal one being that servants could only use a slave in the period between her being used by the masters and her being washed and prepared for her next usage. In other words, the servants were only allowed to use a slut already sullied by the enjoyment of the masters. Knowing this, and delighting in the fact that she was not to be cleaned up for another hour or more yet, the servants gathered round, unzipping their trousers. The most senior of them got first use of the presented cunt, tearing into the unfortunate slave, hanging onto her breast-handles and enjoying showing the more junior staff just how a slut should be treated. Another used her mouth, adding more stones to torture her breasts, much to the pleasure of all of the men. Those not inside her stood around, wanking onto her thighs and hair.

In her heart Anna knew she shouldn't take the dark, perverse pleasure she was experiencing at being treated like this. Men should accord women respect, open doors for them, buy them flowers. But she couldn't help herself. Being reduced to the lowest possible form of servitude, being no longer a person, but instead an attractively presented set of fuck-holes, being nothing more than a toy for male pleasure… …it aroused her as nothing had ever done before. So again she came, as the cocks thrust and the unkind hands squeezed, and she knew she was a whore.

Eventually it was time for her to be cleaned. She was in a sorry state when she was unfastened. Her lips were swollen, from the repeated stretching around big cocks. Her breasts were red and aching from the metal vice, her nipples scarlet. Across her back, thighs and buttocks were innumerable welts from the whipping. Her pussy was sore and inflamed from so much rough usage. And her asshole was still stuffed by the invasive butt plug.

Pusskins led her upstairs, washed her off without a word. Then she was chained to the foot of the bed, naked except for the leather collar, her ankle cuffs and the cuffs which held her arms behind her back. Her wet hair curling damply down her ravaged back. The plug in her young anus was making it ache, but she could not push it out; it was artfully curved so that her muscles helped hold it inside.

"Try and rest," Pusskins told her. "In a few hours you will be fitted with a collar."

Anna wanted to ask her more. Did she mean a collar like her own? But with a flick of her silky tail, Pusskins was gone, leaving Anna to sleep as best she might on the carpet.

CHAPTER 7

Strangely enough she slept well. Maybe she slept with the ease of an animal, now that she had been reduced to one. She had control of her destiny no longer, and so there were no troublesome choices to keep her awake, no more decisions to be made ever again.

Or so she thought. When she awoke her mind ran over the events of the past day. She could feel her clit swelling, her pussy moistening, as she recalled the way she'd been used and beaten. With her arms strapped behind her she could not reach to touch her pudenda, yet she was burning with desire. Getting to her feet she found the chain was just long enough to allow her to reach her Master's chair. Squatting with her feet wide apart over the corner of the chair, she could rub her burning clit against it. She was so aroused already that soon she could feel an orgasm building, and passion made her heedless of the approaching footsteps on the stairs. Suddenly the door was flung open. In came Marcus, and with him, Charles.

"How dare you! Slut!"

And Marcus slapped her hard across her face, knocking her backwards to the floor.

"Lick that chair clean!"

She wriggled onto her knees and did as they bid her, licking her salty honey juices from the smooth leather, the action reminding her again of how intolerably hungry she now was. If she'd been hoping to persuade them to feed her, being caught attempting to pleasure herself was entirely the wrong way to go about it.

Then the men grabbed her by her ankles, pulling her off the floor. She was frightened and cried out, to be rewarded with another slap. There were chains hanging from the ceiling, and to these she was attached by her ankle cuffs. The chains were widely spaced, so she hung there, defenceless and spread, her head just above the floor, her bound arms behind her, her pussy at the height of the men's waists. They stood either side of her, one to the back, one to the front. She could see Marcus's smart shiny shoes, and elegant trousers.

The position had been chosen to afford the men an excellent view of the girl's genitals. With no wool left on the pink labia she was truly naked. Marcus parted her outer lips, and indicated that his brother should observe. The two of them inspected the condition of their property. The clitoris was fat, swollen with desire.

"A bitch in permanent heat," Marcus again remarked, savouring the phrase and smiling unkindly, and both men chuckled.

They inspected the butt plug, agreeing that if it failed to stretch her sufficiently a larger one could always be inserted. Their father's wishes were always paramount. They poked and prodded her newly fucked cunt, noting that there was nothing left now of her torn hymen, she'd been so thoroughly used by so many in such a short space of time.

Then their attention returned to her clit. She didn't understand what they were saying. Something about modification, experimental procedure, insertion, prototype.

"She has a particularly large clitoris, ideal for such purposes."

"And it's cheap to do?"

"Very. Only a few hundred pounds. And the market value afterwards... ...well, who can say! I predict the demand will be extremely high, we should reap a huge return on our investment."

She shivered. It was at any rate clear that they were talking about doing *something* to her genitals, what, she couldn't imagine. She guessed that it had to be something to further reduce and humiliate and control her, and the thought sent delicious shivers of fear through her displayed puss.

Marcus was absent-mindedly stroking her; deeply involved in the discussion with his brother he'd forgotten for a moment what they had caught her doing. Now he remembered that she needed to be punished, and without warning pinched her clit as hard as he could. Anna screamed in shock and pain.

"Now just look at that!"

The men peered at her pussy, chuckling. Anna flushed with shame; she knew only too well what it was they were now observing. The brutal treatment of her clit had made her pussy sopping with fuck juices, and her owners had a perfect vantage point from which to watch every shudder and tightening of her aroused cunt.

"Where's your other slut?" Charles suddenly asked.

"I left her with Jonathan up her arse and Rick Goldstein in her mouth," his brother replied, smiling at the memory. "Why?"

"I just remembered you saying she was getting ideas above her station. I had in mind some entertainment that might bring her down a peg or two."

Marcus laughed.

"Be my guest. I'll send a message for her to be brought over here once they've finished." He picked up the phone to talk to the staff.

The two men walked through to the study, and started discussing business, leaving Anna hanging like so much meat. Before long there was a knock at the door, and Pusskins was delivered, walking a little stiffly. Marcus was pleased to see she already looked a bit less cocky. He'd suggested his eldest brother give her a particularly thorough beating, and the slut's bottom was red raw from lashes.

"All yours," he said to Charles.

Charles was adjusting the chains that held Anna suspended in the air, shortening them by means of a pulley system so that the spread pussy was at the height of Pusskins' face.

"Get to it, bitch," he said, "lick this slut clean."

Pusskins looked as though she'd like to refuse, and Charles reached out and lightly drew the back of his nails along the welts crisscrossing her rear. She shivered and bent her head to her task. The men watched, reclining on the bed and idly stroking their cocks as Pusskins lapped at Anna's slippery clit. Anna was moaning in pleasure. No mouth had ever tasted her before, the sensation was exquisite and electrifying. She wanted to press against Pusskins' tongue, but she could only hang helpless, accepting the stimulation meekly. Pusskins' pink tongue flicked in and out. She really did resemble an elegant little kitten, eating her dinner.

"Of course, Puss, you know what else cats lick, don't you?"

Charles had come alongside, and was removing Anna's butt plug. She breathed a huge sigh of relief as it was eased out of her sore anus. Pusskins froze.

"That's right whore, get licking the slut's asshole." And by way of encouragement he pushed the young girl's face down to Anna's anus, which was pink and swollen from the stretching.

Tentatively at first, Pusskins started to lick. She was tense, but the hole was clean except for the semen that leaked out of it. Tasting maleness she warmed to her task, her tongue licking and working Anna's clit, and both fuck holes, so that soon Anna was mewing with pleasure. Charles reached for a couple of straps and bound the two girls together necks to hips, so Anna's face was pressed into Pusskins' mons. The scant blonde curls smelt strongly of semen.

"You too, udder whore. Get cleaning her up."

Anna started to lick, and realised that she was cleaning up the come of the men who'd just been using the blonde girl, just as she herself was being cleaned. Could there be anything more humiliating than being forced to eat men's semen from another slave's cunt? The taste made her wetter than ever, keeping Pusskins busy licking her juices, and Pusskins too was now very aroused, her slippery juices tasting deliciously sweet to Anna.

Before long the two young girls orgasmed, crying their pleasure in wild, birdlike shrieks.

The watching Masters were rock hard, and impatient now for a female hole to thrust into.

"How about a double sandwich?" suggested Marcus.

"Nice. You want to fuck cunt or arse?"

"Hmmm, decisions, decisions. Arse, I think. I fancy something really tight round my cock. Shall we stuff them with a two-headed dildo, so their poor little pussies don't feel neglected?"

"Good idea. What do you have?"

"This… …or if you want to make them cry, and their assholes *really* tight……?"

"Oh yes! I like it. The blonde first."

Anna watched as Pusskins was unstrapped and tied to the bed, her wrists to the upper bedposts, her ankles to tethers two foot up the lower bedposts, lifting and spreading her legs so her cunt had no defence. Then she saw the dildo. It was a monster, two huge cocks blending in a smooth curve, one into the other.

Pusskins was writhing and moaning and begging.

"No Master. Please Master. It's too big, I can't take it," she whimpered, but Anna thought she could hear excitement in the petite girl's voice, confirmed when she saw how wet her pussy was again. Dripping to be fucked, she thought.

The men took no notice of her protestations, and the blonde moaned and whimpered as the great dildo was forced into her, but was unable to stop herself sighing with pleasure. Charles held it embedded in the wriggling girl, as Marcus lowered Anna to the floor. He lifted her bodily, and hooking his strong arms under her knees spread her legs and lowered her cunt onto the still writhing Pusskins, so that she was impaled on the monster dildo, pushing her down so she had to take the full length of it, sitting astride her sister-slut. Anna wept, it was too big by far for a cunt that had so recently been virgin, but she loved the sensation too; she didn't care that it hurt, she loved being so full.

Her arms were untied, but only for a moment: the two men busied themselves strapping the girls together, face to face, tits to tits, cunt to cunt. They were strapped at the waist, thighs, ankles, wrists, elbows and neck, by thin leather straps fastened so tight that their tender flesh bulged between the cruel bonds. The monster dildo was now even deeper inside the whimpering girls, quite inescapable, forced into each slave by her fellow slut.

The men dragged the double-arsed toy they'd created off the bed, strung it up to the ceiling by its wrists so its toes barely touched the floor. A spreader bar was attached to the trussed ankles, then opened to maximum extension.

The fuck toy moaned in discomfort and humiliation. They surveyed it with satisfaction.

"A hood, perhaps?" said Charles.

"Of course."

And after a moment a black rubber hood was pulled over the toy's head.

The men raised it so it was completely off the floor, dangling by its wrists. They were happy to see how they had reduced the two pretty girls to a fuck object. Each chose a side of the toy; they could no longer see, nor remember, nor did they care, which side was which, and under the tight black rubber the helpless girls had no idea which rock hard cock was being driven into their own anus, which into their slave sister's.

The dildo was filling them so much that their little asses, tight at the best of times, were now even tighter, but the masters just pressed harder until they gained entrance to what was theirs. Deeper they went and deeper, until each man was buried up to the hilt in the tender toy. Then they started to fuck, and wildly too. This was one of the best fucks they'd experienced; the girls were so lovely, so despoiled, so helpless. And the brothers were savouring both their power and the camaraderie of the occasion.

Anna and Clara were in great discomfort, but deeply aroused. They had true slaves' hearts, and a slave is never happier than when she is being stimulated and beaten for her owner's pleasure. They were so full, the men so rough, it was as though they were being beaten as well as fucked, as again and again the men drove their cocks simultaneously into the owned holes. Their clits were exquisitely crushed against each other and against the impaling shaft, that seemed to fuck them itself as it shifted with the rhythm of the men's fucking.

Maybe it was Anna who started to come first. At any rate, as she did so the involuntary bucking of her hips brought Clara tumbling over the edge into the orgasmic abyss, and as both girls climaxed their little assholes squeezed the invading cocks delightfully, so Charles and Marcus shot their loads together deep inside the girls.

Anna felt her Master slip from her fuck hole. There was a few minutes quiet; she guessed the men were adjusting their clothes. Then their muffled voices, discussing a new contract that Charles was negotiating. They were moving away, into the office. She heard the clunk as the heavy door shut behind them.

Silence. The minutes passed, and she became acutely and uncomfortably aware of every aspect of her body's restraint and recent use. The tight leather bonds at her wrists and ankles cut painfully into her flesh. A warm trickle of her Master's semen worked its way down her inner thigh. Her asshole itself was burning still from the stretching. The dildo in her cunt felt intolerably huge, and she squirmed, attempting to relieve the pressure, but as she wriggled this way and that Clara shifted her weight too, equally uncomfortable and equally keen to lessen the penetration. The dildo shifted slightly, as Anna pulled away, but it was thus forced more deeply into Clara, who then strove to lift herself up and off the massive shaft, so now it was Anna's turn to be penetrated even more deeply.

The wordless struggle continued for some minutes, each girl in turn achieving momentary relief only to endure an even deeper thrust as her sister slut retaliated. Soon they were exhausted, and slumped together realising their struggles were useless. In fact, worse than useless as they were now impaled even more deeply than before.

A click of the door opening, bright male laughter. Charles was leaving, and joking about some business arrangement. As he walked past the hapless toy he reached round it, placed a palm on each girl's tail, and pressed his hands together, hard. The toy yelped behind its hood as the dildo forced its way even deeper into the cunts. Both men laughed.

The brothers said goodbye, and Marcus rang the servant's bell before retiring to his office. He was of course too busy to waste time cleaning the slaves himself.

Anna felt hands tugging the straps that bound her ankles and thighs to Clara. None too gently they unfastened each bond in turn, so that finally the girls were only restrained by their wrists above them, the hood still tight over their heads. Sweat trickled down Anna's face and into her eyes. Now her wrists were freed and she struggled to stay upright, unsteady after so much dark torment.

The hood was pulled from her head, and she blinked in the light, her hair plastered to her forehead and neck in sweat-sodden coils. Her eyes met those of the same elderly retainer who had whipped her earlier. The woman looked at her in undisguised disgust, so that Anna flushed in shame.

"Go and clean yourselves, you dirty whores," she said, and with a jerk of her head indicated the bathroom.

The two sluts walked painfully to the bath and Clara turned on the taps. Anna glanced back and was shocked by the expression on the old woman's face. Such a cruel, mocking amusement. She turned away, slumping to her knees on the floor, but a second later heard heavy footfalls behind her. Before she could turn the old woman reached her bony arms either side of her neck, down to her breasts, and grabbed them roughly, digging her long nails into the delicate orbs. Anna cried out and the old harridan clung with her talons to her nipples, pulling up so roughly that the girl was forced to rise to her feet, sobbing in pain.

"There, you little bitch, don't you ever dare sit without permission whilst your betters are standing again".

The witch smiled with evil glee, before turning tail and marching from the room. Anna stood there, shaking and whimpering, until Clara took her hand and helped her into the bath. They washed silently, both sore and shaken. But the hot scented water and their shared predicament soothed them a little. And anyway, thought Anna, the witch might be a free woman, but she was old, and hideously ugly, and no man would want to fuck her. She and Clara might be slaves, but they had been enslaved because they were so beautiful and desirable that every man alive wanted them on the end of his cock.

They dried each other, then made up each other's faces, sitting in companionable closeness on the soft carpet, still naked from their bath. Anna painted Clara's lips in a pretty girlish pink, but rimmed her eyes with kohl; dark slut-eyes, huge and appealing in their vulnerability, like her own. Clara painted Anna's lips scarlet again, so glossy they looked wet. Anna watched Clara dress, in a slutsuit of baby blue rubber that left her tits completely exposed, and wondered aloud what she herself would be wearing.

"You'll be completely naked. You are to be collared."

"A collar like yours?"

"Yes. Don't be frightened. But you must stay quite still, understand?"

She started to lift her long hair, as though to show something to Anna, but at that moment the door opened, and she let the tresses slip back to her shoulders. Their Master entered, flicking approving eyes over Pusskins' sleek curves before turning his gaze upon Anna, who was still sitting on the floor, quite naked except for her leather collar.

She looked frightened, her eyes wide like those of a nervy female animal. He supposed Pusskins had been explaining what was to happen to her. So he smiled at her, to quiet her, and reached a hand to tug at her collar, so she must rise.

She stood, meek and obedient, as he smoothly ran his hands all over her body, caressing, or maybe assessing, every inch of her, but especially her thighs, upper arms and torso. He stroked her neck absently, then felt the cruel marks the whip had left on her back and buttocks, enjoying the way she trembled but held back from whimpering as he touched the sore skin. She remained motionless as he reached around to cup her heavy breasts, weighing them in his hands, noting how the nipples were still deep pink from the torment they had endured. He could tell they were tender, for as he stroked them she held her breath, but now when he cruelly pinched, as had become his custom with this udder-weighted slave, she did not cry out, but like a docile lamb accepted his right to bully and hurt her little body as he chose. There was just the slightest sound of her indrawn breath as he deliberately twisted the hard buds, enjoying her new submissiveness. He motioned to Pusskins, who handed him the arm strapping device she had at the ready. Pulling the slave's arms behind her he again bound her wrists, but this device had half a dozen straps, reaching from wrist to well above the elbow. He fastened them all, then started to refasten them, this time pulling tighter. The slave's breathing quickened in pain as the leather bit into her tender flesh, her arms drawn back far beyond what was comfortable. A final, wide strap went around her waist, again pulled tight enough to hurt, cinching her almost as a corset would and pinioning her bound arms behind her.

He turned her around and inspected her. The bottom lip was wobbling as she tried not to cry, he noted with satisfaction. She looked very vulnerable, and he felt his cock stir again. No time for that now though, he'd be fucking her again soon enough, and whenever he wanted thereafter until he sold her on, the ceremony was important and could not wait.

"Clips!" he barked at Clara, who passed him a small wooden box. He reached inside, and when Anna saw the object he brought out, her swelling tears overspilled and ran in lovely rivulets down her downy cheeks. The clip was of black metal, similar to those used in offices to fasten papers together. But this clip had a fine row of teeth, and as her Master smilingly let its jaws sink tight into one ravaged pink nipple Anna's tears really started to flow. But still she did not whimper, he noted with approval, idly wondering how much pain she would now suffer in silence. He'd eased the first clip onto its target. He let the second clip bite into her with a sudden snap. That broke her. She gave a piteous yelp of hurt, looking at him with eyes so huge and beseeching that he laughed gently, and kissed her full on the mouth, enjoying her confused response as whilst he kissed her, deeply and passionately, he also pulled on a nipple clip, agonisingly hard. For a moment she reacted as she would have one short day before, responding to his kiss with equal vigour, then resisting him as the pain assailed her… …but only for a moment. She was a slave now, becoming more of a slave with every minute of servitude she endured. So instead she offered her mouth to be kissed, pliant and receptive, perfectly and deliciously responsive but not demanding, asking no pleasure of her own, wishing merely to please. And as for the pain she merely trembled and meekly accepted her Master's will. He was pleased, but not yet finished. Reaching again into the box he brought out a third clip, held it up to the tear-streaked face.

"One more clip," he said, smiling, letting the full import of his words sink home, watching his slave grow pale as he reached down between her legs.

"Open," he commanded, and like the well-trained slut

she now was, she edged her feet wide apart, to allow him the access he needed to abuse her.

He manoeuvred the open jaws into place around her clitoris, then watched her face as he let them snap shut, was rewarded by her mouth opening wide in a silent gasp of agony, followed by an involuntary steady whimpering. For whilst the pain when the clips were first attached was intense, neither did it lessen but rather grew, as the nipples and clitoris swelled against the cruel teeth.

The pain was far beyond anything that might be expected to arouse, and yet he could see her pussy lips glistening wetly in invitation to his cock. Her arousal was, he knew, not entirely from the pain, but more from the knowledge of her helplessness and his total power. He was becoming like a god to her, she was so entirely subject to his every whim that she could not help but worship him. After the ceremony was over he would fuck her mercilessly with the clips still in place, he thought. It'd be amusing to see her distress as she was remorselessly pulled towards orgasm with the little jaws still biting her most sensitive, engorged, flesh. But that must wait. He flicked each clip in turn, so her whimpering increased to a yelp, then attached a metal bar, which ended in a handle, to her collar. The bar had the same function as a lead, but it was rigid. It allowed the wielder perfect control of the slave, conferring the ability to direct her head wheresoever it should be required. essential for what would soon be taking place. Clipping an ordinary lead to Pusskins he led the slaves down the narrow stairs, through the deserted hall where the great log fire still blazed, down the wide sweep of the main stairs and out of the front door.

CHAPTER 8

Anna blinked in the bright light. The sun was high in the sky, and full of power, though it was still spring. It was the first time she had been out of the house since she had arrived, and the first time she had seen the mansion by daylight. The building was entirely of stone and larger than she had imagined, with three floors as evidenced by the high, mullioned windows. The roof was flat, with vastly tall chimneys, and small domed towers set atop. It was beautiful, but despite the decoration somehow stark. Maybe it was just the huge expanse of stonework; when Marcus had described the country house as Tudor she had imagined a whitewashed, half-timbered building, mellow lines, a sagging roof with dovecotes. But this ostentatious grandeur must once have formed the home of an exceedingly prosperous family. She had known the Sinclair corporation was tentacular, but still she was startled to realise just how wealthy her owners were. With that sort of money they must have little problem buying silence, she thought, and for some reason, shuddered.

They were led around the side of the house, through an archway, to the stable block which surrounded a courtyard. Her feet were bare and the cobbles were cold and uneven, though Pusskins was trotting along in stilettos as usual. The chill seemed to creep up through her soles until she was full of it, and shivering. A blacksmith was at work in the centre of the courtyard, shoeing a beautiful grey mare, who was wild eyed and nervous. A groom was soothing the creature, stroking her lovely neck with firm hands, and when she settled the blacksmith tapped the new shoe onto her hoof, quickly securing it with a dozen nails. Quite a crowd of gentlemen were watching, many with slaves on leads. Even the house staff were stood nearby in a quiet group. It seemed strange to Anna. It appeared that all the guests and staff of the Sinclair Manor were standing in the courtyard to see a horse shod. But the blacksmith had finished, and the gentle animal was being led away, and yet the crowd made no move. Rather, they turned their heads to look at her.

The blacksmith reached tongs into the furnace. It was ferociously hot, even from yards away the heat was pushing out at her, full in her face. The tongs were gripping a red-hot finger of metal, which the man hammered, the clatter ringing out across the yard, bouncing back from the walls. He held it near a part-circlet of metal that lay on the bench, as though assessing the size; and then, at last, she understood. She had always supposed that Pusskins' collar had some sort of fastening round the back, a hinge, a padlock, maybe. But the object on the bench was a collar, identical to that which bound her sister slave. It had a wide gap in it, so that it could be pushed onto a slender neck, and then a smaller section welded in place to complete the immovable ring of iron. Where the sections met there were thick flanges of metal, each pierced by a hole, no wider than her little finger. It was through these holes that the small red-hot bolt would be threaded, its heat melting the adjacent metal to form an instant and inviolate join.

Her breath was quickening and she felt faint with fear. The Master handed her rod lead to the groom. She was pulling against it in her terror, her eyes wide with panic. But he slid his hand down the rod till he was holding it just inches from her neck, and began to stroke her hair, all the while talking to her in a soft, almost monotonous whisper.

"Hush now m'lovely. Hush now, we won't be ahurting ye. It's just a tiny bit of metal see, and sure it'll be hot, but the rest of the iron will take the heat as quick as you please, spread it out like. You'll feel the glow of it you will, all around, but not so hot as it'll harm you, not a mark. Old Ben has ringed more fillies than you've had hot dinners, he's been collaring slaves for the Sinclairs since he were nowt but a lad, and he learnt his trade from his da before him. He's never burnt one yet, nor will he burn ye. But ye must stay still lass, ye must stay quite still, and not mind the heat or the noise of his hammer. It'll shake you a bit when he hammers the bolt, but it'll not harm ye, as long as ye stays quite still, understand me?"

Whether it was more his words, or the gentle manner of his speech or just the way he stroked her mane of hair, but Anna stilled, and stood meek and placid once more. Another man unbuckled the leather collar she was wearing, and the groom held her instead by her trussed arms.

"We need to put this hood over ye, my lovely. It'll keep ye safe from the heat now."

And he slipped a thick leather cowl over her head. Then he held her firmly whilst other hands pushed the part-circlet around her neck. It gripped snug against the leather. She could feel the panic start to rise again, but the firm hands were always upon her, stroking her flanks and slipping now into her naked puss, soothing her with steady strokes. Someone refastened the leather collar, then she was led forward a few steps. The heat from the furnace blasted against her bare skin. The leading rod was pushed down, bringing her to her knees, then tugged steadily so that she shuffled forward till she felt her breasts press against a cold block of metal. Then it was pulled forward and down, so that she knelt by the block, her face resting upon it, her neck arched and available to the blacksmith. She felt his hands pressing the small section of collar into the gap. It was a snug fit. Then came the sound of more hammering, muffled by the hood but still she felt the panic swell. And again the groom stroked her arse and thighs, talking all the while in his soft voice, though now it seemed to her as though she could no longer properly hear him, or at anyrate understand the words.

She felt the tongs clank against the collar, and suddenly there was a great heat all about her. She would have struggled to rise but yet the groom stroked her, and now she could hear him clear again as his hand petted her bare thigh.

"Still now lovely. Still. Still."

Then came more hammering as the bolt was set true into the collar, and it did shake her but biting her lip so hard she could taste the iron of her own blood she kept still whilst the fierce heat ebbed away, then waited for a moment in fear, hearing the hammering as the second bolt was readied, and all the while the kind groom spoke,

"Still, m'lovely, still."

Then for a second time a clank as the bolt met the collar and the heat rising around her suffocating so she cannot breathe and must escape, but the hand never leaves her flank, the voice is constant in her ear,

"Still now lovely. Almost done m'lovely. Still now, almost there."

And the hammering, so loud close by her ear. And then silence.

Then the rod was tugged up so she rose, then with a quick downward thrust that almost made her fall her head was plunged into icy water. She bucked in panic, the water rushing in between the hood and her face, she will drown she will drown… …but no, she's pulled upright again, the water running in chilling rivulets over her jutting tits. Shaking uncontrollably, a sudden warmth running down her thigh as involuntarily she pisses.

Cold water down her crotch and legs, making her gasp, as someone, the groom again? washes her off.

He's talking to her again.

"All done m'lovely, all done. It's over now little pet, all done."

As he speaks he's unfastening the leather collar, tugging the hood out and off her head.

The daylight is so bright it hurts her eyes. The groom is smiling at her, reaching in his pocket he lifts his palm to her mouth. She sees he has a sugar lump, and it's for her! She gazes at him with adoring eyes, and he laughs as she wolfs it, feeds her another, then smiling gives her a final stroke, clipping a chain lead to her brand new collar, handing her back to her Master with a final slap on her proud haunches.

"You've a fine one there, Sir."

"Indeed. You did a great job, Joe, I could see how nervy she was."

"Aye, well, the quality ones often are, Sir. They're no different to horses, really, the classy fillies need a steady hand."

Marcus reached in his pocket, passed him a note.

"Well thank you very much indeed, Sir! It's not necessary, really it ain't, I loves my work, but much appreciated all the same." And he tipped his hat to the Master.

"Oh one more thing, Joe… …is the name tag ready?"

"Why yes, Sir. I think Ben's put it on the collar already, see there?"

"Oh indeed. Excellent."

With that he led her off, trotting happily alongside Pusskins. She was full to bursting with happiness, every step bouncy and merry. Her heart was rising on a great glad tide, though she didn't quite know why. But it was neither her mood, nor disposition, to analyse, so she luxuriated in her newfound joy. Her Master was smiling, too.

"I think I'll take you for a walk in the grounds," he said, "and then back to the house for some food," chuckling at the last.

Glancing at her face he noticed she'd turned huge piteous eyes to him at the mention of the word 'food' and he laughed more loudly.

"Yes, food for you too, Toy," he said. "Even pets need feeding".

He took them down a path which led to woods. Great beech

trees, smooth and straight, their roots like massive green fingers digging into the earth. It was cooler here, and Toy shivered, her nipples hard as unripe blackberries, tender and aching from the cruel clips. The air was sweet from the bluebells massed upon the ground. Voices sounded, ahead of them. Men laughing, and the softer noise of a whimpering female. Toy felt her clit throb and ache; it was swelling with arousal at the sound, and the clip bit harder.

Rounding a bend they saw a girl dangling helplessly from a high branch, her feet swinging above the bluebell carpet. She was Oriental, maybe Japanese. Very slight, with firm pointed breasts. She was trussed with thin rope that wound across her body, cutting into her tits, binding her arms behind her, then winding down between her legs. Toy realised with a shiver of scared arousal that the rope was pulling tight between the hairless labia, digging right into the delicate pink flesh underneath, so that almost all of the girl's weight was taken by her most sensitive parts. Two men were amusing themselves tormenting her. Toy recognised them as having been in the group that had watched her collaring; they had had no slave with them then. She guessed they had left the unfortunate girl hanging like prepared meat in the wood whilst they'd watched the entertainment. Now they had devised some entertainment of their own: they were tugging on the slave's feet, increasing the pressure on her already crushed clit and crack so that the creature whimpered piteously.

Marcus felt his cock stiffen in appreciation of the delightful scene. He'd forgotten; he'd been planning to fuck Toy as soon as she was collared and was looking forward to hearing her moan as he stroked her tormented clit. There was still time before lunch. He led them past the suspended girl, casually feeling her sweet breasts as he did so, then on a little way, into a clearing. He pushed Toy down amongst the bluebells, looped Pusskins' lead around a nearby branch. Turning back to Toy he saw how pretty she looked, helpless on her back amongst the flowers, her breasts straining upwards, compelled by her arm bonds to proffer themselves to the viewer, her thighs together in a futile and amusing attempt at modesty.

She looked like the doomed servant girl heroine of some period novel, about to be ravished by a heartless landowner, and he smiled to himself realising the whimsy was not so far from the truth. It pleased him to think of the generations of Sinclair men who had been heedlessly taking the virginity of local maidens, girls who'd expected to marry their sweethearts and work hard, keeping house and raising children, instead finding their destiny was far harder: to be no more than cock sluts for all the gentlemen who visited the Manor.

He wondered how many of them had been deflowered in these very woods; some of the older oak trees had rings set into their trunks that were well over a hundred years old, though the Sinclair family business, trading in female flesh reared locally, exporting it for vast profit to rich men the world over, was chronicled as dating back even longer. From the research he'd done it seemed as though the Sinclairs had been stripping, beating and enslaving hapless peasant girls for several hundred years.

His clients sometimes expressed surprise that the business had flourished so constantly. Under successive kings, queens and governments their wealth had continued to accrue, unchallenged. But the answer was simple enough: no judge, no police chief, no politician was against the Sinclairs as they were all so very keen to be amongst their clients. Few men could resist the pleasure of owning a beautiful female who had no other role or interest than to satisfy their every sexual whim, and the Sinclair slaves were more sought after than any others in the world. A Sinclair slave wasn't considered ready to be sold until the only thought she had in her pretty head was how best to please her Master's cock, and that was exactly how the owners liked it.

A large measure of their resounding success lay in the selection of the girls: certainly they had to be beautiful, but more, they had to be sluts at heart from the start, the sort of girls who played with their pussies alone in their beds at night and got wet panties from a kiss. They were easy to seduce, easy to debase, and at the end of their training were hungry to be fucked and eager to please whatever man they belonged to, whether he was an English Lord in his eighties or a fat arab with a penchant for anal sex.

He roughly forced Toy's knees apart, and stuffed his rod into her pink cunt with a single swift stab, savouring her cries as she had to take the full length of his meat. Pounding into her tight pussy as hard as he wanted to, particularly hard today it seemed, he squeezed her lovely breasts as though they were indeed udders, then tugged on the cruel clips. Toy yelped, but still her little back arched, the better to offer him her cock-hungry cunt. He slipped a hand down, found her clit and stroked it. Already engorged, it grew even fatter, the slave whimpering in distress as the clip sunk its teeth deeper into her most sensitive flesh. His stroking was insistent, rhythmic with his hammering into her puss, and soon she came, screaming in ecstasy and pain, whilst looping his little finger and thumb into the nipple clips he pulled on her breasts as though he held her by reins. He pumped her full of his seed.

He was hungry. He removed the clips (they were more effective if used intermittently) then buttoned himself back up, yanked the slut to her feet and hauled both slaves away, back to the house. Toy skipped less merrily than before; perhaps she'd thought that having been collared she would be treated less cruelly, but of course, the reverse was true. The men would keep hurting her because they enjoyed it, and also because it was an essential part of teaching a slave her lowly place. A slave who is regularly beaten and humiliated quickly understands the lesson that her feelings and desires are irrelevant; pleasing men is her sole concern.

CHAPTER 9

Back in the house he took them to the dining hall. Another girl was being thrust under the table to be the luncheon slut, a pretty redhead with a long blaze of silky hair, and ivory skin speckled with freckles. She looked rather classy to be a whore, the sort of girl one would expect to see being waited on at an expensive restaurant, not bound on her knees under a table sucking off over a dozen men. Toy saw her throat convulse as she came close to gagging when the very first cock she started to service was roughly plunged deep down into her, the laughing owner holding her head in his big, red hands for a rapacious face fuck.

The whipping stand stood gleaming, silently ready for the inevitable victim.

Toy's stomach was rumbling at the smell of the food. A waiter took her lead and fastened her at the feeding trough with the other sluts. She was starving, and pushed her shoulders between the haunches like any hungry animal, jostling amongst the other sluts for her share. The food was a sort of swill, as is fed to pigs, the liquidised remains of whatever the masters had been eating the previous day, sweet and savoury all churned up together. It wasn't very nice but the nutritional value was high and the food was cheap, or rather, free, as it would otherwise have ended in the rubbish. As such it was perfect for feeding slaves. If the Masters had eaten particularly well the day before the food was sparse, the slaves went hungry. But this was all to the good, it kept them lean, and thus pleasing to their owners, moreover, it lent a certain urgency to their daily visits to the trough, so that even when the leftovers were plentiful the trough was licked shiningly clean by the slaves' eager pink tongues. On occasion fights broke out, the sluts attacking with nails and teeth, but this was rare. Aggressive behaviour was severely punished, those involved never again having the privilege of unbound arms and also spending the next four weeks muzzled at mealtimes, which made eating so awkward that they could never get their share before the others licked every scrap up. At the end of a month of such treatment they were very skinny, and very keen to please.

Some Masters preferred their whores to be plumper that the Sinclair house-style, which was slender, either full breasted or slight, but carrying no excess fat elsewhere on the body. The Sinclairs catered for all tastes, so some sluts were deliberately fattened, obviously regardless of their personal preferences, generally just until a full bodied feminine curvaceousness, with breasts of maybe forty or forty-four inches, was achieved. Waists were kept slim by keeping the whore permanently encased in a tight corset.

Occasionally a man might prefer his females to be of obese proportions and again, a girl would be fattened to order. Fattening was generally achieved by giving the whore milk instead of water, and adding lard to her feeds.

Toy managed to wolf a fair share of the swill. The process of degradation had been so swift that she never thought once of how humiliating it was to be fed on animal food, from a communal trough, with arms trussed so she could only lap. She was just so glad to be fed at long last. Nor did she mind the slops, but swallowed as quickly as she could, like any bitch. She was carefully licking the trough clean, when she heard shouts of laughter. Looking towards the table she saw the lovely redhead being dragged out by her ankles, her face splattered with come. Like Toy before her she was protesting, and like Toy she was met with a hearty slap. The men were laughing uproariously, Sir Jonathan at the centre. Shooting his semen over the luncheon slut's face must be a regular amusement, an in-joke at the whore's expense.

The trembling girl was strapped to the flogging stand. Toy felt her own pussy grow wet as she saw the struggling slut's tits pulled through the openings in the metal, the lever turned until she was clamped in place by her soft breasts. One of the visiting gentlemen was taking his place in the face fucking chair, clearly a particularly privileged guest. He didn't weight the whore's tits, but simply squeezed them roughly, kneading the delicate white flesh with his large fingers. Toy suddenly realised it was the same man as had so roughly face-fucked the redhead when she was first under the table. He liked to use his women hard. She shivered, but all the same she looked in envy at the trussed girl who was now the centre of attention. A man was pummelling handfuls of the round buttocks, enjoying the snowy whiteness. He stepped aside, making way for a man carrying a braided stock whip. He raised it high, then brought it down on the proffered arse with his full force. The bound girl screamed and bucked, and Toy saw how cruelly the clamped tits pulled as the girl tried to escape her torment. But of course, there would be no escape. And when the man reached his fingers into the creamy labia to see if the slut was aroused, they came out dripping with her fuck juices, much to the amusement of the gentlemen. And so the beating went on, the little arse patterned more and more with the red welts, until the slave no longer bucked, but hung limp and heedless as the blows rained down, mouth passively accepting the cock that filled her to the hilt.

Having flogged her into exhaustion the fucking began, men lining up to drive their rock hard cocks into her tight holes, her asshole and cunt shafted again and again. The whore came, moaning and arching, loving being so stuffed, careless of her degradation. Toy could see the come trickling out of her pussy, a thick river on her slender thigh.

"Hey chaps, look at this one, she can't take her eyes off that slut, what's the betting she's wet again?"

It was Charles speaking. Toy had been so entranced by what was happening to the other whore that she'd not thought to hide her interest. Too late she realised her mistake, as Charles and Marcus pulled her to her feet and half lifted, half dragged her slight body onto the dining table, clearing the dirty dishes to the sides by pushing her into them. The two men each grabbed an ankle, pulling them apart and up, so she was fully spread. She wriggled in arousal as old Sir Jonathan approached to inspect her puss. She knew he'd find her sopping with fuck juices and indeed, when he slipped a finger between her labia it came out wet, an unspoken invitation to them all to fuck her. Sir Jonathan licked his finger and smiled. He thrust three fingers into her little puss hole, then brought them, glistening with her own wetness, to her mouth. Toy didn't have to be told. She opened her mouth and lovingly sucked and teased his fingers, running her tongue over them as she would a cock. Then, to her surprise and embarrassment, the old man bent his head and spreading her lips began to lick her pussy. The touch of his tongue was exquisite. Toy writhed in ecstasy as he flicked her clit again and again with consummate skill. Within moments she felt her body building to orgasm, and then she came, great buffeting rolls of pleasure that peaked repeatedly as she shrieked in passion. She assumed this was a prelude to fucking, but no, now Charles took the old man's place, his head sunk between her soft thighs. Her clit was ultra-sensitive from the orgasm, but writhe as she might she was held so tightly that she could not escape the probing, flicking tongue. The stimulation was unbearably acute, so she moaned and whimpered and yet still she could feel another orgasm building and in a few minutes she came again, arching and screaming because it was so sharp and clear. She slumped back, exhausted. Then she saw Marcus take Charles' place. He took her swollen, tender clit full into his mouth and began to suck on her sweet fruit. The sensation was extraordinary. Little electric tremors passed through her like ripples, as the stimulation overloaded her sensitized clit. And yet as he continued, sucking and lapping at her pussy, circling her clit with delicate precision, again she felt an orgasm build, inexorable inside her, and she squirmed as the pleasure spread through her, whimpering and gasping with the intensity when the wave finally broke.

Surely now they would start to fuck her? Not yet it seemed: as Marcus moved away his elder brother Jonathan went down on her. Spreading her lips wide, pulling them taut so her engorged clit jutted proud, he swept over her puss with the flat of his tongue, spreading the delicious waves of sensation all over her plumped pink flesh. Rhythmically he stoked her, then dived his tongue into her burning cunt, repeating his attentions until eventually she was wrenched to orgasm for a fourth time.

Completely spent, she looked at her four owners with adoring eyes, but already they were turning away, resuming their conversation about oil refineries, letting her legs slump over the edge of the table still spread; she was too exhausted to close them. But she would not be neglected, no: a group of the guests gathered round her, and she shivered as the big, florid man who'd used the redhead so brutally came to the foot of the table. He had no interest in supping on her, he wanted her little body impaled on his huge cock. Grasping both her ankles together he yanked them up above her, pushing them towards her so her tender puss and asshole were raised for him to plunder. He paused for a moment, undecided as to which of her holes to enjoy, then thrust hard into her cunt, so forcefully that she gasped as he sank right to the root in his first plunge. He hammered roughly into her pinioned body, his meat filling the whole of her young puss, pushing down on her ensnared ankles with one hand and with the other manhandling one of her pretty breasts, squeezing the soft orb with his fleshy, rough hand. Helplessly she was brought to a climax in moments, but he was not finished and continued to thrust mercilessly into her tight fuck hole, bruising her swollen clit as he sank himself up to the hilt, again and again. She could feel the swell of another orgasm rising in her, when abruptly he withdrew, but only for a moment. Toy yelped as he forced himself into her tiny asshole in the same heedless manner, pushing steadily into her, making her take all of his hard rod. He continued to pound her as mercilessly as he had pounded her cunt, making no allowance for the inexperience of the young girl he was using, enjoying himself immensely as he felt her muscles gripping his cock and the melting softness inside her. It hurt, and Toy was crying, but unbidden desire grew within her, she could not resist the waves of sensation that flooded through her from the brutal usage, and she climaxed for the sixth time, screaming in mixed pain and pleasure.

Then another man climbed onto the table and knelt over her face, impatiently stuffing her mouth with his cock. Her legs were released and someone else, she couldn't see who, took his place between them and inside her, stretching her cunt with cock once more. Again her ankles were pulled up and apart, but this time they were spread so far that she writhed in discomfort, but could do nothing to stop the inevitable enjoyment of her young body by the gang of big men. When one man finished another would take his place, using her as the sex toy she now was.

Eventually they were all sated for the time being and a servant led her off to be cleaned up ready for the evening's entertainment. He took her back to Marcus's chamber, and through to the bathroom, turning the taps on full so the water thundered into the big bathtub and the room filled with steam. Then he turned back to Toy, unzipping his fly so his long cock sprang out, already fully erect.

"Bend over," he commanded.

Toy had been expecting to climb straight into the sweet waters, she had forgotten that servants were just as likely to use her as gentlemen, whenever the opportunity presented itself. She bent over, resting her hands on the bench that curved round the bath. Unceremoniously he shoved his cock into her pussy, fucking her efficiently so he orgasmed in moments, and withdrew, leaving her aroused but unsatisfied.

Then he fastened her collar to a long chain in the wall, unstrapped her arms, and left.

Toy climbed into the bath and sank back, letting the water rise up to her neck. Her pussy was sore from so much rough use. It seemed strange to think that only a couple of days ago she'd never had a man inside her and now she'd been fucked by dozens, in every possible way; thoroughly transformed from virginal innocent to come-fed slut in a matter of hours. She felt the collar, smooth and immovable at her neck. The knowledge that she was now no more than property scared and excited her. That there was no way back from this dramatic fall in status was confirmed by the obvious permanence of the collar, she was a slave, a fuck toy, an object: her breasts, cunt, asshole, thighs, all had only one purpose: to provide pleasure for men. And this bath, it was not for her own enjoyment, it was just to ready her for more use, to maximise the enjoyment of her owners and their guests.

She started to soap herself, carefully cleansing her holes, shampooing the stickiness of dried semen from her hair and breasts, making herself worthy of her Masters' attentions. Finishing quickly she stepped out of the bath and caught sight of herself in the tall mirror, naked and slender, her breasts so very big, her eyes so very soft and gentle, that the collar looked perfectly fitting, as though she'd be born for this role, could have had no other destiny than sexual slavery. She felt herself grow aroused and would have stroked her swelling clit, delighting in her own body, but already she knew her body was hers no longer.

Never again would she touch herself without her owner's permission, and somehow the thought made her feel deeply peaceful. She finished drying, then painted her face in the way Pusskins always did, with the huge, dark slut-eyes and the red, glossy slut-mouth. Then she repainted her nails, finding a liquid scarlet that matched her lipstick, and carefully applying it to fingers and toes.

Her hair was drying into soft waves which rippled down her back like a dark waterfall, glossy under the lights. She brushed it carefully, and had just finished when she heard the door in the bedroom behind her.

It was Marcus. He smiled when he saw she'd prepared herself.

"Good, little pet," he said, "you're learning fast."

And reaching into his pocket he fed her a chocolate, unwrapping it for her and offering it to her mouth. Toy took it delicately with her soft lips. Instinctively she knew better than to use her hands. Marcus sat down on the bed, pulled her gently onto his lap and stroked her kindly.

"How's your pussy?" he asked her.

"A bit sore, Master."

He pushed her back so that she was lying on the bed, her arse resting in his lap. He carefully spread her labia and inspected her hole, running a finger round it to assess how tender she was.

"You'll do fine for tonight. You'd have to be a lot sorer than that before we rested you. It's pleasant, anyway, to know that a slave has taken so much cock that she's got a continual reminder of it."

Under her buttocks she could feel his rod growing hard again, pressing up at her through the soft fabric of his trousers.

"You may pleasure me with your mouth," he said, lying back on the soft bed, "and your hands."

Toy carefully unbuttoned his trousers and released his proud shaft. She held it with both hands, one above the other and bent her head to lick the glistening glans. In many ways she was still ignorant; so much of her recent experience had been of being used, she had yet to learn her trade. But what better way to be trained than by pleasuring a Master? Marcus instructed her as she worked his cock, and she quickly built her repertoire of skills.

"Tonight you and Pusskins can pleasure me together, and

she can teach you all she's learnt. You'll be schooled in that way and others for several months, until you're as accomplished a whore as can be found. Now, I want to come, and you will swallow every drop, then thank me, understand?"

Toy dutifully sucked the delicious cock. It was so big and smelt so good, she lapped and sucked and tongued the perfect organ until she felt the spasm of her Master's orgasm, then swallowed his load with gratitude.

"Thank you, Master," she said, wholeheartedly.

"Now lick me clean."

"Yes, Master. Thank you, Master."

And she bent her pretty head to the task.

Marcus sighed in satisfaction. He really did enjoy his work. What occupation could be more pleasurable than training a beautiful young girl in the complex art of pleasing men? The soft hair draped over his thighs, her white breasts, still enticingly whip marked, brushed against his balls as she concentrated on her task. When she was finished she looked at him, ready to serve him in whatever way he should command.

"Lick my asshole, slut."

He rolled over. Immediately her soft hands were tugging at his trousers, pulling them down to bare his buttocks. He did nothing to help her. She had to learn, after all. He felt her pause. His arse was bare, but his asshole was out of sight between his hard, muscular buttocks. If he'd wanted to adopt a more open pose he would have done so, she reasoned, correctly intuiting what he wanted. He felt the cool of her palms spreading his cheeks, then the sweet warmth of her hot pink tongue was lapping at his hole. His cock stiffened again, and the whore knew her job without having to be told, working her mouth and tongue over the whole of his genital area, licking and sucking his balls, tonguing his asshole, burying her little face in the fragrant hair at the root of his cock as she sucked and licked at him.

Shrugging his trousers completely off he crouched on all fours, permitting the slut full access to his cock. Soon he was rock hard once more, her mouth slipping between his cock and asshole and balls, already skillful at balancing the pleasure between them, stimulating each area with exquisite licks and sucks, fondling with her hands when her mouth was centred elsewhere. Nor did she rush him to orgasm with rough strokes, but held him suspended in deep pleasure for a long time, till finally he'd had his fill, and grabbing her little head between his two strong hands sank himself deep in her throat, shooting his load into her.

He lay back, gratified, and smiled at the slut. She looked ridiculously happy, and he laughed to see how well she suited her whoredom. He was ready for a nap. Pulling her to him he was quickly asleep, her soft cheek resting on his curly groin.

Toy slept deeply, as contented as any bitch on her Master's bed.

CHAPTER 10

She awoke to find him stirring beneath her. He stretched happily, and looked at the clock.

"Nearly dinnertime. Tidy yourself carefully, you are to be displayed tonight."

Toy carefully repainted her lips and wiped a smudge of kohl from below her lids, then added a little more around her eyes. She brushed her long tresses so they gleamed. Her Master opened a drawer next to the bed and reached inside. Not needing to look he found what he wanted: two clamps to screw onto her sweet nipples. Toy sat passively as he fastened them upon her, tightening the screws until she whimpered. He handed her a heap of glossy, scarlet, rubber clothes, and told her to dress. First stockings that ended mid thigh, then a garment like a swimsuit but with holes for tits and genitals, so that nothing important was covered, only displayed. Scarlet rubber stiletto boots. Finally a rubber hood that completely encased her head, with only a hole for her hair, which hung out in a long ponytail. There were holes in the hood at the nostrils so that she could breath, but no mouth hole, instead there was a soft gag that sat on her tongue like a flaccid cock. There were no holes for her eyes.

She didn't like the hood. It was frightening to be unable to see. The Master clipped a lead to her collar, and led her carefully down the stairs, through the hall where she'd first been stripped and enjoyed. She felt the heat of the fire on her exposed flesh as they passed by. Then down the passage to the dining room.

Marcus entered the room, returning the friendly greetings of his colleagues and clients. The tall, clear Perspex stands were already in place he saw with satisfaction, one either side of the table. He handed the slut's lead to a waiting servant, then supervised the trussing. Toy was pushed to the floor, and strapped in a brutal hogtie, ankles and wrists together, bound by tight black leather straps. Then she was lifted onto the stand, a silver-striped pole which ended in a small, transparent, curved platform from which protruded an inflated rubber dildo. She was pulled and pushed onto it, unable to utter more than muffled whimpers with the gag in her mouth, until her spread perineum rested on the platform, the dildo deep in her cunt. Chains from the ceiling led to her collar and bound limbs, ensuring she remained upright. A soft rubber butt plug was roughly stuffed into her anus through a hole in the supporting platform, screwed firmly into place. She made a delightful sight, her creamy young skin gleaming in the fire and candlelight, the red rubber shinily gracing her lovely curves, her huge tits with clamped nipples jutting forward so attractively presented to all comers. Marcus motioned the servants to connect the tubing that ran to the mouth gag, butt plug and dildo.

The dainty redhead who had earlier been used as the luncheon slut was being mounted on the twin pole. Dressed identically, the girls formed a pretty pair of matching ornaments for the diners, the hoods rendering the female forms pleasantly anonymous, simply sexual toys to amuse. There was little left to distinguish the two females; Toy's udders apart, there were only subtle differences: the colour of the manes of hair in the ponies, the ivory skin of the redhead and a certain slender delicacy of her arms and thighs.

Suction cups were being fitted over the naked breasts. A few more connections, then the hydraulics system was ready, and the pump switched on. Tremors shook the displayed slaves as the dildos stuffing their cunts, assholes and mouths swelled with air. They would have cried out as their tender pussies stretched to accommodate the now huge shafts penetrating deep inside them, but their mouths were gagged by similar devices, no longer lolling soft, but hard and filling their tender spaces. The suction cups pulled the tits like grabbing hands, elongating them into cones. Toy felt her pussy rush with fuck juices as she was stuffed and tugged.

Then, abruptly, the suction released its grip on the girls' breasts, the dildos slackened. But the respite was only momentary, again the dildos swelled, again the suction cups squeezed. The sequence was repeated: relax, swell, relax, swell… …the helpless girls were being thoroughly fucked by a machine. Each time the dildos swelled they grew ever so slightly bigger, mimicking a cock thrusting deeper and deeper into vulnerable female flesh.

Marcus adjusted the controls. The machine was now fucking at full force and speed, the cunt-dildos stuffing the girls like a huge, rough man, their little assholes and mouths similarly used. The suction cups squeezed the tits like cruel, heedless hands, working the soft orbs like a milking machine. Indeed, Marcus chuckled to himself, the apparatus had been modified from one used to milk the Manor's herd of jersey cows.

The gentlemen stood about in companionable groups, sipping their aperitifs and making jokes about the whores. They gathered round the stands, the Perspex platforms giving them unimpeded views of the huge, swelling dildos. The platforms had holes through which the clits jutted, plumped by arousal as the young girls were rhythmically stuffed. The men carelessly flicked the sensitive organs, laughing as the sluts shivered with desire, unable to protest. Toy felt something smooth and icy cold against her clit; it was the edge of a man's wine glass. Noticing her shiver of desire he trailed it repeatedly back and forth over her swollen bud. It was enough to push her over the edge into orgasm, her whole body shaking as she reached an intense climax, the machine stuffing her without pause.

The men would have known she'd peaked even if she hadn't been shaking like a storm-battered leaf, because of another amusing aspect of the design. Tiny electrodes inside the dildos detected the involuntary contractions of an orgasming cunt, relayed the signal so that now the first stripe of the stand was brilliantly lit up. The men laughed uproariously, as though someone had scored a goal, and as the machine continued its inexorable fucking they took turns at teasing the exposed clits, licking them, rubbing them with ice cubes from their drinks, pinching them. Blaze, the little redhead, stiffened in ecstasy as she too was transfixed by orgasm. Then the food was brought in, and someone had the bright idea of fastening clothes pegs to the whores' swollen clits, so that they wouldn't be neglected whilst the gentlemen enjoyed their meal.

The remorseless machine-fucking was irresistible. Within minutes both girls had climaxed again. As their flesh was now exquisitely sensitive from orgasm, the swelling dildos inside them were almost beyond bearing, but there was nothing they could do, they had to take it. They were only playthings after all. If their mouths hadn't been stuffed they would have been screaming their ecstatic abandon with full voice, any modesty they once had, any sense of shame at their obvious enjoyment of their humiliation, long since abandoned. Both girls were truly born to be whores.

As Toy orgasmed again the men started taking bets on which girl would reach most climaxes. The clothes peg was painfully removed and she felt a soft wetness at her clit. Two servants had been assigned to hasten the stuffed girls to orgasm; they stood by the poles, lapping away at the presented nubs, soon to be rewarded by their quivering and jerking as the sluts came yet again.

So the evening wore on. The time between the orgasms grew longer, as the girls gradually became exhausted. After several hours they slumped limp on the poles, almost unconscious, still being stuffed by the machine but long past responding to it. Even cruel pinches of their little clits brought no reaction. The ornaments had been well-matched: the two teams had drawn level.

The machine was switched off. There was no response from the sagging bodies as they were lowered to the ground, unstuffed and untied. Pulled to their feet they staggered, then collapsed. So the gentlemen had the servants strap them together, arse to arse, thigh to thigh, neck to neck. Tight leather straps were buckled around them, biting in to the pale flesh. Their waists, thighs, ankles, wrists and upper-arms were bound together. It was delicious to handle their unresisting limbs; they were as compliant as sex-dolls but delightfully real.

Their wrists were brought together and fastened to a chain that hung from the ceiling, pulled high so their dangling toes just skimmed the floor. The men paused to admire their handiwork, another pretty double-fuck toy had been created.

Someone took off his belt, lashed it with full force into the naked breasts, one side, then the other. The toy barely twitched. Again and again he brought the hard leather down in stinging blows, whilst his colleagues rubbed their hard cocks through their trousers, then started unbuttoning and unzipping their flies. A spreader bar was attached to the unresisting ankles, then lengthened to maximum extension, the pussies perfectly accessible to the thrusting cocks that now wanted to enjoy them.

The fucking began. The girls could only hang there, bound and still blindfolded by the rubber hoods, as cock after cock thrust into their spread pussies. They had no idea who was fucking them, they were long past taking pleasure from the shafts that pushed into their tight holes. Each man was enjoying himself using them, and that was the point. It was a salutary reminder to the sluts that no matter how much they loved to be beaten and fucked, the point of such usage was not their pleasure, that was irrelevant. The point of their enslavement was male pleasure. The world they had entered was divided into the godlike creatures who owned them and their lowly selves. They existed to serve, and for no other reason.

Come ran down the toy's legs, pooled on the floor. One after another the guests enjoyed the soft cunts, until all of them had had at least one side of the object, many of them both. Lighting their cigars they moved off to the drawing room, where they'd chat and drink whilst maybe watching a little more entertainment.

Now it was the turn of the servants. Not that the girls could tell who was using them. It was just more cock shooting more come deep inside them. They were sore now, and the semen burned hot on the delicate, ravaged flesh as it trickled out. Again and again they were fucked, until every male member of the house staff had been inside them, their fellows meanwhile clearing away the dishes.

Finally they were lowered to the floor. But there were still men nearby for whom they could provide pleasure. Still strapped, still reduced to a single fuck toy, they were carried off, one man holding the spreader bar, another the trussed wrists. Doors banged, then a cold breeze blew, icy on the bare skin. Nipples clenched to tight buds. Then through another door, and a close warmth, thick with the smell of animals and the sweetness of hay. They heard the familiar clank of chain as again they were dangled from the roof, then without pause more cocks took turns at their sweet cunts, thrusting so hard they would have gasped if their mouths hadn't still been so stuffed they could only moan. Toy bit down hard as a particularly large meat rod was rammed into her in one swift movement, her breasts roughly squeezed by the man who was at the same moment fucking her slave sister. She had no idea she was being enjoyed by Joe, the groom who had handled her so gently when she was being collared, her tits assailed by old Ben, the blacksmith. Joe thrust into the toy as hard as he could, enjoying his turn at mastery. There was a time to be gentle with a whore, and there was a time to let her know she was just a cock-slut, and Joe had no trouble in distinguishing the two occasions. He would enjoy breaking in these two fillies and no mistake, he thought, as he hammered the tight hole.

A few more men enjoyed them. The stable lads and farmhands took their turns. And then at long last there were no more cocks wanting pleasure from the bound bodies. Again they were taken down, carried a short distance, and again the wind blew icy on their bare flesh. Cold cobbles under Toy's breasts as they were dumped on the ground. Rough hands untying them, stripping off their slutsuits and hoods, until the girls found themselves naked excepting only their iron collars, sprawled in a heap on the cold stone of the courtyard. It was deep night. The stars wheeled in the heavens above them. Toy saw a tall figure, black against the lit barn, then yelped in shock as she was blasted with freezing water. The two girls clung together as they were remorselessly hosed down, all traces of spunk washed from their thighs, tits, hair. Toy yelped louder as she was seized by her sopping mane and the nozzle of the hose unceremoniously stuffed into her sore cunt, then quickly withdrawn and pushed into her little asshole. Blaze was similarly cleansed. The girls had been expecting the sweet baths and softly carpeted rooms that had always before followed the men's enjoyment of their lithe bodies, but something had changed; what, Toy did not know.

They were dragged to their feet by their collars. Toy recognised the groom who had steadied her whilst she was collared, but his face was shut, no kindness in his eyes now. They stood together shivering as he fastened their wrists behind them, clipped chains to their collars and led them back into the barn. Without a word he fastened the chains to a ring let into the wall at the end of a stall, then left them there, stabled on rough straw between two of the horses, and without a backward glance went to his bed.

CHAPTER 11

Toy slept deeply, until the bright spring sunlight fell fierce on her lids. She stretched stiffly; her arms and legs ached from the bondage of the day before. When she rolled over she realised her pussy was still sore, not surprising really, considering how many cocks had enjoyed her. She felt a swell of pride at the thought; lots of men had found pleasure in her yesterday. She looked down at her lovely body, her full breasts marked by the lash, the bruises where she'd been roughly handled, her slender waist, her naked mons. It was a strange thing: in a way the men were working to remove her innate intelligence, to rework her as the animal she was inside, and yet her intelligence was sharper than ever, but entirely focussed on her new role. So now, looking at her marked body she didn't see herself as she would have just a few days before. Instead she was able to see herself exactly as her masters would, feel their pleasure in her enslavement. She was like a fine instrument, attuned to play only one note, but to hold it with exquisite skill and accuracy. She was degraded, that she knew, but she exalted in it exactly as her owners would, because so much of herself was now subsumed in them.

Blaze was stirring. She was one of the most beautiful girls Toy had ever seen, and she gazed at her, almost in awe. Such a wondrous thing is true female beauty, freely given with nothing held back, given for ever, to a man or men. The dark red hair fell down over her shoulders in soft, lustrous waves. Her skin was pale as milk, pure white where the sunlight fell upon her, delicately freckled with speckles as on a sparrow's egg. Her breasts were full, but lovely hemispheres with little pink nipples, not udders like Toy's own. Her mons was as naked as Toy's, but her secret inner lips protruded dark from her plump outer labia; whore's lips. And the whiteness of her sweet flesh was so prettily marked by the lashing and belting and fucking of the previous day that Toy felt her own lips grow wet. Blaze opened her eyes wide, deep green they were, the colour of seaweed that is still underwater, vivid, glowing. She smiled at Toy, and Toy smiled back.

Toy wriggled over to join her, and the girls lay against each other, enjoying the smell of the sweet straw, the musk of their own fresh clean young bodies, the softness of their girl-skin.

"What will happen next?" said Blaze.

"I don't know. I know nothing. I've only been here… …two days, maybe three."

Toy felt confused. Days, nights, nothing was clear now, all blurred into one vast sensate ocean of feeling, thrusting cocks, lashing whips, tumultuous orgasms. It was as if she'd stepped from one world into quite another.

"I'm not sure how long I've been here," Blaze replied. "Maybe two weeks or so?"

"What were you before?"

"Before they made me a whore, you mean? Oh, I was at college. I was doing a dissertation on local history. I came up here to ask if I could see round the house."

"What happened?"

"They showed me round. Every room seemed to have a girl, being whipped, or being tied and fucked. And yet they all seemed so… …peaceful, somehow. As though they were quite at home. Content. I was going to go, but then there I was in the hall, and old Sir Jonathan, he told me to kneel. I don't know why I obeyed him, but I did… …it just seemed right, somehow… …fitting. And he took out his cock… …I'd never even seen a cock before! He was so big! He rubbed it in my face, told me he was my Master, told me to suck… …so I did. And I liked it. Then they beat me, and whilst they beat me they played with my clit until I came, and I found I liked the beating, too. I didn't know I would like it, but they seemed to know, they seemed to know almost as soon as they looked at me."

She turned to look directly at Toy, with her huge, green, bewitching eyes.

"I think we are born to be whores, you see. Only we don't know it, until they show us, show us our selves, our true selves. But somehow they know, they know right from the start."

She shivered, though it was warm in the stable, the space full of light. Dust motes were dancing in the sweep of sunlight, crazed and random, moving with no purpose. Toy shivered too; she was caught up in something too big to understand, buffeted by powers she couldn't comprehend. Still, the stable was warm. She snuggled closer to the other girl, nestling together like animals in a den.

Metal shod feet clattered in the yard outside and the big barn door swung open. A man stood there looking down at them. The light behind him, Toy could see only the bulk of him, knew nothing of his features, but then he stepped forward and a shaft of sunlight fell across his face, and she saw it was the groom, Joe.

"Now then, m'lovelies, let's be having ye."

Both girls wriggled to their knees and quickly stood. By now they knew better than to be slow in response. Joe's words had been gentle enough, but they could hear the steel threading through his command and had no intention of courting a beating.

He was eyeing them appraisingly. Standing so close to Toy that his belt and trousers brushed against her hip, he ran his hands along her limbs, assessing her strength, perhaps; she did not know. Then his rough palms traced over her shoulders, buttocks, inner thighs, the calloused skin scratchy against Toy's softness. She stood meek, and did not flinch nor try to pull away, but held still whilst his fingers brushed over her breasts, the thumbs rubbing over her nipples repeatedly till they stiffened into jutting buttons. Then his hands moved down to her asshole and cunt, already slippery in response to his touch, and she suffered herself to be penetrated by the thick fingers of both hands, first one in her ass and two in her cunt, then having ascertained her size, two in her ass, four in her cunt. She moaned a little at that, but if he heard her he made no sign, but continued his business, methodically examining the property. He squeezed her cheeks to open her mouth, looking at her fine, white teeth and stretching her lips uncomfortably wide with his fingers, as though deciding just how big an object she'd be able to suck upon.

Abruptly he was done. Wiping his hands on a cloth that dangled from his belt, together with some implements that she could not guess a use for, and a whip, whose use was all too apparent, he moved on to Blaze. The delicate redhead stood as still and meek as Toy, but like a classy horse she stood taut, shivering slightly as the hands that inspected her roamed with proprietorial confidence over every inch of her flesh, sizing up her mouth, pressing into her pussy and ass with no more concern or emotion than a man might show when checking the health of a mare. Watching the male hands on the acquiescent female flesh Toy felt her pussy grow wetter yet, and unthinkingly she moved forward, gently nudging her head against the shoulder of the man in a spontaneous plea for attention. He glanced at her in amused surprise.

"Patience little whore, they'll be something stuffing your wet cunt soon enough, don't ye worry."

She stepped back, abashed. So he thought that was what she was after? But what *had* she been wanting? Her face reddened, realising he understood the depths of her desire better than she did herself, though if she'd been able to be objective about it, she would have seen this was quite unsurprising. After all, though he was still a young man Joe had been handling whores for most of his adult life, some ten years or so, whereas Toy had only been a whore for a matter of days.

He was finished with Blaze now, and had moved over to the wall, where hung an assortment of reins and bridles for the horses. Perhaps he would be taking them for a ride, thought Toy, imagining cantering around the estate, like some modern-day Lady Godiva, on the comely dappled grey mare in the next stall.

Joe returned, and slipped a bridle over her head. Toy was so startled she pulled sharply away, to be met with an angry, 'No!' and a harsh slap across her backside. She didn't need telling twice, and stood compliant, submissively waiting whilst he fastened buckles, adjusted straps, until the headgear was properly fitted.

It didn't hurt, but fitted snugly and securely over her face and neck. The straps were of strong black hide, but trimmed with softer, finer leather so that they did not chafe. They held in place blinkers, that had just the same function as those on a real pony; she could see, but only a narrow strip straight in front of her. Her mouth was still free, but not for long: Joe carefully selected a bit of smooth iron, slipped it between her lips, buckled it firmly in place. The metal lay heavily against her tongue; it tasted like blood.

Next came the harness, straps that led down from her shoulders, between and either side of her full breasts, pushing them together and meeting in a wide waist band whence other straps led down next to her naked pussy lips, around her upper thighs. Straps at her back wrapped tightly round her arms, trussing them neatly out of the way so her tits stuck out in a pleasing fashion, her shoulders well pulled back. On her feet high stilettos.

Joe stood back to admire the effect; she would make an excellent trap pony. He tethered her to the wall, and turned to bridle the sorrel. She was nervy, trying her best to hold still, but tense, frightened. He stroked her flanks, letting his hand slip between her legs to find her slippery clit, and worked her steadily and firmly, standing behind her so she could feel the hard bulge of his cock through his work trousers, and reaching his other hand round to her front to gently squeeze and play with her tits. He brought her to a climax in minutes with the efficiency of an expert mechanic tuning an engine. Relaxed and adoring, the delicate creature stood calmly now whilst he fastened the bridle over her sweet face, slipping his fingers into her mouth, so she tasted herself on his hand. That always seemed to steady them, he wasn't sure why, but it was a trick he'd learned from old Ben and it'd not failed him yet. He put an iron bit between her pink lips, buckled it into place.

The dark bay was pulling against her tether, clearly disgruntled. Jealous, he thought to himself, chuckling, what a cock-hungry slut that one is. He looked at his watch: he was still early. Leaving the sorrel bridled but unharnessed he unzipped his trousers. Coming up behind the dark bay he felt for her hole. She was ready, as he'd known she would be; he pushed the full length of his huge cock into her tight cunt in one single practised movement. She gasped in shock, but immediately arched her little arse towards him, so as to take him as deeply as she could. He fucked her steadily, reaching to fondle the tits and clit as he had her. In a minute she was orgasming, shrieking with full voice. He shot his load deep into her hot puss and withdrew, returning his attention to the sorrel.

She was perfectly submissive as he strapped her into the harness, adjusting it carefully so that it was snug round the tits but not over tight. When he pulled her arms behind her and strapped them into place she looked superb. The stilettos completed the tack. He took both ponies by their reins, and led them out into the chill of the morning.

The sun was still low, and most of the courtyard lay in deep shadow. But the patch of cobbles in front of the stable was in full sunlight, and above them the sky arced, pure and blue as a dunnock's egg. A little trap stood ready, a homely affair that was just used for training, slightly shabby, but well-made and serviceable enough. It was Joe's own, and he enjoyed running ponies in it, pretending he owned the elegant fillies that the Sinclairs stocked.

He harnessed the two whores between the shafts. They were both shivering in the fresh air, but a quick trot would soon stop that. Climbing onto the trap he gave a practiced double flick of his long whip, catching both mares nicely on their naked rumps. They started, a little panicked, understood what was expected, and set off.

At first he took them slow, letting them get used to the weight of the trap, the pressure of the harnesses, the high shoes, but they settled in well enough, and he soon decided to hurry the pace up, letting the whip lick them to a trot. He drove them round the estate, admiring the fine curves of their bodies, now glistening with perspiration; they were unaccustomed to being worked. He practiced manoeuvring them, teaching them to turn with a pull on the reins, and was pleased with the speed at which they learnt. Really they made a very good pair. He wished very much he could own two such himself, and idly dreamed of days spent driving the trap, and nights spent filling tight young slave cunt with his meat, but no, he was just a trainer. Still, they were his to train and fuck for several weeks now, and he'd turn them into a perfect pair in that time. Hopefully they would be sold on as a pair, but he knew all Sinclair sluts had pony training, wherever they were destined to go, whomsoever they were destined to please. Some owners would never use them to pull a trap or cart again, but even so, it was an essential part of the training of a Sinclair slave; no girl ever forgot being used exactly as an animal is used, it worked better than simple whipping and banging for teaching a whore her lowly place.

He flicked his whip harder, testing out how fast they could run, and the trap rattled merrily along, gathering speed as the sluts strove to go faster with each expertly directed lash.

They were panting now, heaving with the effort, and their backs were running wet with sweat. He wheeled them sharply around with a firm tug of the bit into Toy's soft mouth, then drove them full tilt back towards the house, lashing them again and again so as they belted into the courtyard like the wind and pulled to an abrupt but tidy halt in front of the stable. Sir Jonathan Sinclair was waiting for them.

"Good morning, Joe! That was a cracking speed. Do they handle well?"

"Yes indeed, Sir, I've not trained a finer pair. They're both so young and straight limbed and dainty like, they don't put a foot wrong and they're learning quickly."

"I'm pleased to hear it," the old man was checking the bits, probing the mares' tender lips with his fat-knuckled fingers, "and such pretty fillies, too."

"Aye. Classy-like, both of 'em. Are you wanting one now, Sir?"

"Not just yet. Shaft them yourself and give them a thorough whipping, then send them up to my rooms midmorning, after you've got them cleaned up. About ten, perhaps?"

"Certainly, Sir, ten o' clock it is then."

Sir Jonathan ran a proprietorial hand over the still heaving udders, pinching the pink nipples hard so that both slaves gave a soft whimper, then strode off to the house. Joe unfastened them from the trap shafts, led them into the barn, and removed their bridles and harnesses.

He plucked a handful of fresh hay from the manger and started to rub Blaze down, calling for a stable lad to see to Toy. He was only a boy, maybe eighteen or nineteen, with dark curls and a cheeky smile. Despite his youth he was stocky, with a barrel-like chest and thick, powerful thighs. As he rubbed the sweat from her smooth flesh he looked her full in the face, his eyes seemed mocking; they had none of the hopeful tentativeness with which a boy usually gazes upon a lovely girl. Toy understood the look, and the casual, knowing way his hands roved over her most private parts: he was one of the many who had had her the previous night. When he had finished drying her off he pushed her down flat on her back in the straw, unceremoniously pulled his cock from his bulging trousers, spread her knees and had her for a second time. He finished too quickly for Toy to orgasm and she felt cross and frustrated to be used in such an offhand manner by a youth. Somehow inherent in her submission had been an expectation that it would be to older men, men for whom she had an innate natural respect; it was mortifying to be forced to serve a callow youth. Something of her sullenness must have showed in her pretty face, because the boy was glaring at her.

"You'll show me proper respect, whore!" he said, and before she could reply let fly with his whip, bringing it snaking over her creamy thigh and catching her clit, hard, with the tip. Toy yelped as streams of pain seared through her pudenda. The young man smiled, and repeated the lash with equal precision; this time Toy screamed. Joe looked up from where he knelt on the straw, his shaft deep inside the moaning sorrel, who was obediently crouched on all fours, her knees on a straw bale so that her arse was presented high: she was halfway to standing on her hands. Without breaking the steady rhythm of his deep fucking he laughed to see the hapless Toy, struggling to protect her clit from the onslaught:

"That's right Thomas, teach her a proper lesson. Hang her from the roof, spread her legs with the wide bar and let her have it right on the nub."

Thomas had a mean smile on his face as he followed the instructions. Toy was whimpering and pleading with her young Master, but it was too late, pity would not move him now. Besides, he would enjoy hurting her.

Soon she dangled from her wrists, her toes swinging free above the floor. He started to attach the spreader bar and she cried piteously in discomfort and fear. Soon she was immobile. He reached for his whip and then paused, hanging it from a nail at the end of the stall. Coming up to her so close that she felt the hard bulge of his cock pressing against her through his trousers he started to caress her with a brutal thoroughness, stroking her nipples until they were stiff, wandering over her breasts and thighs. He bent down, and fastened her swinging ankles to the wall behind, then harshly rubbed her clit till she was moaning, and he could see that it was well swollen. He picked up his whip.

His first blow caught her square on the nub. Now she was spread her labia did nothing to soften the impact. Fastened to the wall, unable to move or even swing from the blow, she took the full force of his considerable anger entirely on her most sensitive spot. She screamed in pain and terror, and he laughed and lashed her a second time. She was still screaming when the third blow caught her, licking viciously around one tight pink nipple. Then the fourth, again on her clit. Then the turn of her other nipple.

Toy had sustained many lashings since she'd entered the Sinclair mansion, but none before had been inflicted with such merciless cruelty and accuracy. Between sobs she tried to beg him to stop, but he paid her no regard. She looked over to the groom for help, but he was still steadily stuffing the redhead. Besides, she realised in shamed horror, he was watching her beating with obvious enjoyment.

As the man continued to whip her she understood how wrong she had been not to accord him the respect his sex and power was due, she must honour all her Masters. Although he was young he was already finely attuned to the nuances of slave training: he saw the new respect in her eyes, and that she had stopped her wild begging and instead was striving to submit with as much meekness as she could muster. He stayed his hand, and bent to inspect her bruised flesh. There wasn't much damage he saw with satisfaction. Joe and Ben had taught him well; how to whip to inflict maximum pain with minimum real damage. She'd find walking painful for the rest of the day, and it'd be a while longer than that before she'd take much pleasure in being used, but in a few days her clit would be perfectly healed.

His cock was rock hard; he'd very much enjoyed beating such a lovely girl. There was no disrespect in her eyes now, not a shred. She looked almost worshipful. Unzipping his trousers he thrust into her again, ignoring her gasps as his hard rod bruised her abused clit, and in three strokes shot her full of his spunk. Withdrawing he lowered the chain that suspended her, and wiped his moist cock off on her tits. She had been used, in a manner even more casual than before, but this time she had learnt her lesson. When he untied her she half-knelt, half fell to the floor at his feet, kissed them reverentially and with bowed head sweetly intoned, "Thank you, Master."

Both men chuckled in pleasure. Breaking slaves in was a job like any other, but it held its own, special, rewards.

Joe set to, beating Blaze as instructed by old Sir Jonathan. There was no call to beat her, she had behaved with impeccable submissiveness, meekly accepting the touch of cock and whip, but the old man knew his business, he'd specified a thorough whipping and a thorough whipping was what she would get. She was dangled from the rafters, and Joe laid into the delicate body with a lusty stroke, sending her swaying like a luscious pendulum with every hard blow. When he'd finished and was satisfied he'd done a good job, as confirmed by the tracks of her tears that flowed freely down her velvet cheeks, he pulled both girls out to the yard, and held them by their tethers whilst Thomas hosed them down, soaking them with cold water, cleansing their hair, tits, thighs, then, as Joe had done the night before, forcing the spurting hose into cunt and asshole. In a matter of minutes both sluts were clean and fresh. They were given some time to tidy themselves, to dry and brush their long tresses, then their arms were strapped behind their backs, chain leads were clipped to their collars, and the exquisite pair was led barefoot through the yard, and into the house by a back door. A house servant took their leads and with an unnecessarily rough tug, pulled them after him, towards the suite of rooms occupied by the Master of the house, Sir Jonathan.

CHAPTER 12

They stopped by a grand doorway on the first floor. A soft knock, and it was opened by another servant, or maybe she was a slave, Toy was uncertain. She was unbound, and dressed normally, except that the elegant cream cashmere sweater that fitted her so beautifully had two perfect, round holes, through which her large, satiny breasts hung, naked and accessible. With a courteous smile to the manservant she took their leads and led them into an antechamber, clipping them to a stand, somewhat like a hat stand but far heavier, that stood in the centre of the room. Apart from that one item, there was no furniture. Without so much as a glance at the nervous sluts, she left through a doorway ahead of them, passing through quickly so that the girls had no more than a momentary glimpse of what lay beyond.

The room they were in was warm, the carpet so soft and plush beneath their naked feet that its opulence was almost ostentatious. A faint hint of perfume hung in the air, sweet, almost cloying. There were paintings and arty photographs on the walls; Toy looked at them, and shivered. She had thought before that the old man seemed to have a particular taste for cruelty, and the images that surrounded her seemed to confirm that. Girls bound, gagged, stretched on beds or hung from beams. Everywhere rope cutting deep into delicate female flesh, everywhere thighs spread and pussy lips stretched around dildo or fingers, and everywhere the whip. One particular painting caught her eye. A large breasted girl, her head loosely hooded. Standing barefoot, her arms behind her, likely tied. Seeming somehow very alone… …maybe that was just the way the figure did not fill the whole of the large canvas, but seemed to float in the centre of the plummy background, lost. But what caught Toy's eye, and made little shivers of fear, or perhaps it was actually arousal, tingle along the length of her supple spine, was the way the girl's breasts were trussed. Fine rope pulled tight around the stems of the generous udders, so that they were cruelly pinched into taut orbs, the nipples jutting erect and vulnerable. And the tip of a whip lash lying snake-coiled on the bound breasts added more than a touch of menace. And yet the girl stood so meek and passive. Even with her face covered Toy could see there was no fight in her, rather complete acceptance of her pain and humiliation. That was why it was so frightening, she thought, turning away, and realising with a sudden start of shame that her fuck juices were dribbling down her bare thigh.

She had been so absorbed in the painting that she hadn't heard Sir Jonathan enter the room. He was standing quite close in front of them, eyeing Toy with a knowing expression, his mouth twisted slightly up, into a smile that held no warmth. He let his gaze flick slowly to her glistening thigh, then to the painting of the breast-trussed slut, then to Toy's tits, then back to her face, deliberating showing her that he had seen her arousal, and knew exactly what had inspired it. Toy blushed in confusion, and he laughed out loud. He unhooked their leashes from the stand, and led them into the room beyond.

It was a bedroom, of sorts. There was a great four poster bed, with huge carved posts of dark old oak, as old as the house. The carving was obscene: giant phalluses sprouting from goat-men impaled tiny maidens, bound females with dangling breasts took men in their mouths and cunts, girls dangled by their ankles as their arses were whipped. Oh, the Sinclair tradition was an ancient one, alright. It gave Sir Jonathan Sinclair untold pleasure to use sluts in this bed, knowing that his father, his grandfather, his great-grandfather... ...and so on, right back for seventeen generations... ...had each been doing just the same before him. An unbroken line of sex slave traders, whipping, fucking, degrading pretty girls, shooting come on their faces and stuffing them with cock, for over four hundred years. It was undoubtedly a dynasty to be proud of.

There were other furnishings in the room, some of them with clear and common purpose: a desk, table, several chairs. But there were also things that Toy didn't recognise: a tilted table-like object, strange stands. The walls were dark red, covered with an old embossed paper, and oak panelling, almost black with age.

Sir Jonathan chained the young slaves to the foot of the bed, undressed and lay back on the velvety coverlet.

"You may pleasure me," he commanded, "and be sure you do it to my satisfaction, else the consequences will be severe."

He smiled to himself. Of course, no matter how well the girls performed their duties the outcome would be the same, but they needn't know that. It would add to their concentration on the task in hand if they believed that by working hard they might avoid a beating.

He settled back, closing his eyes, feeling the mattress shift slightly as each girl climbed up, one either side on his feet. There was the shortest of pauses, then he felt the delicious softness of a plush young mouth on his cock, a hot wet tongue on his balls. His mind drifted, floating in the luxury of the tender flesh that existed entirely for his pleasure, the sluts sucking and licking, flicking their tongue tips against his glans, paying their utmost respects to the swelling cock in their certain knowledge that this rod ruled them, enjoying and tasting it as though it was the most delectable of ice creams. Whores for such a short length of time, and already so expert! He inwardly congratulated himself on managing such an excellent training facility, world renowned; in fact, world leading, and not by a small margin.

He was rock hard now, and wanted to stuff a tight wet hole.

"You," motioning to Blaze. "Open your mouth. You, my asshole." This last was to Anna.

Pliant as ever, Blaze opened her little mouth wide, tensing as he quickly filled her to the hilt. His pubes scratched

116

against her lips, his balls dangled over her chin. Toy leant forwards. With her hands still firmly trussed behind her she could not part her owners buttocks, so was forced to press her face hard against them, butting him like an animal, pushing steadily until she felt her outstretched tongue touch his puckered flesh. She licked obediently, horrified to find her pussy growing still wetter with desire, not because she enjoyed licking the old man's anus, but because she was so aroused by her utter degradation. Before long he climaxed, sending some of his load spurting down into the redhead's belly, pulling out so that her face also received a thick hot splattering of his come.

He lay down, quite comfortable, with his groin still resting on Blaze's little face, completely covering her. Then he rolled onto his back as though using the girl's face as a cushion.

"Clean me, slut."

Toy obediently bent her head and licked the spunk-matted pubes, the soft shaft, the wrinkly balls, pitying poor Blaze who was being used so unreflectively.

The old man reached to yank on a bell-pull that dangled at the bedside. A tinkle sounded close by, and a door opened, the bare-titted servant appearing.

"You called, Sir?"

"Yes, Rebecca. Kindly take this slut back down to Joe. Tell him she has failed to satisfy." Toy could hear a chuckle in his voice, his amusement at his own lie, saw it reflected in an unkind smile on Rebecca's beautiful face. He was sliding off Blaze, pushing her off the bed.

"Certainly, Sir. And the other one?"

She didn't even bother to look at Toy.

"I'll be seeing to her myself."

"Very good, Sir." Rebecca was smiling outright now. Toy trembled, understanding that she had somehow drawn the shorter straw, and that Rebecca was pleased about it. Perhaps Rebecca was jealous of her breasts; her own were large and lovely, but not as full, nor as perfectly firm, as Toy's own. Or maybe it was the lustrous length of her dark hair. She couldn't guess, but she knew enough to be frightened.

The woman left, leading the sorrel whore by her leash. Toy was left alone with the old man. He swiftly dressed, then motioned for her to come and stand by him. He buckled a leather cuff round one wrist, then the other, reached to pull chains that dangled from the ceiling, clipped her wrists so she stood, feet together on the soft carpet, arms high above her head, but splayed a yard apart. He bent and cuffed her ankles, fastening them to chains that led to iron rings set into the floor. Now she was standing with her feet apart, her body and legs forming a narrow X. He pressed a switch on the wall. Slowly, with a grim rattle of iron on iron, the chains began to wind up, wrapping around spools that were out of sight, above the ceiling, under the floor. Toy felt herself lifted off the floor as the arm chains shortened, her arms forced wider apart. At the same time the ankle chains were shortening, so her feet which had been comfortably placed maybe a yard apart were pulled further and further open. Soon she was stretched, no longer a narrow X but a wide one, suspended taut as a violin string. He sat comfortably back in an easy chair, watching the machinery do its work.

Toy started to mew, though more in fear than discomfort, and was flooded with relief as he pressed the button again, bringing the chains to a halt. He stood, towering above her, despite her feet being well clear of the ground. He stuffed a soft gag into her mouth, buckled it tight behind her head, so that the leather bit into her cheeks. She was still mewing softly. He squeezed a bulb that hung from the gag and she felt a rubber cock grow to thick life in her mouth. Reaching for a whip he lashed her puss with full force; an open mouthed cry escaped past the gag. He squeezed the pump again. Her mouth now felt as stuffed as if a huge cock was using it. He lashed again; she could only moan piteously.

Satisfied that the slut could now neither speak nor cry above a whimper, he blindfolded her, then pulled a heavy leather hood over her head, strapping it tight at the throat.

His cock grew rock hard as he looked at her, fully stretched, naked, accessible; totally under his power, helpless to hinder him using her pretty flesh to satisfy each and every whim. He pressed the button once more, and watched her carefully. A spasm of shock rippled through her; she had thought he had her as tight as he wanted. Not so; that was why he had gagged her. He alone would be the arbiter of how tight the chains would be pulled, her feelings on the matter were irrelevant.

Toy felt herself stretched until she would have screamed, but her mouth fully stuffed, could offer only a helpless groan of protest. The chains clinked and ground, slowly pulling her wider. Then he must have pressed the button again, for all movement stopped. A hand slipped between her open thighs, the fingers slipping between her labia to fondle her pussy. She already knew she was dripping with fuck juices; the hand wiped itself dry on her tits.

There was a pause, the noise of something heavy being moved, dragged into place below her. After a moment she felt something pressing at her pussy. Not a cock, this was very cold and hard as rock or metal. The dildo gradually rose into her, quite slowly, but steadily. It was steeply tapered, so as it sank deeper it stretched her cunt wider. She could only whimper as the monster slowly stuffed her, within a minute she was stretched wider than ever before, helplessly impaled on the huge object. She burned with desire. Still it rose higher within her, until she felt the cool of its hilt press hard against her inner lips. Next it was the turn of her asshole. Again the hard chill and the irresistible pressure, her tight anus forced to take the cruelly large plug. She squirmed in involuntary resistance, but it was futile; soon she was stuffed as never before.

She felt something scratchy against her breasts, hands

adjusting, tugging. Suddenly she felt her breasts squeezed as though fingers were encircling them and pressing hard, but as the line of biting pressure continued, increased and deepened almost unbearably, she understood what was happening. Her breasts were being trussed, exactly like the girl in the painting. Fine rope wrapped around them, pulled tight, digging into her softness, forcing her gentle titties into taut hard balls of owned flesh. The cord was tightened to her owner's satisfaction, then he took his hands away.

Bound, stretched, stuffed and helpless, unable to see what would happen next, unable to utter more than a pathetic mew, any tears she might cry hidden by the hood, the slave could only wait in fear for her Master's next act.

It seemed an age that she waited. What he was doing she had no idea. Maybe he was just watching her, enjoying her degradation and helplessness, savouring his power. Maybe he was talking to a client in another room. Maybe he was pulling on his cock, enjoying her flesh without blessing her with the touch of his organ. She did not know. Then, all at once she felt hands caress her aching breasts, stroking tenderly, gently rubbing her nipples into hard nubs, a mouth, licking and circling as a hand slid down her smooth belly to rub her clit. She was getting close to coming, would have arched her puss towards him if she could but move, her slut juices tracking a familiar trail down her soft thigh, when abruptly the touch ceased.

The briefest of pauses, then fire shot through her nipple as a clamp was clipped into the tender flesh. Then her other nipple suffered the same heartless treatment. But worse was in store: with a flash of pain that made her bound body buck, a clamp closed its teeth into her bruised clit. There was a flicker of cold against her breasts, something attached to the clips, pulling softly. It felt like slim metal rods were hanging from her nipples. Then another was hung from her clit.

The slut was trembling, and Sir Jonathan unzipped his trousers to ease the uncomfortable pressure on his swollen cock. He took one of the larger weights, slid it into place on a nipple rod, and smiled as he saw her flinch. Next the other nipple, and then the clit. Oh, she really didn't like that, she didn't like that one bit. He chuckled at the muffled cries and began steadily piling on the weights enjoying her feeble attempts to pull away, no more than flickers of movement, stretched as she was into helplessness.

More weights. Her bulging, strapped breasts were swollen and pink now, amplifying the torment of the weights on her nipples. Her clit was already sore from the expert ministrations of young Thomas, he was being particularly cruel to choose such a punishment at such a time, but the lesson that her body was but a toy for male pleasure was one that needed to be drummed into a slave until it was as automatic as breathing, and the more a slave was aroused by pain, the harder she must be punished to make that lesson perfectly clear. Unfortunately for Toy she got aroused at extremely rough treatment, so it was necessary to be exceedingly cruel in order to teach her how irrelevant her feelings were.

Besides, he was enjoying hurting her. He added some more weights.

When her most sensitive flesh was abused to his complete satisfaction he reached for a whip, and laid into her with full force. The impact of the blow made her body sway and the suspended weights swing, nicely maximising her torment. He let the lash snake over her buttocks and thighs, stinging her pale flesh into red welts. Then lashed her front, enjoying her muffled yelps as he flogged her breasts and pudenda.

He used so much force his arm soon tired, so he rang the bell pull, and passed the whip to the lovely Rebecca, who began her task with obvious enjoyment. She was a strong woman, and able to beat the slave for a long time without tiring, and each lash bit harder than his old arms could manage.

The sad little mews coming muffled from the hood made him chuckle some more. Yes, the slave wouldn't forget this lesson in a hurry. She'd been pliant enough before, but now she'd be completely broken into her new role and would just need occasional reminders that her pleasure and feelings were unimportant, as she continued her training as a sex toy.

Eventually he decided she'd been flogged enough; he always took great care of his property, and would never instigate or permit treatment that might lessen a pieces value. He sent Rebecca from the room, and left the slut in her bondage whilst he did some work, chatting on the phone to a few, select clients who needed to be honoured with direct contact with the company president. When he was done he glanced at the immobile slave, and felt his cock stiffen at the sight. Her breasts were looking uncomfortably swollen, and the weights were dragging. Time for a taste of the carrot, he thought, and unclipped the clamps from nipples and clit. Her sigh of relief was audible despite the gag and heavy hood. Then he removed the butt plug from her asshole, and lowered the iron dildo that had been filling her young cunt. He started to stroke her breasts.

The slave was one of the best he'd broken in. A merest touch of his wrinkly hands on her bound breasts and he could feel her arousal start. It was delicious how much ill treatment she enjoyed; one of the hottest whores he'd handled. The combination of the uncomfortable trussing and his mild touch was enough to make her pussy freshly wet, as he found when he slipped his fingers gently into her opening. It was also delicious how tight her cunt remained; despite being brutally stuffed only moments before, she gripped his solitary finger as strongly as most cunts gripped a cock.

He was rock hard now. He unbuckled the hood and

removed the gag from her mouth, but left the blindfold in place. He steadily stroked her nipples until she was moaning and trying to offer him her cunt.

"You may speak, slave."

"Thank you Master." The response was immediate, and exactly as required. He intensified his stimulation of her nipples so that she would know that she was pleasing him.

"Have you any feelings you would like to express to me about the punishment I meted out to you?"

"I thank you for it, Master." His cock twitched at her words, a quick learner indeed, she was a whore by instinct sure enough.

At that he bent his head and sucked upon her nipple, making her tremble with delight.

"What is your sole purpose?"

"To give you, and any others you choose, pleasure, Master."

She was having trouble talking; the words came out interspersed with little gasps of desire.

"And if it pleases us to hurt you?"

"I wish only to please you, Master."

"Do you consent, then, to my using your body in any manner I wish?"

"Of course Master. I belong to you."

"Excellent. You please me, slave."

He was slackening the chains till she stood, a little shaky, on her two feet once more. Then he released her arms, and her ankles, though leaving them cuffed. She was weak, and he lifted her light body easily onto the bed, laying her on her front, clipping her wrist cuffs together so her hands were fastened behind her once more.

Toy's bound breasts ached exquisitely under her. Sir Jonathan was rubbing her pussy, bringing her juices to her asshole. She lay submissive and unresisting whilst he gently pressed his shaft against her tight, puckered hole, slowly entering her, gradually burying the whole length of his cock inside her arse. He started to fuck her with a firm, deep rhythm, his weight on hers further pressing her bound breasts, the movement of his fucking pulling them like a strong tide, back and forth over the velvety coverlet. The sensation was delectable, the rubbing of her nipples alone might have brought her to orgasm, combined with the thick rod in her ass it was unavoidable. She climaxed uttering wild little shrieks and her spasming asshole brought her Master to fulfillment. He lay still in her, stroking her bound udders, then pulled away.

"I need you to sign something."

The words seemed nonsensical, jarring echoes of her former life. She was no longer Anna, she was a toy, a pet; how and why would her Master wish her to sign anything?

She sat up, a little awkwardly as her hands were still bound. He unclipped them, handed her a pen and sheet of paper.

She started to read it.

"Just sign. In your old name."

She did as she was commanded. He took the paper away, re-clipped her hands and rang the bell pull. Rebecca appeared, her footsteps soundless on the plush carpet. Her eyes flicked over Toy's lash-marked body, rested with malicious amusement on her trussed breasts which were now aching and swollen, hard and reddened. Deliberately, by the tiniest flicker of her eyelashes she drew Toy's gaze to her own lovely breasts, swinging free and full, unblemished; her own. Toy flushed in sudden shame, whilst Rebecca tugged sharply on her lead, pulling her to her feet, and led her back to the house staff.

CHAPTER 13

Jonathan Sinclair Senior filed the signed document with the others concerning slave number AR453W. When a slave was sold the dossier would be passed on. Partly it was just for the new owner's amusement. There was an album, with photos firstly of her as an untouched girl taken covertly at the office and around the building: working, swimming, eating in the canteen. Then there were photos of her having her pretty lace dress ripped from her dainty body, photos of her losing her virginity… …the whole of her gradual degradation and reduction in status from a free woman to a sex toy had been carefully recorded for her owner's pleasure.

Also, there was a set of videos of the same process; when she came to be sold they would be presented as a boxed set of ten, beginning with her defloration and ending with her branding. Six were complete, a seventh in the making. All of the torment which she had just undergone was recorded. Probably she would see it herself some time, owners often liked to humiliate their slaves by letting them dress as servants, then showing a video or two to the assembled guests, then having the slut whipped and fucked. It was pleasant to let the girl imagine she was held in some small regard and then to remind her she was just an owned whore by showing her herself being used, then treating her as she was born to be treated.

But other documents in the dossier were for more serious purpose. Inoculation certificates to satisfy the export authorities, a certificate of ownership, and a consent form. It was the consent form that Toy had just signed. On the rare occasions that an owner was challenged it was always easy to placate the police: all the owner had to do was show them the consent form, and sugar it by allowing them full use of the slave for an hour or two. Then the most belligerent policeman would be fully satisfied that nothing untoward was taking place, and if he had sufficient funds would often even order a Sinclair slut for himself. Several such policemen had banded together with their colleagues, unable to afford the full cost themselves they would buy a girl in a joint purchase. It was easy enough to recoup the initial outlay, all one had to do was chain her up in some cheap apartment and charge friends for their use of her. And a slave was so much more amusing than a free whore!

The consent form read:

I, Anna Lockett do hereby give up entirely all my rights as a free woman, and agree voluntarily to become a slave. My body is the property of my owner (for details see attached certificate), and I consent to serve him sexually in any manner he so desires, including serving sexually any other person to whom he should give, lend or sell me. As my body is the property of my owner he may also whip, bind or torment me as he sees fit, and he has total authority to give, lend or sell me to any other person to treat thus. I have no right to protest at my treatment at any time, I exist only to serve the man or men who own me.

Signed, Anna Lockett.

Joe laughed at Toy when she was led back into the stables. "What's been happening to those udders of yours, now just see the state of 'em!"

Looking her in the eye, he roughly squeezed both her bound breasts, shivers of desire coursing through her, swelling her clit, despite the tenderness that made her gasp.

His face was suddenly intent, serious. With a practiced movement he unzipped his flies with one hand, the other still kneading her tit, pulling the nipple and digging his fingers into the taut orb. Then he was inside her, his cock filling her up, pumping quite slowly, but very deep, as he lifted her by the thighs, spread her and pressed her up against the wall of the barn, letting her own weight deepen the fucking. She moaned in helpless desire as his fingers enjoyed her little buttocks, and they came together, the man grunting his lust, the slave mewing like a she-cat.

She had been so lost in passion that she hadn't noticed that Thomas had appeared, was standing near, watching. As Joe lowered her Thomas moved forward, and pushed down on her shoulders so she fell to her knees to meet the huge rod that was jutting from his trousers. She opened her mouth, (it was automatic by now, whenever a cock came close to her face), and he thrust inside in that mercilessly way he had, almost choking her with the force of his thrust and the size of his penis, holding her head to better drive into her, savouring the way her eyes opened very wide with startlement and the effort of accommodating so much man.

He spurted a thick blast of semen into her, pulling out as he did so in order that it would splatter her face as well as filling her mouth. She swallowed down what she could, dribbles coming from her mouth and trickling onto her chin, greedily licking them up.

Joe was getting the harness. He slipped it over her, buckled it firmly, fastened the bit between her lips. Her face was still messy with come, her breasts still trussed. Then he led her out of the stable door into the dazzling light and hitched her to the trap, next to Blaze who was shivering in the cold, her pink nipples jutting like sugared candies, fresh welts gracing her smooth belly. A flick of the whip, and they were off.

They spent several hours learning immediate response to the subtle signals of whip and voice, trotting the paths around the grounds till they were exhausted and dripping with sweat. At last Joe was satisfied and let them walk back to the stable, where they were washed and fed and allowed to rest. Not until the evening were her breasts unbound, and when they were they tingled so painfully that she rubbed them against the straw strewn floor, like an animal scratching, for with her arms behind her she could find relief no other way.

They were under his tutelage for five weeks. Each day they were trotted, learning to turn in an instant, building their strength so as they could gallop at full tilt without soon tiring, learning to wait, patient and still, whilst their masters chatted or smoked. Each night they slept on the straw, each day they were fed slops from a trough. They were beaten regularly, but there was no pattern to it. At least once a day they were whipped, more usually twice. One day Joe must've been in a foul mood for some reason, for he lashed them no less than four times, and each beating was worse than the last. But now Toy knew what torment awaited at the hands of Sir Jonathan she strove hard to offer herself to be beaten in much the same way as she had long since learnt to offer herself to be fucked. And Joe would use it as a threat, just little hints, but she understood well enough.

"So are you wanting another trip indoors?" he'd say if she didn't behave quite to his liking. And so when the whip fell towards her round buttocks she'd arch her back, welcoming the bite of the lash, showing her willingness to be chastised. And if they whipped her slim thighs she would spread them to give them the most sensitive flesh, parting her knees and pushing her pussy forwards, though she yelped when the lash bit her sweet mons.

And each day she was fucked, thoroughly, casually, by whoever happened to be around. Always by Joe, every day, and likewise Thomas. But just as often by one or more of the other men; other stablehands, the field workers. Occasionally the kitchen staff would walk over to the stable for a joke and a beer, and have her at the same time.

It was delectable to be so thoroughly owned, and more than once she came just from the beating alone, especially if she was allowed the taste of cock in her mouth at the same time. She loved them using her mouth above anything else, loved being on her knees as to a king or a god. She thought of the spunk that splattered her, messing her hair, coating her sweet breasts, as holy water, anointing her. She lapped it hungrily, and would lick it carefully off Blaze, her sister slave.

The days wound on. An irregular tapestry of whipping and fucking, the regular long hours of training. The two girls spent much of their time harnessed together, and were never out of each other's sight. They didn't talk much. Somehow they were journeying to a place where talking wasn't really necessary, or appropriate. But they were as close as litter mates, sleeping entwined, soft breast resting against smooth thigh, or cheek on buttock, tangled together like the contented animals they truly were.

One day Toy was standing harnessed to the trap after the usual practice, the sweat running in little rivulets between her heaving breasts, for Joe had worked them very hard, when a man came up and began running his hands over her tits and belly.

"They've not ringed her yet?" he called out to Joe, slipping his fingers between her lips to stroke her clit.

It was Harry, one of the field workers, a man she didn't see that often, which was a relief because when she did he always liked to put far too large a dildo up her pussy whilst he had her ass, or almost as big a dildo up her ass whilst he had her pussy.

"Oh, it's all in hand, they'll be ringing the pair of em…
…aren't they a pretty pair, just?… …They'll be ringing the pair of em tomorrow. Would ye like to see it? I can give ye a shout if ye can spare the time."

"Aye, do that."

The next morning the sky was dark, overcast. Toy could smell rain in the air. After the whores had been fed their slops, Joe took a small pot of ointment down from the shelves. It had a strange scent, reminiscent of menthol, that wafted to her sensitive nostrils as soon as he opened the jar.

He dipped his fingers into the pot, then holding her easily immobile by her bound arms, he rubbed the salve into her nipples. Toy felt an icy chill biting into her, which spread out from the place the salve touched, so the centre of her breasts felt frozen. The cold was so hard it hurt and she whimpered, but Joe just dipped his fingers in the jar again and rubbed more ointment into her nubs, which were hard and erect, from the chill and from his touch.

Next it was the turn of her clit. She squealed and wriggled in his arms as he rubbed a big dollop of the ointment against her exquisitely sensitive tissue, but he just held her all the tighter as he massaged with all four of his fingers, repeating the process twice more.

Toy had been close to orgasm from his touch, but something had happened to her; although she could feel from the pressure that his hand was still spreading her lips, fingering her clit, her clit itself could feel nothing. Both her nipples too, felt frozen and numb.

Experimentally the groom dug his nails into her little nubs. She didn't even pull away, let alone yelp. He did the same to her swollen clit. Nothing. The ointment was very effective. It certainly needed to be; she would receive no other anaesthetic for the procedure. He dragged her out of the stable into the yard, then into the blacksmith's workshop nearby.

Ben looked up as they walked in, flicked approving eyes over her full breasts, noticing how the nipples gleamed from the oily salve.

"On the table with her, thanks Joe."

There was an odd-looking table, as high as her chest but with a narrow, short top, the legs splaying away from the top at a slight angle. Joe dumped her down on her arse on it and proceeded to strap her limbs to the table legs. Her head dangled down at the end, ignored. The table was exactly the right size so that her open lips were on display at the lower end, her full breasts, the glistening nipples jutting proud, at the other.

"I'll let the Masters know she's ready. Oh, and old Harry. He never likes to miss a show."

Chuckling, Joe left.

It must've been nigh on an hour before he returned, soon followed by Harry and a handful of other field workers. Ten minutes later Marcus arrived with half a dozen of the guests. They gathered round the spread whore, fingering her tits and pussy.

"I like to check they be properly numb in the cunt before I starts," said the old blacksmith, and bending his head he gently tested the slut's clit between his teeth. Toy felt a whiskery face, scratchy between her smooth thighs, fingers spreading her nether lips, then a slightly uncomfortable pressure, but no pain. He was not biting hard enough to cause damage, nevertheless, if a girl was bitten like that without the prior application of the salve she'd have screamed the house down.

"Aye, she be dead down there alright," Ben announced in satisfaction, and went to fetch the ringing tool.

Strapped on her back with her head dangling down, Toy could not see what was happening. She tried to lift her head to look, but one of the guests had noticed how well presented for fucking her mouth was: digging his thumbs into the corners of her mouth so as she could not bite he started to fill her face with cock. It was a wise precaution: Toy felt the chill of cold metal against her pussy, then the jaws of the tool bit home, driving a fat gold ring through her most sensitive flesh. The salve had deadened her enough to take away a great deal of the pain, but still it hurt. She would have cried out if her mouth hadn't been in use, as it was she bucked uncontrollably, the movement speeding the orgasm of the man using her face so that she was rewarded with a generous spurt of thick come. As she swallowed it she felt the heat of another cock against her face, and dutifully opened her mouth so as to aid the man, who then drove

131

himself deep into her throat. At that moment she felt the chill of metal again, this time against her right nipple. Before she even had time to steel herself against the pain the ring was shot home, seconds later her left nipple was ringed.

Now all three of her most tender places were throbbing with discomfort and pierced by thick gold rings. She had had no say in the matter; her masters had wanted her ringed and so she had been. Marcus ran his hands over her in satisfaction as his guests gathered round to fuck her face. Ringing served a dual purpose: it made a whore even more controllable that she already was, but also, aesthetically it was very pleasing: a pierced girl displayed her status so obviously; no-one but a slave would have a ring through her clit. With that in mind there was one more ring to be inserted. Old Ben waited until all the guests had finished using the young girl's mouth, then went round to her dangling head and again cold metal shot through her flesh. This time it was her nose that was ringed, not at the side, as girls sometimes chose to wear body jewelry, but through the tissue that separated her nostrils, the way an animal is ringed. The small ring was quite unobtrusive, nevertheless it was a subtle but decisive indicator of her status to anyone who saw her, even if perchance she was clothed.

Once inserted the rings could not be removed unless the metal was sawn through by a hacksaw. Anyway, there had never been any call to remove a slave's rings, anymore than anyone would wish to remove her collar.

The weather had changed whilst Toy was inside. The sun was now quite fierce, the sky full of a tumult of clouds moving fast under a strong wind. As she was led away, her shameful finery glinting prettily in the sunlight, she passed Blaze being led by Thomas. She was, of course, next for Ben's eager attentions. The little bay's eyes widened as she saw the thick gold bands that decorated and further enslaved her sister slut. Joe saw her gaze, and in amusement tweaked Toy's left nipple ring, pulling her breast into a high peak.

Toy whimpered, Blaze trembled and Joe and Thomas laughed.

Joe tethered Toy in the stable then went to watch the second filly receive her banding. Half an hour later Blaze reappeared, as pale as snow from the shock but, much to the delight of Thomas, glistening between her legs in arousal. He casually fucked her on all fours, pulling on her new rings as he did so. Her submissive nature was so alluring.

The rings needed to be turned each day, and to his glee this chore was assigned to Thomas, who took great pleasure in the slaves' little mews of mingled pain and pleasure as he twisted the fat bands.

Chapter 14

One night Toy was woken by an insistent tug on her leash. Joe was standing over her, a long strap in his hands. The old leather gleamed in the glow from the oil lamp, polished by years of use. She started to sit up, but he pushed her down again, so she was laid on her back, the straw scratchy against her buttocks. He pushed her thighs up close to her body, then slipped the strap around, so it went around her waist at the back and under her pulled up knees at the front. Then another strap, this one around her back in the same fashion, then over her calves, so her legs were strapped tidily out of the way, her pussy and asshole totally available.

She could hear the sound of men talking and laughing, and when Joe lifted her bodily in his arms and carried her out of the stall where Blaze still slept, she saw that half a dozen of the grooms and stable lads were gathered, drinking beer. There were bawdy shouts of approval when they saw the trussed whore, and big Harry reached out his huge, reddened hands to take first turn. He was sitting on a bale of hay, and his beefy arms were so strong that he was easily able to hold her aloft as he slid his thick shaft into her. Toy felt again like a blow up sex doll, being so held and used. She could take no active part in the fucking, strapped as she was into total passivity, slid back and forth on the long, fat cock.

He enjoyed her slowly, pausing when she began to moan in pleasure and asking for a gag to silence her.

"How's about I silences her with my cock?" said Thomas, and so Harry let her slip down to rest against his legs, still deeply inside her, whilst Thomas knelt and rammed his meat into her mouth. Only the littlest murmurs of her pleasure could creep out now her throat was so full, so when she came they knew it more by the sudden clutching of her cunt around the big penis that so filled it. Harry shot his load into her tight puss, then Thomas filled her mouth with thick come, and then she was passed on to the next man.

As they handed her round she saw Blaze being carried in. She was bound in an extreme hogtie, very tight, and with a cord leading from her ankles and wrists to her thick pony tail, so that her head was pulled back, her pretty tits displayed to best advantage, her sweet little nipples as inviting to the tongue as strawberry jellytots, the fat gold rings offering plenty of scope for teasing. Her ivory skin looked very lovely in the lamplight, almost transparent in its delicacy, marked on breast and belly by red welts from her most recent beatings.

Toy was being laid on her front in the straw, so one of the smaller men could kneel behind her and easily fuck her up the rump. Despite his diminutive stature his arms were taut and wiry, his rough fingers digging deep into the soft flesh of her upper arms, and his cock was huge. Toy moaned as she had to take him, it hurt to be stretched so wide. And yet she was aroused almost to orgasm by submitting to such a big rod, that wonderful sensation of being more stuffed than one could imagine possible. There was something very reassuring about being full of cock, she thought, and it was lucky she had such an attitude, because just then another man slipped his lap under her head so as to stuff her mouth with his swollen member.

The two girls were passed round the group, used in various ways. It was a pleasant night off for the men.

They had been talking about how easy the girls were to control, and Pete said,

"Even easier I hear, when they've had this dark 'un modified."

"Aye, and it shouldn't be long now, they've got a surgeon lined up, they've got the device working reet. Can't wait to see it in use."

They all laughed. Young Thomas said,

"Where do they cut, exactly?"

And she was lifted from where they'd left her,

ignominiously face down in the straw, and dumped down on her back in the centre of the group.

Joe knelt over her, his naked balls dangling against her face, and spread her labia wide with his two palms.

"See that?" He was pointing with his thumb to her clit, giving it a casual flick.

"That's her clit. That's where it'll go. The clit's the heart of any slut. Control her clit, you control her totally. Of course, you can do it anyway, with whip and tongue and clips... ...but this'll be tidy, you see. The no-hands method."

Again they all laughed.

Toy shivered, she had no idea what they were talking about, but it was frightening to be discussed like that.

After a bit more fucking the men departed, heading their separate ways. Joe was too tired and mellow with beer to stable the two whores properly, leaving them lying still trussed on the floor of the stable, whilst he went to sleep in his comfortable bed.

Toy slept badly, as did her sister slut. The bonds were too tight and besides, the stable was cold without another to snuggle close to. She was glad when the first light of dawn lit the inky sky to turquoise, and not long after heard the familiar footsteps of Joe in the courtyard. The door creaked open, and she saw his bulky shape, black against the lightening sky. He came into the stable and reaching down laid his rough, warm hand against her cool thigh. He grimaced, knelt down, unstrapped her. His eyes looked red and bleary. She was shivering and stiff, and lifting her in his great arms he carried her through to the stall, putting her down very gently. He reached up to one of the baskets that contained bridles and bits for the real horses, pulled down a blanket, threw it over her. It stank of horse sweat, but it was thick and woolly, and soon she was warm again, quickly falling asleep.

When she awoke it was midmorning. She knew at once by

the light, by the way the sunlight fell in a narrow patch just inside the window. The stable was warm from sun and horses, so she pushed back the blanket, realising with a shock of surprise that she was entirely unbound. Blaze was snuggled up close to her under the same blanket. She was still fast asleep. Her arms were unbound, but her collar was fastened to her chain as usual.

Anna knew at once that Joe had made a mistake, that he had intended to tether her too, but tired and hungover he had forgotten. She remembered his grimace. Although he treated the pair of them hard, although he whipped them daily and fucked them with no regard for their pleasure, sating only his own appetites, he was nevertheless a good groom. He cared for the fillies, not as the people they had once been, but as the animals they now were. Just as he never neglected the health of his four legged horses, so he never neglected the health of his whores; never, that is, until last night. Tired and sozzled by too much beer he had left them without seeing to their basic needs. Left them to shiver and stiffen. Then he had woken at dawn, full of guilt, made amends for his neglect and gone back to sleep off his hangover. And in his hurry left her free.

She walked to the window, luxuriating in the movement of her arms which were so rarely unbound. The courtyard was silent. This was very strange. Usually by this time of day the place would be humming with life, servants seeing to the animals, kitchen staff making slops. And then she remembered a snatch of the conversation from last night. A day off. The Sinclairs' had given all their staff the day off, a token of thanks for their devoted service. That was why Joe had bothered to come and see to the whores at crack of dawn: he knew he wouldn't be there for the whole day. She stood by the window, straining her ears to catch any sound. Nothing.

Her heart thumping, she looked down at her welt-marked body. She ran her hands over her full breasts, touched her own pussy for the first time in weeks. She felt gloriously wicked, and more than a little frightened. She had believed herself to be totally subjugated, happy in her simple role of sex toy, happy to be an owned whore, existing only for male pleasure. But since she had first arrived at the Manor, since she had first stepped into the great Tudor hall, to be stripped and fucked by over a dozen men, not for one moment had she been free. At times, brief though they were, she had been unbound. But always in the company of her owner, or under the sway of the lovely Pusskins, or alone but behind the locked doors of Marcus's suite. Now she was free, completely free, and she felt quite different; fearful yes, but, overwhelmingly, heady with excitement.

She turned from the window, unsure what to do. The dappled mare in the next stall gave a soft snort, and all of a sudden she felt entirely clear. Quickly she searched the stable. Was there anything her she could wear? All she could find was a scruffy old towel. Still, it was better than nothing, she wrapped it around herself and crept to the horse. The great beast knew something unusual was afoot; she snorted her impatience as Anna opened her half door, but was meek as could be when Anna gently took her bridle and led her to the stable door. Anna took a deep breath, and pushed it open, the creak it always made sounded far, far louder today; but Blaze did not even stir. Even if she had, what would it have mattered? Anna felt a pang of guilt at abandoning her beloved friend, but her resolve was unquenchable. In one easy movement she mounted the grey mare and they trotted quickly out of the yard.

She had neglected to saddle the horse, not wanting to waste time and risk discovery. It didn't matter. She had loved horses since she was very small, but stuck in the dreariness of the children's' home she'd rarely ever even seen one. When she had escaped, as she saw it, to her little bedsit and her secretarial course, she had been delighted to find a horse stabled not far from where she lived. The spoilt teenager who owned the animal was too lazy to care for her properly, and more than happy to agree to Anna's suggestion that she muck her out in exchange for free rides, so every evening after college or office, Anna rode the mare, slowly out past the allotments, out through the park, through the old oak woods and on, into the country. She has an instinctual affinity with the gentle creatures, and learnt to ride as naturally as most learn to walk.

So she rode bareback, her thighs warmed by the great body beneath her. She chose a path that she knew took her quickly out of sight of the Manor, into the woods, trotting the mare along as fast as she dared. So often she had trotted this path herself, as a bound slave, a pony-girl. She commanded the animal she rode with the utmost gentleness, and the slight pressure of her heels against the mare's sides was all that was needed for the horse to obey her.

The woods stretched for miles, and it was midday when they left the cover, coming at last to open fields. Above them the sun was beating down from a pure blue sky. It had been chill in the woods, but the air over the fields was soft and mild, despite the breeze that caught at her hair. They reached a brook, and Anna dismounted so both she and the horse could drink.

They were on high ground, a green promontory that ahead sloped gently down through fields to a wooded valley. To either side the ground fell away more sharply, too sharply for her mount to negotiate. Far below a river snaked, vivid blue. She could just hear the sound of the rushing water. Beyond the river, she could see a church steeple proud above the trees: a village, and a village meant people, and people meant safety.

She re-mounted the mare, and was about to urge her down the slope in front of them when the horse turned her head, catching the breeze, and uttered an anxious whinny. Twisting round her heart beat suddenly went wild when she saw what was troubling the mare: four horsemen were emerging from the wood, a scant five hundred yards behind them.

"Fly, girl! Fly!" as she spoke she kicked her heels against Bess's sturdy flanks, and flattened herself against her neck, clinging on for dear life as the beast took off at a gallop. She heard a shout from behind her; they had been spotted.

The mare sped down the path. The ground was good and firm, they raced at full tilt. But soon behind them Anna could hear the thunder of hooves. They were almost at the river. The towel that she'd used to cover her nakedness slipped from her slight form; she hardly noticed but drove her mount onwards, kicking her heels roughly now in sheer panic.

And then she was aware of a rider to her right, and moments later Marcus was abreast of her atop the black stallion, Jet. He reached down from his taller steed and grabbing the reins brought both horses to a halt.

The girl in front of him presented a very pretty picture. Her long dark hair windswept, her cheeks pink as apples and her full breasts heaving both with panic and from the hard ride. Not to mention her slim, creamy thighs spread to encompass the stocky mare, her naked mons sweet above the dappled grey back. His cock was rock hard, and he made a mental note to add 'slave hunting' to the many amusements he already provided for his guests. It was certainly delightful to run such a lovely quarry to ground. It seemed to appeal to some very primitive and ancient instincts in a man.

Jonathan, Charles and Joe were not far behind him, and his two brothers were already pulling their swollen shafts from their trousers. Of course, the whore must be punished, and he would enjoy thinking up a particularly humiliating punishment for her, but first things first. He unzipped his flies and his own huge cock sprang out.

On the bank of the river was a tall oak, conveniently equipped with a sturdy horizontal branch about ten foot above the ground. He took hold of Toy's wrists, pleased to discover she was trembling with fear, wound cord round them, deliberately making it tight enough to bite into her soft flesh, then urged his horse forward to the tree, leading the mare with them. He tied the other end of the cord to the big branch, so the slave was sitting astride her horse, her hands above her head, pulling up towards the branch above her. Then he rode round behind the mare and gave her rump a hefty blow from his crop. In pain and surprise the mare bolted, and the whore slipped from her back, to dangle from her wrists a foot above the ground, just as he had intended.

Her breasts were swinging prettily, so he sliced into them with the crop, the sweet white skin marking easily into satisfyingly angry red welts. He chuckled at her cry of pain. Riding behind her he saw her lovely little ass, so naked, so defenceless, and again his crop sang through the air, and again the slut cried out.

But what they really wanted was to plunge their cocks deep into her pliant body. All four men dismounted, Joe tying the horses to another tree. Marcus and Charles took first turn, Marcus holding her full breasts as though they were convenient handles with which to pull the dangling toy onto his rod. He stuffed himself into her tight hole in one swift movement, discovering to his amusement that she was as aroused as ever, his cock greeted by the delectable contractions of her pussy that was always ready and willing to please. Charles took her hips and pressed his shaft into her tight anus, making her gasp; he was a very big man.

The brothers rocked her back and forth between them in a steady rhythm, like lumberjacks wielding a saw. As Marcus thrust in, Charles pulled out, as Marcus pulled out, Charles buried his cock to the hilt. Toy couldn't help herself, she was loving every thrust. She was close to orgasm when suddenly Marcus said,

"Oh no you don't!" shooting his load deep into her cunt, at the same time tugging cruelly on her clit ring. Both men pulled out of her, Charles splattering her buttocks with his seed.

She was moaning in frustration; she'd been so close to orgasm, but the abrupt removal of stimulation coupled with the pain from her clit ring had left her horribly dissatisfied.

They beat her some more, taking it in turns to lash her with the crop. Arousal began to build in her again, her clit was swollen with desire as she yelped and swung in response to their blows. But again, before she could orgasm she was cut down, forced to her knees, and her mouth unceremoniously stuffed with Jonathan's cock, whilst Joe wanked over her face, Marcus tying her wrists behind her with cruelly tight turns of the cord, strapping her arms together to right above her elbows.

When they had all come Marcus said to her,

"You want to orgasm, don't you?"

"Oh yes, Master, please Master."

"Well you shan't. You've put us to a lot of trouble running off like that, all for no reason. You like being a slave, don't you? You signed away all your rights, didn't you? You know we own you and, deep in your heart, you know that all this," he flicked her nipple rings and collar, "was meant to be. You were born to be an owned whore. You have misbehaved abominably, and I'm sure you'd agree, though of course your opinion is anyway irrelevant, that you deserve to be thoroughly punished."

She had to admit he was right. Now she was bound again it felt so natural, she couldn't think what madness had taken hold of her.

"I'm sorry Master," she bowed her head, humble and ashamed.

"Well sorry is not good enough." He lashed her with the crop so she squealed again. "Your punishment is only just beginning. You are mine, your cunt and clit are mine. You reach climax only as I see fit. And at this moment what I see fit is that you learn again that you exist for the sole purpose of providing men with pleasure."

And he brought the crop down hard on her bare buttocks

so she yelped and whimpered.

He could feel his cock stirring again. It really was most fortunate that the whore had been stupid enough to attempt to escape. He was thoroughly enjoying her punishment. Of course, they could have punished her just on a whim, but the fact that she deserved it and knew she did added a deal of piquancy to the situation. Yes, he'd have to make 'slaves' escapes' a regular feature of Manor entertainment. It'd be easy to encourage a slave to make a bid for freedom; a little idle talk of some particularly cruel humiliation that was planned, (he had heard from Joe that they had been discussing Toy's clitoral modification in her hearing), a subcutaneous radio tag so that she was easily trackable, a horse available but no saddle……… the whore really had made a delicious sight, riding naked and panicked in front of his galloping steed. He sighed with satisfaction. One of the delights of his family tradition was the way each new generation of slave owners brought his own special touches to Sinclair slave training. It was his great great grandfather who had designed the whipping stand, complete with the tit vice, it was his own father who'd invented the luncheon slut ritual. And now he would add to the repertoire of humiliation and enjoyment by incorporating slave hunts into the guests' entertainment.

The slave was now looking thoroughly meek and obedient. Joe was getting the fine chains from his saddlebag, and clipping them to the rings in her udders, nose and clit. The weight dragged at her tits, then when Joe pulled on them, lifted her nipples so her tits were pulled into conical peaks. The groom carefully arranged the chains, so that the one from her right nipple led to Marcus's horse, the ones from her clit and nose to Jonathan's, the final chain from her left nipple to Charles'.

Toy had imagined that they would make their way back up the hill, towards the Manor hidden in the woods above. She was shocked and startled when the three brothers, riding abreast, set their horses to ford the stream. For a moment she paused on the bank, but the lash of Joe's crop falling in a stinging blow across her naked buttocks combined with a tug on her clit and nipples as the chains tautened; she yelped and stepped down into the water.

At first it only came to her calves. But by the time they were halfway across she was wading through water that reached to mid-thigh, so icy it took her breath away. She struggled across, missing her footing and stumbling into deeper water so that suddenly it was up to her mons and she whimpered as the cold enveloped her sensitive clit.

When they reached the other side she was shivering violently, but her owners were unconcerned. She was going to be taught a lesson she wouldn't forget in a hurry. And anyway, the sun was hot now, she would soon dry off.

They walked up the bank, made their way through a gate and into a lane which led into the heart of the village. It was now quite clear: the men had no fear of being seen. On the contrary, they were intent on parading their captive through the streets, for the pleasure of the locals and the humiliation of the slut.

They turned a corner; a man was walking towards them along the street. He doffed his cap to the gentlemen then stared at Toy, grinning broadly, letting his eyes feast upon her ringed udders and naked mons. Joe caught his eye and dipped his head towards the whore, smiling pleasantly in open invitation. The man, who was about forty or so, thickset and swarthy, with large, work-coarsened hands, needed no second bidding. He walked along next to Toy, fingering her stretched nipples, probing her pussy which was immediately slippery from his attentions. Then he stuffed one fat finger into her little asshole and she had to walk along like that, her cheeks burning with shame as he wriggled his finger inside her to deepen the penetration and to hear her moan in supplication.

They reached the main street, busy with people out

shopping and chatting. Within a minute there was not another female in sight, young girls, portly matrons, mothers: all scurried away. The men, on the other hand, must have spread the word, for soon there were crowds of them, standing leching at the pretty bound girl as she was paraded in front of them. The swarthy man on her left still had his finger inside her anus, and he started to thrust with it, to the wholehearted approval of the crowd which whooped with glee and yelled bawdy incitements for him to 'stuff her hard'. The streets were lined with stalls for it was market day, and the greengrocer came walking over to her right. He was holding a fat courgette which he waved at the excited crowd. "Stuff the slut!", "Ram her hard!" Holding her by her buttock he pressed it firmly against her pussy and she gasped as the cold, smooth length of it slipped inside her until his large fist was right up against her hole. It was uncomfortable to walk whilst stuffed by such an unyielding dildo but she had no choice in the matter: the horsemen kept on riding. They seemed to have a certain purpose and she shivered as she wondered where they were taking her.

There was now a sizable group of men walking next to her. Hands roamed all over her, squeezing her breasts, pinching her ringed nipples till she yelped, massaging her clit. There were so many men and so many hands that she could not be sure who was slipping his finger in to join that already in her ass, whose hands were probing the entrance to her cunt, enjoying the feel of the solid shaft stuffed up inside her, nor even whose fingers were pushed into her mouth, perhaps aiming to ensure every hole her slight body possessed was full. She stumbled along, often more dragged than walking, lost in a sea of men. Many had already unzipped their trousers and hot cocks brushed against her thighs, pressed against her little buttocks. She could no longer see where they were headed.

Joe chuckled to himself as he rode behind, watching the

whore disappear under so many eager male hands. His own cock was rock hard again. They had almost reached the square, and some of the townsfolk were preparing the stocks. The riders halted and he slipped down to take charge of the slut. The men playing with her stepped back respectfully so he could unclip her from the chains, then he wound his right arm into her thick mane of hair, and frog-marched her forward.

The stocks were on a small platform. She was wriggling in panic, but she was so tiny it made no impact on him. Besides, he knew she wanted it, really. He felt her pussy: wet of course. She was desperate for a good fucking and looking around him at the crowd of men, cocks jutting erect from unzipped flies, he was absolutely sure she'd be getting one.

He unbound her arms, noting with pleasure how the tight cord had marked her, then lifted her up. Someone helpfully raised the gate of the stocks and he pushed her head into place then held her there whilst the gate was lowered and padlocked shut. Now she was on all fours, her head through the solid wood wall of the stocks, quite unable to see anything that might happen to the rest of her body. Black iron manacles snapped shut with satisfying finality around her wrists, and then her ankles, pulling her thighs open.

Within seconds she felt the hot pressure of the first cock against her asshole. She had no idea which of the men was intent on using her thus, only that it was not one of her owners, for the three brothers sat, aloof, on horseback, watching with mild amusement as the gangbang began. Then horrified she saw them turn away; they were abandoning her to the attentions of the village men. The cock at her ass was large and finding it hard to gain entry. She felt her buttocks yanked apart by helping hands and then the man slid into her. She whimpered with pained desire as she had to take his full length, loving the way he filled her so completely. She didn't care that it hurt a little, she didn't care that she was a mere sex toy: she loved cock, and she arched her back the better to receive it. The action did not go unnoticed: men whooped and slapped her ass, and the big cock inside her pounded even harder.

In a few more thrusts he was spurting her full of his come. As soon as he slipped out another cock entered her. This time it was her cunt that was to be enjoyed, the huge rod shafting into her in a single stroke. She flushed with shame to see the men standing in front of her, watching her being used when she herself had no idea who was inside her. They gathered close about her and she realised that the platform brought her face to the height of their cocks. Half a dozen swollen shafts pushed from the open flies, she could smell the musky scent of them. She licked her lips and felt her pussy rush with more fuck juices. At that moment a voice said,

"Let's use her whore-mouth too."

And a second later a cock was pushing against her sweet lips.

She opened wide to take it and was shafted deep in her throat by an organ so large that she was scared she'd be choked by it. The two men using her began to thrust in rhythm, and arousal built so fast inside her that when her mouth was filled with jetting semen she too was close to climaxing. But her owners had issued clear instructions: a rough tug on her clit ring brought such sudden pain that the orgasm was lost to her. The men pumped away and quickly filled her with their come.

No sooner had those two finished using her than they slipped away from the tender mouth and pussy that would have caressed them still, would have held them far longer and cherished them back to hardness. And now other cocks were taking their turn at the proffered holes, using her remorselessly and with great pleasure, and when they, too, had spent their seed into her warm body, still more took their place.

She could not see beyond the genitals that pressed against her face; when one man left her mouth he was followed so quickly by another that she only glimpsed thighs, pubes, cocks, testicles, saw nothing of the square or the street or the world beyond. The scent of men was so strong she was drowning in it, intoxicated. Her lips were chafed by the rough pubic hair that, again and again, rasped against her face as cocks thrust into her throat. Her anus was burning from so much penetration, her cunt likewise. And yet still she wanted it, still she would have hung on to each cock a little longer, just a little longer, forever maybe, loving each cock as though it was the last that'd ever take her. And though her flesh was burning with so much use, her desire and frustration burnt even fiercer, for each time she started to peak the possessing cocks quickly withdrew, and her clitoris stung as dominating hands twisted or pulled at the controlling ring, so the fuckings were not illuminated by the bright starbursts of orgasm, but instead by the hard clear light of pain.

It was nightfall before they were all done with her, or maybe they were not done with her at all, but it was just that Joe decided to call a halt. At any rate, the fucking stopped, and the men fell back. Revealed, the chill of the night air swam all around her, tightening her nipples to hard buds, covering her pale thighs with goose bumps. The groom stepped forward and unlocked the padlock that held the gate of the stocks shut, then lifted the heavy wood, freeing her neck. She was so stiff she could not move, but slumped helpless till he grabbed her by her thick hair and yanked her unsteadily to her feet. From somewhere they fetched a hose and she was washed down, inside and out, just as she had been so many times before at the Manor, but now her cunt and asshole were being cleansed in full public view and she flushed with the shame of it.

Joe left her standing shakily by the stocks, quite unbound for a moment but as far from free as it is possible for a woman to be. She could not raise her eyes to those of the men who surrounded her, rather she looked down at the ground, at the puddle of water from her washing. She was again wet through, and shivering with cold.

Joe returned, leading the saddled mare, but the saddle looked odd, something protruding from it, something as thick as her wrist, a hand span high. Joe bound her arms behind her back again, mounted his horse and reaching down to hold her under the arms, lifted her onto her mount, carefully settling her onto the fat leather dildo that stood proud from the rest of the saddle. She whimpered to find herself so full once more, when her pussy had already been so roughly and thoroughly used, but he paid her no heed, just strapped her in place by her ankles, thighs and wrists so that she should not fall.

One of the townsmen held the mare's reins whilst Joe went into the inn to tell the Masters they were ready for the off. Half an hour later, amidst shouted jocularities and in apparent high good humour, the three gentlemen emerged from the pub, kissing fond farewells to the local tarts who'd been amusing them. With barely a glance at the trussed, stuffed Toy, they mounted their horses and set off towards the Manor. Joe lashed the mare to get her trotting after them, and it was no accident that more than half of the blow landed on the rump of the slave.

CHAPTER 15

The ride back seemed far longer than the journey there. They kept to the valley roads, which wound between the close-knit hills, trotting steadily along so that the great dildo filling her cruelly-used puss jiggled and pressed at the tender flesh. When they reached a straight section the three riders ahead spurred their mounts to a gallop, and Joe let Toy's horse taste his crop again: hard, and again, harder; so that the stung mare bolted into a gallop. Toy cried as the possessing shaft bucked into her with every movement of the animal under her, the relentless pounding of the saddle against her clit speeding the orgasm that engulfed her so powerfully that she shrieked her ecstasy as she was carried along. The men paid the whore no heed.

Above her the heavens wheeled, a deep bowl of black velvet, sparkling with so many stars that the hugeness of revealed space dizzied her. All her life had been lived in the city, trapped under the flat orange plate of sky with the other two-legged animals who never gazed upwards for there was nothing to see. On a clear night she had sometimes tried to peer between the glow of streetlights, counting no more than a half dozen points of starlight in the opaque mass. They had seemed such poor, sorry creatures compared to the immeasurably brighter glitter of the city plain which spread around her like spilt treasure.

Now she saw their true glory she was awestruck. How tawdry her city life with its cheap glitz when compared with the natural rhythm and exaltation of which she was now part!

They had reached the driveway to the Manor. It twisted up the steep hillside, lacing between the trees, steadily gaining height. The horses were tired and they made their way quite slowly. They reached the top as they left the cover of the wood, and before them, at the end of a long level stretch of meadow, loomed the dark bulk of the mansion, brooding over the moonlit countryside. Toy shivered.

The horses quickened pace as the gentlemen spurred them to a final gallop. Joe's crop clipped Toy's thigh and then the mare's rump, and again the horse set off at full-tilt, and again the dildo fucked her easily to climax. She was ashamed at her own pliability and would have hidden the orgasm, but she could not help but cry in passion. The brothers dismounted by the wide sweep of steps, and Joe led all the horses round to the courtyard.

He left the slut shivering on the mare's back, the dildo burning within her cunt, whilst he saw to the other beasts. Only when Jet and the other stallions were comfortably stabled for the night did he turn his attention to Toy and her mount, but rather than release Toy from the saddle that still shafted her, he undid the saddle from the mare. Then lifting it down, the young girl still bound in place upon it, he rested it on a mounting block whilst he saw to the horse.

Toy sat shaking with cold and exhaustion. It was many minutes before Joe returned. When he did unstrap her he was gentle, lifting her slowly off the dildo and carrying her slight body held close to his own, into the warmth of the stable. Blaze was there, tethered in her usual place. There was food in the trough, and the oil lamp spilt soft yellow light over the straw where she would sleep. Joe laid her down, and clipped her collar securely to the chain. He fastened anklets and manacles around her limbs, and these too were attached to chains. There would be no more escapes. Then he settled himself between the two whores, idly caressing their long hair with his two rough hands.

"Ye silly creature," he said to Toy, stroking her steadily, "bet you be right glad t'be home, ain't ye?"

In answer, Toy just snuggled closer into his strong warm body, rubbing her face enquiringly against his crotch. Joe chuckled in amusement and pulled out his cock, already half erect. With happy gratitude Toy bent her head and licked carefully along the length of his shaft, then ran her tongue round his glans with dainty precision. Her chains clanked softly as she worked. The groom leant back against the straw bales with a contented sigh.

Toy stimulated him with all the skill her weeks of slavery had taught her, bringing him to the edge of climax and then keeping him hovering there, silent in his ecstasy, until in the end he grasped her head in his big hands and thrusting deep into her throat, filled her with the benediction of his come. She thankfully swallowed all of his semen, meek as a lamb and overjoyed to be servicing his cock once again.

Her Master bade her eat, and she hungrily wolfed slops from the trough whilst he permitted the bay to lick him clean. By the time she had completed the task to their mutual satisfaction he was hard again, and this time it was Blaze's throat he pumped into, Toy watching carefully to see what new skills she might learn. When he had shot his second load into the willing redhead, he silently gestured for both whores to clean him, so they bent their heads together over his matted pubes, and two pink tongues lapped and sucked at him, until his hair glistened fresh in the mellow light. He left the girls curled together drowsy on the straw, and went off to sleep in his comfortable bed, but not before his wife had performed the same service for him. Happily, she was also a girl who knew her place.

The next day dawned drear but mild. A constant light rain fell from before daybreak, and the slaves slept late, lulled by the murmurous thrumming on the tiles above them. It was still drizzling when Joe arrived to harness them to the trap, and he sat in relative comfort, bundled in a waxed jacket, a tarpaulin over his legs and his face shielded by his cap, whilst they pulled him around the manor grounds.

Their pale skin was quickly shiny wet, their hair hanging down their backs in dark, twisting ropes. The rain made rivers between Toy's breasts and buttocks and trickled, icy, into the cleft in her mons, running over her clit like the cold fingers of an old lover. Joe put the pair through their paces with relentless efficiency and did not spare the crop, whose stinging slices sent a fine spray of mist from the whores' haunches. He worked them so hard that they grew hot despite the ceaseless rain, a slight steam rising from their heaving breasts as they trotted past the sodden vegetation.

Eventually he was satisfied with their performance and drove them back to the courtyard, leaving them in the care of two young stable lads whilst he went to see to some business at the house.

The boys were not much older than the slaves they were drying off. Although they had on previous occasions helped feed and groom the sluts, neither of them had ever been alone with a naked female before, owned whore or free. Joe had not said they were allowed to have them, but there again, he had said nothing to the contrary. They conferred together as they brought in the slops, and decided that silence must mean consent.

The elder boy would have Blaze, his blonde brother enjoy Toy.

The younger boy tentatively approached the dark-haired slut.

"Will you spread your legs for me?" he asked uncertainly.

"Not like that!" his brother interrupted him, derisory. "Like this!"

And then to Blaze:

"On your knees, whore, and get sucking my dick! And if you don't do it real good I'll beat you till your ass is red raw."

Instantly Blaze dropped to her knees in front of him, and nuzzled at his zip in a mute request for him to open it, since her hands were bound behind her in the usual fashion. The lad smiled triumphantly at his brother, then eagerly opened his flies and his cock proudly pushed out. Blaze took his bulging manhood between her sweet lips and at that moment he came, some of his ejaculate shooting into her ready mouth, the rest spattering her face in thick gobbets. She looked so good like that that the younger boy, Todd, losing his shyness, came forward and wanked over her, spurting his semen to add to that which already decorated her.

Matt was quickly finding his feet as a new whore-master.

"Lick her clean!" he ordered Toy, who dutifully wriggled over and carefully lapped the mess from her sister-slut's face. Watching them the boys soon grew rigid once more. As she finished the task the younger lad decided to try his hand.

"On your backs, whores, legs spread as far as they'll go! And let's see you raising your hips to ask us to fuck you."

He barked the command, and the next moment the girls lay side by side on the barn floor, lifting their hips and wriggling in invitation, just the way girls always did in his late night dreams.

The boys smiled at each other in outright glee, then dived into the pliant female flesh. This time they were able to last longer, and it was the cunt squeezes of the whores' own orgasms that brought them both to climax. They lay heavily on top of their mounts, not bothering to take their weight off the slight bodies under them. Never had they imagined such bliss as can be found in the deeps of a girl.

"Fuck, that was good," said Matt, the elder, if only by ten months. "Shall we take their asses now?"

Already he was pulling Blaze up onto all fours. His cock was but half stiff, so he rested against a straw bail whilst she sucked it for him. Toy did the same for Todd, carefully licking all her juices from his shaft, loving the way it grew huge again so quickly in response to her ministrations. Now he had grown in confidence he was handling her roughly; he suddenly pushed her face away from him down into the straw, so that she was knelt with her bottom in the air. He pressed his cock against her puckered hole whilst his brother watched, the bay still mouthing his cock. She was tight, he could not gain entry.

"Push harder," his brother advised, "just keep it hard against her, as hard as it takes for her to let you in. That's it. That's it... ...ah, now you're in her! Keep on, get it all the way in, make her take every inch!"

Toy whimpered as this advice was followed. She was still sore from being so well-used the day before, and the cock in her was enormous, surprisingly so for such a young man. When she was completely impaled he began to shaft her very roughly, huge waves of delicious pressure echoing through her ass to her cunt and clit so that soon she was moaning in ecstasy, whilst still she gasped in pain at his roughness. Her orgasm seared through her, and she screamed as he seemed to sink still deeper into her yielding flesh. He had not finished, and pumped harder and harder at her trembling body.

Matt had been watching the performance with growing interest, and now he went over to join Todd.

"Can you lean back? Lie with her on top of you?" he asked.

Todd shifted position so he was flat on his back on the straw, holding the squirming Toy around her waist and shifting her back and forth on his long organ. Matt was remembering a favourite photo in one of his well-thumbed porno mags. He took hold of each of her slender ankles in his strong hands and lifted them towards her neck, at the same time pressing his swollen cock into her nicely presented cunt. She took the full length of it with a tiny cry of protest. The two brothers could feel each others cocks through the girl's ringing muscles. It felt good. She was whimpering again, but what the hell, this was what she was for. Matt thrust harder.

Despite being bruised and tender, Toy could not help but adore the two young cocks sinking up to their hilts inside her. She felt almost unbearably full, and she was loving it. The older boy was using her as hard as he could now, and each time he dove into her it hurt a little, so that tears were spilling down her pretty face, but her submissive nature was so strong that being treated this brutally only heightened her arousal. Each cruel thrust seemed to sink right to her heart, the heart of a whore. She knew she was nothing, just a toy to amuse, an animal to ride for pleasure, and her lowly status made her hotter still. All men are gods if you are but a plaything; she knew she was honoured to be fucked by the boys, she worshipped them in silence as they ravaged her soft body.

"You! Come and sit on her face!" Matt barked the command at Blaze, who obediently crawled over and began to lower herself over Toy.

"Not that way. Turn round!"

He wanted the pretty whore facing him. The pungent wet pussy was pressed hard against Toy's mouth, as Matt brought his weight down on Blaze's shoulders.

"Now bitch, lick that cunt good." Toy found Blaze's fat clit, and began to lick it with hard flicks of her stiff tongue, then dipped into the girl's sweet hole, enjoying the taste of the moaning slut.

Still thrusting into the lithe body under him the boy knelt up, and began to kiss the sorrel whore, stroking her lovely breasts very gently with one hand. With his other hand he reached for Toy's tits and dug his fingers in as hard as he could, twisting and pinching the delicate orbs so that her yelped response was clear despite her mouthful of cunt.

"Todd! Hurt the bitch! Be as rough as you can! You like it, don't you slut? That's it, take her tits and make her cry, the whore loves it."

It was true. Being so used and hurt and humiliated made her half crazy in her arousal. She saw how tenderly and soothingly the young man stroked Blaze, whilst both brothers hammered into her as unkindly as they could. As Todd took her nipple rings between thumb and forefinger, pinching and pulling her breasts into absurd towers, she was blasted by the deepest orgasm she had ever felt. She did not pause in her licking of Blaze's clit, and the men did not pause in taking their pleasure.

They continued using her as though she had no feelings, or rather, none that mattered, until they had both come, filling her holes full of their spunk. Blaze was close to coming but they had lost interest in that part of the game. They were drunk on newfound power. They slipped out of Toy and hit upon the fine idea of tying her from the rafters, strung by her ankles. Using several turns of rough rope around each ankle they hauled her up, then Matt reached down a couple of whips from the wall rack, threw one to his brother.

"You go round and beat her ass. I'll let her have it on the tits and belly."

As he spoke he lashed towards her, the stinging blow leaving a burning red welt across the pure white skin of her right breast. She bucked and swung, totally helpless. He matched it with another on the left, this time taking careful aim so that the taut nipple felt the lick of fire. He could see the gleam of her wet cunt in a warm shaft of late afternoon sunlight; his cock stiffened with the knowledge that she was turned on by his pitilessness.

The first blow hit her round buttocks as the third landed upon her tits. The agitated slut writhed helplessly in her attempts to avoid the blows; both young men felt giddy and exhilarated to hold a girl so entirely in their power. And the great joy came from knowing she was totally acquiescent; the Sinclair slaves were girls who loved to be savagely used. Matt and Todd had both heard the whispered stories: from their friends' older brothers, from men at the inn, from their father himself. Stories of girls who would come just from being beaten, girls who had decided, quite freely, to dedicate their whole existence to providing men with pleasure, by offering up their beautiful bodies to be mercilessly fucked and beaten. Girls who revered all men as gods. And now they had two such to play with!

At this moment Joe walked in. Toy saw him first, for both young men were intent on the beating, enjoying the patterning of welts with which her fine flesh was now crisscrossed, and Blaze was watching them in their work, both aroused and horrified. Toy knew the groom's face so well that even upside down she could see that his eyes twinkled with approval as they flicked over the scene, lingering on her heavy breasts which had been so cruelly treated. As he walked forward the boys suddenly became aware of his presence, halting in confusion, but he waved a reassuring hand to them to continue, and again the stinging blows licked her tormented flesh, now with renewed vigour.

He looked her over, then fetched a couple of things from the shelf, and motioned that they should pause, whilst he strapped onto and into her a be-dildoed chastity belt that had thick shafts that probed deep into her pussy and asshole and then he filled her mouth with a fat ball gag . Now she was completely stuffed and he smilingly nodded for the beating to continue.

As the blows rained down once more, some landing on the impaling belt with such force that they made the dildos thrust deeper into her, she felt herself beginning to come. To her shame and horror muffled moans of pleasure squeezed from behind the bulbous gag, and the men all laughed, knowing quite well that she was climaxing. Joe undid his trousers and wanked off over her tits, the hot, thick spray of semen dripping from her nipples, trickling over her face. Even then they did not stop the beating.

Toy was almost unconscious by the time they let her down. She was dragged outside by her hair, hosed off with icy water inside and out, then tethered securely in the stall, fastened by her collar as always with her wrists behind her back. But now her ankles were also chained. Not on long chains as they had been the night before, but with shorter tethers, so that although she could wriggle and shift into various positions she could never close her legs, her lean, milky thighs were pulled always wide open, completely exposing her naked mons.

For the next two weeks she was not beaten at all. The red welts all healed completely, so her body was perfect and pristine once again. Each day Joe put the pair of fillies through their paces in the trap, but the two whores were now so well trained that only the tiniest tickle of the crop was needed to command them. In the evenings, in fact at any time, Joe and other men would fuck them. Sometimes a gentleman would hail them as they pulled the trap, and Joe would stop and partially undo the harnesses, so he could enjoy one or other girl.

And Blaze was still beaten. Oftentimes Toy would lie tethered on the floor of the stable, always now with her ankles chained apart, watching her sister slut crying and wriggling as she was whipped. It made her wet.

She was fucked more than ever now, as any man entering the stable was greeted by the sight of her spread legs and defenceless pussy, and the prospect of ramming her full of cock was irresistible. Half a dozen of the field workers took to coming to the stable for their lunchbreak, taking it in turns to hammer into the bound girl. One would shoot his load into her, pull out, and immediately another man would take his place, leaving her pussy swollen with desire.

One evening Marcus came to inspect her. He was pleased to find her quite unmarked; he had an amusing little scenario planned, a belated punishment for her escape attempt. He handed Joe a bundle of garments, then settled back on a straw bale to watch her arrayed in her finery. First she was laced into a cruelly-tight black leather corset, that was cut to lie under her breasts, with straps in triangular fashion to frame them nicely. Suspenders led to shiny black rubber stockings, her feet encased in gleaming black ankle boots, the heels so high she could only totter. Long, black, rubber

159

gloves graced her lower arms, which were then strapped behind her with seven straps that cut into her flesh from wrists to above her elbows. Blaze painted her face, giving her huge dark eyes and a glossy scarlet mouth. Her breasts bulged forwards soft and vulnerable, and it came as no surprise when Joe fastened clips to her already ringed nipples, that bit into her delicate areolae with small sharp teeth, making her gasp. To these were added weights, and yet more weights on her nipple rings. They dragged her tits down and made fresh tears prickle her eyes. Finally she was fitted with her bridle and bit, the tang of iron sharp against her tongue.

Marcus led her away, teetering over the cobbles to the dark doorway of the house. He took her up the stairs, then paused in front of the door to the great hall. Toy felt a sudden chilling blast of deja vu; they had stood like this not so many months back, when he had first brought her to the Manor. She had been a free woman then, about to be handled and used with no regard for her feelings, turned into a plaything to satisfy male lust. The eyes that flicked over her trussed flesh held the same cold, appraising intent that had governed them then. As before, she shivered. This time he noticed the shiver, and smiled. There was no warmth in his smile, just pleasure in his ownership of such a fine whore. He turned and opened the door.

A group of men stood chatting near the fire, the brandy they swirled in elegant crystal glasses bright with reflected flame, a haze of cigar smoke in the air, so at first she could not clearly see their faces. As Marcus led her forward they turned to survey the evening's amusement, and Anna felt her blood turn to water.

Every face was familiar from her former life. In the centre of the group was her doctor, a man in his forties who made no attempt to hide his arousal as his eyes trailed slowly over the pretty young girl in front of him, lingering with obvious pleasure upon her naked mons and weighted nipples. To his right were a couple of lecturers from her college, one salaciously licking his lips and staring at her breasts, the other's eyes fixed on her pussy as he started to unzip his flies. On his left the sleazy fat face of the manager of the food store where she had worked part-time to make ends meet. He was a man she had always been scared of; on her first day the other girls had warned her that when she was alone he would likely coerce her into sucking his dick, same as he had all of them, but she had managed to protect herself from his advances. Until now. He was openly chuckling to see her thus presented, and rubbing his bulging crotch. Next to him......

Anna gasped as her eyes met those of Carl Johnson who had lived in the bedsit next to hers. An ugly, brutish young man, about 6'6" tall and grotesquely overweight. She had never felt at ease when he'd passed her on the narrow stairs, sensing a deliberateness in the contact when he'd brushed against her, the heat of his podgy knuckles against her cool thigh in her little summer shorts. Now he leered at her naked breasts, almost drooling as he took in her tormented nipples and denuded pussy. An obscenely thick shaft was already jutting from his open trousers, rock hard and ready to have her.

She took an involuntary step back, halted by the warm bulk of her owner, Marcus, who reached round and gave her nipple chain a sharp tug of admonishment so that she whimpered in shock.

"So you used to watch her play with herself, Carl?"

One of the men was questioning her former co-tenant.

"That's right. I bored a hole in the wall one day when she was at work. Used to get a smashing view as she stuffed half her hand into herself. She always was a slut. If you people hadn't brought her here for training she'd soon have been selling tricks for a fiver just for the fun of it. Dirty whore."

They all laughed.

The doctor moved forward and started to gently stroke her breasts. The other men gathered round, encircling her. Marcus backed away, and bidding the men a pleasant evening he left the room, abandoning her to the attentions of his guests with a chuckle.

The doctor tugged roughly on the nipple weights so that she yelped in pain. At the same time she felt the firm pressure of a finger against her anus. She didn't know whose it was, and she squirmed as it started to twist and thrust into her.

The lecturers reached strong arms around her and lifted her off the ground, large fingers digging into her firm thighs, pulling them open. The doctor moved aside, and she saw that Carl Johnson had settled himself comfortably in a large leather armchair. They carried her towards him, her legs spread, her glistening pussy offered to him like some rich fruit. Right to his lips they carried her, then he bent his head, and drank in the scent of her womanhood. She felt the warmth of his breath upon her pulsating clit, and moaned in supplication as his tongue darted out to taste her. He licked her clit in quick circles, working his way around it then dipping into her sweet cunt, again and again and again. Whilst he teased her burning pussy other men were stroking her breasts, fondling her nipples, pinching them into tight pinnacles. The finger that had chosen to invade her ass pumped in steady rhythm.

As she approached climax the obese man stopped and smiled at her. He seemed to be waiting for something. She sighed in disappointment as the orgasm ebbed away. He raised a quizzical eyebrow then bent his head and licked once more. Quickly she was brought to the brink again. Again he stopped, again he looked at her, his lips curled in a smile of satisfaction at his own power. This time she understood. Flushing with humiliation she began to beg, for she knew that was the only way she would be given release. She had to beg these honourable men to grace her unworthy flesh with their great cocks, she was an owned whore, and only by showing true appreciation would she be permitted to come.

"Please fuck me, Masters. Please fuck me."

The men chuckled in pleasure, lowered her to the ground.

Strong hands were pressing down on her shoulders. As she sank to her knees someone said, "Carl first". Then right in front of her face was the fat man's swollen dick. Opening her mouth to receive cock was now as automatic as opening it for sustenance. As she parted her pretty lips the huge member was stuffed swiftly into her mouth, plunging to the root in one movement so she gagged as her throat was stretched wide to take the man. Rough pubic hair grazed against her soft lips. Someone was squeezing her full breasts as though they were indeed udders, but she couldn't see which of the men it was, her face was pressed into the rolls of belly fat of the young man using her.

Again and again he pulled his shaft almost out of her throat, the better to relish the pleasure of its tightness gripping all of his considerable length. She was finding it hard not to gag, and the spasms of her throat rippled delightfully around the invading organ. Again he drove into her, then rested like that a moment, his balls hanging softly against her chin and neck, her nose full of the scent of him.

She had assumed he'd climax in her throat, but he wanted all of her. He pulled out, and the strong arms lifted her again, holding her arms and legs which were pulled firmly open. She saw that it was her lecturers who were so assuredly parting her legs, the store manager and the doctor holding her arms. Inexorably her light body was lifted and slid onto the shaft that still glistened with her saliva. He felt huge inside her, and to her shame she moaned in pleasure as he started to fuck her. He used her with deep, jarring, thrusts, that both hurt as his cock was so long, and at the same time sent vast waves of arousal through her slender frame. Within moments she felt the start of an orgasm building in her very depths. He hammered away as she came, screaming her pleasure. He was near to coming himself, but as he reached his peak he pulled out of her cunt, and splattered his thick semen all over her pretty face, roughly forcing her mouth open so that she got a good load of the sour fluid. At the same time she was pulled upright and felt the pressure of a cock at her anus, and had to suffer the entry of the doctor.

He lifted her onto his cock, and held her pressed close against him, squeezing both her tormented breasts. Like that she sank down onto his shaft until it penetrated her fully, her body weight supported almost entirely by the invading rod so that she whimpered, helplessly. The other men now had an unimpeded view of her ass-fucked, sweating flesh, the big tits gleaming with perspiration. The lecturers were reaching for her tit-weights, yanking them with cruel pleasure so that she whined in pain. Still her cunt burnt hotter with desire, as ever, her body was a traitor, and she moaned with desire and joyously welcomed each wonderful cock.

The store manager stepped forward and pushed his cock into her cunt, digging his fingers deep into the soft, creamy flesh of her weighted breasts. The two men inside her then began to thrust in rhythm, enjoying the feeling of each others hammering shafts through the delicate dividing flesh of the girl, who swooned with ecstatic passion in their arms. Very soon she came once more, providing her owners with delicious pleasures as her pussy and anus tightened around their penetrating organs in exquisite rhythmic waves.

The store manager climaxed, and the doctor held her firmly in place so that the next man could slip easily inside the slut. She was so lost in passion she was not clear which men were using her, she knew only cock and orgasm. Her sense of self was drifting from her. Someone pulled a hood of soft leather over her head; it was strapped tightly around her neck and then she was alone in the pungent dark. The cock that still wholly filled her ass seemed to impale her so deeply that all her attention was now focussed on it. The man was no longer thrusting into her, but instead letting her weight bring her full knowledge of his fat organ. She was repeatedly burning hot, then shivering with icy cold in an uncontrollable physical response to being penetrated so deeply and unnaturally. As she whimpered, not so much in pain, more through being so utterly overwhelmed, the damp leather slickened between her lips.

A man had been inside her cunt, enjoying her with staccato thrusts that ended with a hot splattering all over her breasts and belly. Now her front hole was empty. She squirmed as her legs were pulled more widely open, powerless to prevent the cock inside her little anus from reaching even deeper into her body as she did so. She anticipated another cock in her cunt, and gasped in shock when instead she was granted a bolt of fire right on her clit. If fucking a helpless girl gave these men pleasure, beating her at the same time could only increase their delight.

She could hear their merriment as blow after blow from the unknown implement found its way to her very centre. Yelping and bucking in pain she could nevertheless do nothing to prevent them exacting such fitting revenge upon her. Revenge for scorning them, for failing to worship their undoubted power, back in the long lost days when she had been free to choose.

Every so often she was spared the full force of a lash to her clit as her labia protected her from all but the most accurate of blows. But this flaw was easily remedied. She felt their hands on her mons, her labia stretched wide apart, then brutally strapped into place with fine cords that encircled her thighs and were pulled so tight fresh tears sprang from her eyes.

Now the target was clear, and no blow missed. As the relentless beating continued the cock in her arse resumed thrusting, and hands mauled her tormented tits.

Quite overcome by the sexual and sensory overload, she pissed herself.

"You dirty bitch!" the words were indignant, disgusted, but the voice was thick with enjoyment. The beating stopped.

A fat finger pressed enquiringly into her pussy. She had no idea whose it was, and yet her pussy hugged it as tight as if it had been the penis of some tender lover. A second digit was brought to join its fellow. And then a third. She felt very full now and couldn't help herself: she pushed against the invading hand in pure lust. A fourth finger.

Only when the thumb was pressing against her stuffed hole did she suddenly understand what was about to happen. She moaned in panic and arousal, but the men just chuckled. The hand was hard now against her stretched opening. She felt herself being opened wider than ever before, tears ran freely down her face as the big hand forced its way inside her cunt. And then it was all inside her, and her pussy lips were hugging a man's wrist. She had never felt so hugely, overwhelmingly full; the sensation was overpowering in its eroticism. The combination of the width of the invader that she had no choice but accept and the delicious humiliation of her full knowledge of the situation brought a blasting orgasm within moments. She shuddered and moaned and cried in ecstasy and shame.

They were shifting her into a different position. With cock still deeply stuffed in her little ass and her pussy over-full with the possessing fist she was being turned and lowered. Something hard under her knees; and yet it was not the chill of the stone flagged floor. She guessed that they were placing her on the low wooden table. The heat from the fire felt intolerably strong against her right side. She felt hands at the blinding hood: a flap was being opened, fingers probed her mouth and obedient as ever she sucked them tenderly. Then she felt cock pressing to enjoy her mouth, and for the first time pulled back in the shock of surprise as she realised not one but two cocks were seeking entrance. She realised the men must be standing facing each other- she herself was on her knees, bent forward- and then hands pressed down on her shoulders so that her mouth was thoroughly stuffed by the two fat cocks.

Her lips were stretched wide to take them. She willed herself into total passivity, so that the men might penetrate her as deeply as possible. The sweet musky scent of the men's pubes, the complete fullness of her ass and cunt and mouth, the certain knowledge that she was now as stuffed as a girl could possibly be and that it was a good thing that she was enjoying it, because no-one would have taken the slightest notice if she had objected...... all this combined to bring her instantly to orgasm. As she shook with the force of her pleasure the cocks inside her responded with their own spasms of climax, and suddenly her mouth was so full of glutinous come that whilst she did her best to swallow it all she could not help but let some of her Masters' precious fluid drip from her lips. At the same time the cock in her anus thrust harder and deeper than ever inside her, before filling her with yet another load.

The three softening organs slipped depleted from her slender body. But the fist, so deep inside her, focussing all her attention on her poor, stretched pussy, remained in her cunt. She was pulled upright, and carried a short way across the room. Hands at the leather hood. Bright light, dazzling her.

When she grew accustomed to the glare she saw she was looking at a girl, the most beautiful and most degraded she had ever seen. Lovely full breasts, tormented by weights that pulled on the sweet nipples, jutting forward as the arms were trussed behind the back. Huge dark eyes that looked back at her with such complete acceptance of their state that they seemed more animal than human. A pretty red mouth, puffy and bruised by use and dripping fresh semen. And above all, a man's wrist emerging from an owned pussy.

The store manager, for it was he, lifted his arm so that her weight was taken entirely by the fist by which she was subjugated, the men around him just holding her a little so as she would not topple.

She saw the girl in front of her, legs dangling helpless as she was raised in the air, and at last recognised that the owned beauty was herself.

They were pulling her hair to hold her head back, to make sure she got a perfectly clear view of herself impaled on the Master's arm, a vision of a girl completely subject to the will of men. The sight of herself, the realisation of just how lovely an object she presented and her dark joy at being owned combined to bring her to orgasm yet again, her cunt clenching wildly against the store manager's wrist.

Whilst she shook and shuddered and moaned they still held her head back, making her watch herself come.

Then the hand was pulled out of her and she was strapped on her back to an arched whipping stand, legs splayed and tied to the wooden legs of the stand, arms likewise, head dangling. And they beat her and beat her and beat her, heedless of her cries for mercy, deaf to her pleas for cock, not belt, until they were too tired to lash her any more.

They re-buckled their thick leather belts with the satisfaction of a job well done, and went off to eat, leaving her still strapped helplessly in place. Her legs wide, her naked pussy on full view, her reddened labia showing how thoroughly she'd been enjoyed and the myriad of welts on her sweet breasts showing how thoroughly she'd been chastised for being such a whore as to take pleasure in her use.

CHAPTER 16

If Toy had been meek before it was as nothing to the total submission with which she now delighted her owners. The merest touch of a male hand on the fine swell of her buttocks would have her arching her spine, pushing her ass towards the gentleman in mute request. She was like a she-cat that was somehow permanently in heat, always ready to be fucked, seeking no reward, happy to be used.

They kept her stabled alone now, separate from Blaze. It was because she had capitulated so quickly and completely to the will of men; her submissive nature was so strong that she'd been reduced to the state of contented animal, and thus perfect slave, in almost half the time of an average Sinclair whore. Blaze was meek, but still had some way to go before she was ready to be branded. Toy, on the other hand was more than ready. Running his hands lightly over her smooth white flesh Marcus thought with satisfaction what a high price this slut would bring him, and what a delightful business the slave trade was. The overheads were tiny compared with the profit made, mother nature did such a good job supplying the raw material. He slipped his fingers between her lips. Deliciously wet and inviting, as always. He was sure that Sinclair Precision Components would have many more serious competitors if the ability to spot natural submissives was not such a rare gift. It would be no good at all enslaving girls who at heart wanted to be free, sooner or later it'd have brought the law down on the firm. All his girls were natural whores; if anyone had been so silly as to bother asking if they were willing to be treated thus he'd have got an immediate confirmation that they were indeed utterly compliant, in the shape of two sweetly spread and offered thighs. Few men had this gift of knowing which girls would relish servitude. All of the Sinclairs knew by certain instinct which pretty maidens to ensnare and that was the source of their now huge wealth. Utterly easy for them, nigh on impossible for others.

The whore was pressing hopefully against his questing fingers, but he was too busy right now to grant her the pleasure of his cock. He unzipped his trousers and with a few swift pulls on his penis spurted his come across her neat bottom. If she was disappointed, (he knew with certainty that she was), she knew better than to show it. He turned away, thinking, not for the first time, how a whore come-splattered in such a pleasantly casual manner was rather reminiscent of an object upon which a tom cat had marked his territory. Yes, ownership was a pleasant state, he really did enjoy it. He'd make arrangements for the branding, and then they'd see about getting her clit and nipples implanted with those new devices.

Brandings were an important event on the Sinclair estate. Everyone would be in attendance, from the lowliest field workers to old Sir Jonathan Sinclair himself. There were nine girls in the batch this time, all delightful creatures that would please any man, though Toy was undoubtedly the prize possession.

The day dawned bright and warm. In the gardens the roses were in full bloom and their scent wafted sweetly over the courtyard. Joe got Toy ready himself. There was little to do for a branding: the slave was traditionally naked and barefoot to show her without artifice. He'd washed and combed her lovely hair which was longer than ever now, brushing against her buttocks like a gleaming cape. The rings through her nipples and nose would sparkle decoratively in the bright sunlight, the clitoris ring would look especially appealing as it jutted from her naked crack. All that remained for him to do was to oil her. The oil was expensive and luxuriant, made from rose petals grown in some hot, distant country. On a sudden whim he decided to take her to the rose garden and do it there.

She walked along, meek and silent on her leash, her little legs having to trot to keep up with his great strides, her wrists bound together behind her back. She really was very tiny. Which added to her appeal, of course. And so utterly feminine, with those huge wobbling breasts that jiggled so prettily. If she understood what was to happen today she showed no sign of nervousness. Probably she just didn't know; no-one would have bothered to tell her after all, there was no question of asking her permission. The days when anyone would ask this girl's permission before doing what they wished to her sweet body were now long gone. In fact, the idea seemed as humorously absurd as asking a car's permission before affixing a personalised number plate. He chuckled at the whimsy.

There was a small rowan tree in the garden. He tied her wrists to it, high above her head so that she had to stand on tiptoes. There was no real need to bind her, he knew she'd stand and passively accept whatever he might mete out, whether that be the soft caress of oily hands, as today, or the harsh cutting bites of his whip. But she looked particularly delightful when bound, and also it pleased him to make her suffer discomfort.

He poured oil into both his big palms, and cupped each over a delicious round breast, massaging the liquid into the glowing skin with the flats of his hands. The rings pressed this way and that under his steady movement. The nipples were taut buds, hard as buttons. She was moaning as though already close to coming. He realised it was a while since he'd petted her: male pleasure was the sole goal of sexual activity at the manor, probably her recent shaftings had been too brief to grant her the release of orgasm. All the better: the more frustrated a girl was, the hotter she was. It'd be a fine thing when she was modified and her owner had total control over her pleasure.

He oiled her back, carefully lifting the thick curtain of hair away so that it wouldn't be sullied. Her muscles were fine and well-defined from the daily trap work. She was in perfect condition. His hands slipped down to her buttocks, kneading the pliant flesh with the total confidence of power. She was moaning very loudly, trying to splay her legs further open but unable to do so as her wrists were tied too high. She was desperate to be fucked, but he would enjoy denying her that satisfaction. Still, his cock was rock hard in his trousers. He'd use her mouth, later, and that way gain his own pleasure without furthering the whore's.

He began to oil her slender thighs, his big hands easily encircling them. He ringed her leg just above the knee, with the full span of his spread fingers, then worked his way up to the top, enjoying the creamy softness of the skin close to her groin and the way she trembled with unsatisfied desire. He let one finger brush with infinite gentleness against her labia, casually, in one movement with his massaging of her thighs, and chuckled at her sharp intake of breath. She was on the very tips of her toes now, trying desperately to spread for him, to invite him inside. He'd whip her for her insolence, but he didn't want her marked today, he wanted the crowd to see her at her most lovely and unspoiled.

Joe took great pride in his work as a whore trainer. On the rare occasion that a branded slave had been foolish enough to shame him by misbehaving with an owner she had certainly regretted it when returned to his care for a dose of... ...re-education. His wrath had been awesome. As far as Joe was concerned, any fault in the slave's performance was a direct reflection upon him and his skill. No girl had ever failed to please a second time.

But he could be as gentle as he could be cruel. And as he stroked the sweet flesh of the trembling whore he knew that this slave was one of his most exquisite creations. She would fetch an enormous price, and he looked forward to his cut with pleasure. It had been a proud day last month when the Sinclairs had decided to pay him a percentage of the profits; before then it'd been a plain wage. Now he had a financial investment in the outcome of each training, to match the investment of his pride. He would probably have saved his earnings to buy a slave of his own, but he had no real need. He had the same fine eye for submissive girls as the men he worked for, and had made sure to marry a lass who was ready to serve.

Whilst they were still on their honeymoon he had brought his subtle skills as a trainer to bear upon the innocent girl, and now, whilst she was still ostensibly a free woman, who wore clothes, bought the shopping and cleaned the house just like any other village wife, she was totally subjugated, and loving it. Whilst other men were greeted by a quick peck on the cheek after their hard days work, Joe had a daily blowjob to look forward to each evening, as he settled back on the sofa watching the football and eating the delicious food his wife had spent the day preparing. Occasionally he'd bring friends back with him to share a beer. He wouldn't share his woman with them; after all, she was his wife, but he would insist she strip and service him as usual, in front of them. He enjoyed seeing her blushes. She knew better than to be hesitant; if she was tardy about displaying her body with so many eyes upon it, if she didn't dance so provocatively when told to go through the normal routine, he had occasionally responded by letting his mates handle her whilst she sucked him. Then she really did blush, cheeks pink with humiliation whilst unfamiliar hands stroked her breasts or even slipped into her pussy as she got to work. The memory made him even harder. He was having a few of the lads back tonight as it happened, to celebrate the branding of the latest batch. He wondered what he could ask his wife to do that would make her hesitate. Of course: he'd make her spread her lips and walk round the room, showing her wet pussy to all his friends. That was a big step beyond anything he'd asked her to do before, and he knew for certain she'd baulk at the idea, maybe even ask to be let off. Loving it really, of course, and when she obeyed and spread herself they'd all see just how much she did love it. And as punishment for her hesitancy he would be perfectly justified in letting the three of them fumble with her whilst he used her mouth. He did so enjoy seeing her blush with shame. Perhaps he should let one of the boys bring her to orgasm. Oh, that'd really humiliate her. He chuckled at the thought. She was a tricky female to bring off, needed a particular knack. She'd actually had to show him her own technique, which considering how much experience he had was quite remarkable. Once mastered, she'd been easy to bring to climax quickly every time. He'd had a mischievous thought: he'd use one of the sluts' clits to demonstrate the fingering needed to bring his wife to a quick and resounding orgasm, teach all the lads just what was needed. Then tonight, whilst she sucked him, he'd get them to bring her off. Not only would she be humiliated by him, her husband, seeing her ecstatic pleasure in another man's touch, she'd have the additional shame of knowing that he had shared her most intimate sexual needs with his friends. And of course, later that night, once alone, she would accept a beating with true humility, knowing that she most certainly deserved it for such a whorish response. Sometime he must have her blindfolded, he thought, and let them use a pre-heated dildo on her. She'd think she was being shafted by cock, she was far too inexperienced to notice the subtle difference in texture between rubber and flesh. Idly he wondered how she'd respond if he let her believe he was sharing her with three of four friends. Quite certainly with enough disobedience to justify a thorough whipping and some torment of her lovely tits. He smiled to himself. Life was truly good.

Whilst he thought his hands steadily massaged the dangling whore. She was still arching towards him, up on her tiptoes, legs as spread as she could manage. A mute plea for a thorough fucking. What a truly delightful creature.

He stepped back to admire the flesh so prettily presented. The full breasts, round as melons, hung ready to be squeezed, glistening now with the oil that emphasized their rich curves. The nipples raspberry pink and punctured by the fat gold rings, such a clear sign of servitude. The small high buttocks, so firm and smooth and the slender thighs, with such soft inner skin. The belly, very slightly rounded and with such an endearing little navel. Truly exquisite. The face too: those eyes, still so young and somehow innocent despite her training, and the full, plush mouth, that seemed designed to receive cock. He glanced down, and smiled to see the clit ring peeking teasingly out from between her slightly parted, denuded labia.

On a whim he slipped a finger between her nether lips and brought it out, glistening. He held it to her mouth. Obedient as always she licked it clean.

Toy suckled Joe's finger wishing fervently that it was his cock. She was electric with desire, her skin still tingling from the touch of his steady hands. Whilst he had massaged her he had seemed abstracted, his mind elsewhere. To be so casually stroked and fondled, like a cat petted whilst the owner talks on the telephone, had driven her to distraction. She yearned so desperately for the plunge of his hard cock into her pussy. Or her asshole. Or her mouth. She didn't care how he used her, she wanted to be used. Now she licked and lapped at the fat digit in her mouth with all the careful consideration and expertise she would apply to a penis, any penis. Maybe if she reminded him how delightfully she could pleasure a man he'd enjoy her mouth then give her cunt a thorough shafting. She hadn't had an orgasm for days. All the men who had used her, and there had certainly been plenty, had been hurrying around, working harder than usual. She supposed something special was going on, but she didn't know what it could be.

So all her recent fuckings had been swift thirty second jobs; a body as pleasant at hers brought men off very quickly, so was ideal recreation for men in a hurry. She'd probably been used by more individuals over the last three days than in any other similar period of time since her enslavement started, but not one man had taken enough time to allow her own orgasm to reach fruition. When she was free she'd masturbated every day, often more than once. (She flushed with shame, remembering how she'd unknowingly given Carl Johnson such agreeable entertainment). But now her hands were always bound, so she was unable to pleasure herself. And anyway, she knew it was forbidden. Her body was the property of the Sinclairs; she must not touch their property without express permission.

And yet… …she was so frustrated. She squirmed as she dangled helpless from the tree, pressing her mons forward against her trainer's thigh in the hope he would use her. She knew she was now so deprived that even a few seconds of cock using her cunt or ass would have her screaming with orgasm.

Joe smiled to himself. She was hotter than he'd ever known her. Thinking back he realised it was probably four days since anyone had taken enough time inside the whore's body for her to reach orgasm. All to the good: the more reminders a slut got that she existed entirely for the purposes of male enjoyment the better. The more she pressed towards him, silently begging for sex, the stiffer his resolve that she would not come and the stiffer his cock at the thought of how he'd enjoy her quite one-sidedly.

He untied her wrists from the rowan tree. He could feel her eagerness, her eyes were excited. Swiftly he retied her wrists behind her back, then glanced around. He wanted her on her knees, but he didn't want her grass stained when she was soon to be on display at the branding ceremony. He led her to a spot by a grassy knoll where the spent rose petals lay so thick upon the ground they formed a carpet of perfumed pink and gold, and pushed her to her knees.

Unzipping his flies, he slipped his bulging penis into her sweet mouth.

She sucked him delicately, using all her skill to keep him

hovering on the edge of orgasm. This was, of course, how she'd been trained to service a man. But today he was suspicious of her motivations. He thought it likely that she didn't want him filling her mouth with spunk, for she was so hungry for his hard cock to use her cunt. She was greedy for her own satisfaction.

That would never do. He leant back, enjoying her work, the delicious movement of her lips along his shaft, the light stroking as her heavy breasts trailed against his thighs. But when he'd had enough, and he wanted to come, he simply grabbed her head and with great roughness shafted her throat as though it was her pussy, bringing himself to a mind-blowing climax in a dozen hard thrusts. Then he pushed her away, and did up his trousers, smiling so knowingly that the slut flushed with the shame of discovery.

He looked at his watch, it was time they were getting along back to the courtyard. By now preparations would be complete and the first of the batch of newly finished slaves would be arriving. He liked seeing their faces when they realised what was going to happen.

He looked Toy over. She was perfectly beautiful as ever, maybe even more so than usual as her face was attractively flushed from exertion and frustration. He'd come deep in her throat, his semen immediately swallowed, so there was no messy dribble emerging from the plump red lips. She looked ever so slightly resentful, but that was no matter. It was part of the art of training to mistreat the slave in subtle and unpredictable ways so that a slight spirit of rebellion would enthuse her owned flesh. All the more pleasant to beat or brand a girl who did not accept her servitude with absolute equanimity.

He pulled a brush from his pocket, and groomed her long mane which had become untidied as she worked. Then he tugged on her chain lead and led her towards the end of her journey.

The courtyard was bustling with activity when they returned. Joe saw Toy's eyes take in the scene with curiosity and maybe a whisper of anxiety.

Benches had been arranged in tiers for the servants so that all would have an unimpeded view of the entertainment, whilst the Masters and their honoured guests would watch in total comfort from velvet upholstered chairs that had been carried out of the manor for the purpose.

To one side was a portable shackling system: a thick iron bar supported at each end by wooden uprights. Rather like a clothes rail in a dress shop, but far heftier and quite immovable now it was complete, as the uprights were themselves fastened to the stone mounting block and watering trough that were permanent features of the courtyard. Even if all the whores should panic and run in the same direction, something the silly creatures never had the sense to do, the bar would not topple, nor even move an inch.

Along this rail were already tethered half a dozen or so lovely naked girls. Each one had her arms firmly tied behind her back, each prettily bobbing pair of breasts glistened enticingly with the same sweet oil. Every lovely nipple was pierced by identical, fat, gold rings, all labia were naked of hair, and poking cheekily out from between them all was another fat, gold ring of ownership.

The dull metal collars round the sluts' necks were chained to the immovable bar. There was not even the slightest possibility of escape.

The girls were clearly agitated about something. Toy was fastened amongst them, the chain tethering her being rather short so that she was forced to stand quite upright and close to the thick bar above her. Joe looked her over, approvingly, she thought. He seemed about to go, but then turned back as though remembering something. Reaching between her legs he found her clit and gave it a sudden vicious squeeze, so hard that she yelped in shocked pain and tears started from her eyes. He smiled, looking her full in the face, and she knew she was being punished for seeking her own pleasure in the rose garden, and she knew the punishment was well-deserved.

Some of the serving maids from the house were already seated on the stands, close by where Toy stood. They'd seen what had happened, and were now laughing and pointing and demonstrating to each other how Toy had yelped in shock, they were giggly and excited, looking forward to the show. But what was the show to be, Toy wondered to herself.

Her eyes followed those of the other sluts, to the centre of the assembled throng. It was similar equipment to when she'd been collared, (her heart beat faster as she remembered that terror): a blacksmith's furnace, blazing away so that no one could stand within yards of it. She could see the bright orange of the fire that nestled inside it. And a row of three of the arching whipping stands, so beloved of her Masters: curved oaken devices with splayed legs over which a slut could be bent double then strapped firmly in place. Most whipping stands just had four integral straps, to hold a girl helpless by her wrists and ankles. These were more elaborate, with straps waiting to be buckled all the way up legs and arms, and even round the waist. Any slut thus restrained would be unable to move even a fraction of an inch. Now all that was missing were the girls, and it didn't take much thought to realise that she and the lovelies tethered to either side of her were the intended victims. Uneasily she pulled at her chain. The collar dug into her soft neck, insistent. If there had been a time when freedom was an option it was now long gone.

The bar was now replete with girls, nine in all, shackled in line like market animals. The stand of servants was full apart from the first row, which was presumably reserved for those who were still busy with final preparations, bustling here and there, smiling and confident. Joe was settling himself on the front bench.

Suddenly the chattering ranks of servants hushed and at the same moment rose to their feet: the gentlemen were arriving. A dozen or so wealthy-looking men, mainly in late middle age or older, but some younger ones, too, being shown to their places by the ever-courteous Sinclair brothers. Typical Sinclair clients. And old Sir Jonathan Sinclair, leaning slightly on a fine cane, still an imposing figure; was sinking into the central chair.

When all the guests were seated the rich old man gestured to the servants who sat back upon their benches. The air felt tense with excitement, somehow reminiscent of a hunt. There was somehow the same feeling of permitted barbarity, of pleasure that all know is wrong, but nevertheless, gloriously allowed, as though through some overlooked loophole in moral law.

Sir Jonathan Sinclair stood up, and the quiet deepened.

"Good afternoon everyone," he was smiling round at the other gentlemen, "I am delighted to welcome you to our Manor, and to the entertainment we have planned for you. I hope you shall find it amusing."

There was an appreciative murmur of chuckles from the guests and staff.

"As you all know, my family business is the production of best quality female sex slaves. By the time one of our girls is sold she is an exquisite creation: the delights that mother nature so copiously provides have been artfully augmented by the Sinclair trainers to produce a beauty who is totally ready to serve her owner. Once the process of subjugation is complete the sluts are branded with our insignia and a unique identification number. The branding is permanent and serves a dual purpose: firstly, to impress most forcibly upon a slave that she now has no more status than the lovely animal to which we have reduced her, secondly, as a mark or quality control and certification of authenticity to ensure each slut reaches an appropriate price should an owner wish to re-sell her. Of course, the procedure also provides capital amusement for all of us, which is why I have invited you here today. Let the entertainment begin!"

Toy finally understood what was about to happen as the first girl was led out. She was a pretty young thing, about Toy's own age, with thick blonde curls tumbling down to her shoulders, and plump white breasts. A trainer bent her over the first of the arching stands, and started strapping her in place. He was fastening the straps very tightly, so tight indeed that Toy could hear the girl whimpering as each buckle was secured. Her delicate flesh bulged from between the black leather bands which striped her limbs. Her breasts hung down like bells through the holes designed for that purpose, and in between fastening straps the trainer casually stroked them, as though to comfort her.

Once she was properly secured, the multiple straps ensuring she could not move an inch, except only her head which dangled down, hidden by her mane of curls, the next girl was led forward. A tiny delicate oriental slut, with gorgeously smooth skin of golden olive, and shiny black hair. Toy could see she was trembling, yet meekly suffered herself to be led to the stand and strapped tightly in place without protest. Her spread thighs and naked pudenda must have looked a fine sight to the gentlemen with their ringside seats; Toy noticed that old Sir Jonathan and several of the guests were idly rubbing their bulging crotches.

The final enslaved innocent of this first batch was a dashing beauty who was likely of Eastern European descent. Her hair was as black as that of the little japanese girl, but hung in thick waves from her proud head. She was tall, maybe 5' 10" or so, and very slender in the waist, but with rich, full hips and big breasts that were nevertheless high and pert. The word 'thoroughbred' slipped unbidden into Toy's mind, and she realised with a sort of excited horror how apt it was; all these girls, whatever they had been in their former lives, were now simply lovely animals. Well trained animals that would bring whoever owned them much pleasure.

It was degrading, inarguably. But also intensely erotic for a submissive such as herself, and she knew her pussy was running wet yet again.

The final straps were being fastened round the graceful white arms of the tall girl. She was too proud to whimper, but each time the trainer buckled one tight her head gave the tiniest of jerks. The man's face had a cruel smile that frightened Toy, and she suspected the beauty was being strapped especially tightly for no other reason than his sadistic pleasure. As if in confirmation he fastened the final bond, then reaching for the helpless dangling tits pinched the nipples so hard that the girl's head reared right up in shock. But still she did not cry out.

Old Ben was ready with the branding irons. With neither hurry nor fuss he walked round to the blonde's side, carrying the hot iron in a heavily gloved right hand. He smiled happily at the gentlemen, then pressed the iron against the smooth buttock. The blonde head jerked up and the unfortunate girl screamed. The whole of the audience laughed and cheered, the servants whooping in glee. Now Toy understood why the whores were strapped so tightly: the immobility meant that the brand would leave a clear, sharp imprint on the property, as you'd expect with such high-quality merchandise.

Next it was the turn of the little Japanese girl. The branding iron came down, her head bucked, she screamed. She also pissed herself. The crowd whooped its satisfaction once more. Toy knew they'd take especial pleasure in the girl's inability to control her own bladder. Glancing back at the blonde she realised that she too had urinated in shock. She hadn't noticed before as she'd been too intent on the screams and the reaction of the crowd.

Now the proud Slav would receive her mark of product

quality. Ben was thoroughly enjoying himself, grinning from ear to ear. The iron pressed firmly down on the perfect white orb, and the beautiful girl, who could easily have graced the catwalks of Milan and Rome, screamed and bellowed like the injured animal she was. She also pissed herself even more spectacularly than the other two whores, provoking much merriment from the ecstatic crowd.

The three were then unstrapped and led away. Each had her eyes downcast in shame. Each had a fiery red 'S' and a code number indelibly imprinted on the swell of her left buttock.

The next three girls were trembling and mewing. Toy was one of the final three, and as she watched the others bound she realised with horror that she really needed to piss. With a sickening sense of betrayal she remembered how Joe had given her a big drink of fruit juice this morning. At the time she'd thought it a lovely treat, but recalling how he'd refused to allow her to urinate since then she knew it had been an entirely deliberate act to ensure she was humiliated by losing control as the other girls had. By the pressure in her bladder she knew that when she succumbed it'd be a real fountain, far more impressive than even the Slav whore's waterfall. Her face burned with shame at the thought.

This time the victims were a slender black girl with absolutely huge breasts, a tanned blonde with long, straight, silky hair, and a delicate redhead who was as petite as the oriental slut but had an even slighter frame. Her tiny breasts barely hung through the holes in the stand, but that didn't stop the trainer squeezing them roughly, with resulting cheers of appreciation from the servants. Toy noticed that whilst he was quite gentle with some of the girls, stroking the blonde's full udders with a reassuring touch for example, he had been particularly cruel to the Slav and the redhead. They had in common that almost indefinable air of quality, that had made her think of the most precious racehorses. She felt a chill as she realised that she had that quality too.

She had never recognised it in herself until that night when, brutally fist-fucked, they'd made her watch her own violation in the mirror. In that moment before she had understood that she was looking at her own body she had recognised the same ineffable quality of thoroughbred.

The girls were all in place now. Down came the branding iron on the hard buttock of the black girl. Down it came on the page three blonde. Down it came on the lovely redhead. And all three reared their pretty heads and screamed, and pissed themselves in sorry puddles. They looked down at their feet as they were led away, truly subdued at last, mere products for male amusement.

With sheer terror Toy realised that her turn had come. But to her surprise one of the wooden stands was being taken away, the remaining two shifted closer together as though it was no longer needed. And yet there were still three girls remaining, chained to the bar. Herself, a very plump girl who had clearly been deliberately fattened for some man who preferred plenty of flesh and an Indian girl with huge, sad, dark eyes and a perfect, classic figure.

As the trainer came for them she shrank back, hoping that she was the one that might escape the terrible ordeal and humiliation. The trainer led the Indian girl to a stand, and strapped her in place. She was moaning and crying, and beseeching the man to stop, in a language that no-one understood. The trainer was gentle with her. As soon as she was completely immobile he reached for her parted labia and began to stroke her. Soon she was gasping with pleasure, as his thick fingers slipped in and out of her helpless pussy. He was asking her something, requesting her compliance maybe, Toy wondered.

Suddenly the girl lifted her pretty face and called in a thickly accented voice, "Yes! Yes! I submit to you!" and then moaned as an orgasm washed over her. The trainer wiped his fingers clean on her presented buttock, and returned to the two remaining chained girls. Toy pulled back as far as she could, but when he ignored her and instead unchained the fattened slut she felt a surge of disappointment that was close to misery. If she was not to be branded, why was she here then?

The fat girl was being strapped now. Some of the servants were jeering at her, laughing at her fleshy body. The poor girl was pink with shame. She'd been quite slim when she'd first been brought to the Manor, but a prospective buyer had identified her as exactly the sort of whore he required, and she'd been fattened to his precise specifications like so much meat.

Down came the branding iron on the Indian girl. Up came her head, screaming, her piss puddling between her legs. Down came the iron on the fattened girl. Up came her head, as her screams rang out over the courtyard. And again that puddle of piss.

Oh, how Toy felt for those girls as they were led away, so shamed their hair hid their faces.

The two remaining stands were removed. Surely this couldn't be it? She felt so let down. But the crowd was not moving, instead all eyes were upon her. Every single one of the seated company, every servant on the benches, every rich man in the upholstered chairs… …each one was looking right at her. And then she saw they were bringing on a new stand. This one was slightly different from the others, the legs far more widely splayed so as to spread a whore's thighs more widely apart, and at the front just one leg, to which both arms could be strapped.

The trainer came to get her.

She was trembling with fear, and as he unfastened her from the bar she pulled shrinking away. The crowd roared but she didn't hear them, she just kept trying to escape from the man who was smiling so cruelly, and pulling her towards him by her chain. In a quiet voice he said, "This is going to really hurt."

It was too much. In total panic Toy tugged away, her metal

collar digging hurtfully into her tender neck. But with practised ease he pushed her around, grasped her bound arms together with his own dark muscular right arm, and frogmarched her to the stand. The crowd roared its approval.

He forced her, still struggling, over the wooden frame, strapping her wrists together to the single front support, then tugged her thighs wide open, strapping her ankles to each wooden leg. She knew old Sir Jonathan was seated right behind her, enjoying the pleasant view of her legs, so spread that her labia were also open. She knew that he must be able to see the way her lips were glistening from her arousal at seeing the other sluts branded. She was not really surprised to feel a cock suddenly rammed into her defenceless pussy as the trainer continued to strap her into immobility.

The straps were fastened cruelly tight, the trainer tugging on the strong leather restraints with all his strength, so that they cut deeply into the helpless girl. All down her legs went the straps, then down her arms. All the while the cock pushed roughly in and out of her. Finally the strapping was completed. She felt the trainer's scratchy hands on her dangling breasts, then almost yelped as he attached weights to her nipple rings which pulled her sweet breasts into long cones. With a sudden hard thrust Sir Jonathan finished using her. He felt her painfully elongated breasts and decided they were not tormented enough, clicking his fingers to the trainer, who added more weights. Then still more. He was finally satisfied when Toy was audibly weeping with the pain.

He moved away from her. So did the trainer. She knew what must happen next, and she was determined she'd not piss herself like all the other girls. Her face was close to the ground and her nostrils were assailed by the acrid stench of the urine there.

Nothing happened.

Then she was aware of someone close by her again, and

the next moment she was screaming in pain as the iron seared her servitude forever upon her owned flesh. Still, she had managed not to piss. Her bladder was full to bursting but she had concentrated every ounce of her strength on not letting go. She had won a small victory over the Sinclairs.

Or so she thought. What poor Toy did not yet know was that she was a particularly special slave. At most once a year was a product of such superlative quality manufactured, and any such product has to receive some sort of gold mark. In this case the mark of superior quality came in the form of another brand, a small crown shape that was applied just underneath the standard Sinclair S and the whore's identifying number. Toy had thought it was all over. Slumped and just waiting for her straps to be released so she could walk off with her head still high, unlike all the other girls before her, she was totally unprepared for the second blast of pain on her poor bottom. She reared her head, screamed like an animal, and let loose a huge waterfall of piss that had the whole courtyard laughing and cheering.

And still it was not over. Men gathered round her. She could not see their faces, only their feet. They were congratulating Sir Jonathan on an excellent afternoon's entertainment, complimenting him on the beauty of the sluts. She winced as fingers trailed over her freshly burnt brand mark, remarking on the clarity of the lettering.

"May I?" said a deep male voice, and she heard Sir Jonathan reply, "But of course!"

Then a cock was pressing hotly against her puckered asshole, having trouble gaining entry: the pain in her rear made her tighter than ever. But no matter, he forced his way inside her and began enjoying her with long slow thrusts. Of course he would not have been asking her permission. No man would ever ask her permission again before penetrating her. It would be her owner that would be asked, the final stage was complete. She was branded property, now.

After that man had finished another took her, then another. All the guests wanted to sample the best the Manor had to offer. When finally she was unstrapped she was shaking and stiff. Joe took her by the lead and led her back to the stable. She kept her eyes down cast all the time, she didn't want to see the laughing faces of the servants, especially the female ones.

"Congratulations Joe, a fine piece of meat."

She recognised the purring female voice.

"Pull her head up. I want to see what she look like, now."

And her head was yanked up, so she had no choice but to meet the amused eyes of Rebecca. Beautifully dressed in a transparent silk blouse, her breasts slipping sensuously free under the soft material, she looked Toy's humiliated body up and down, chuckling at the tits, still tormented by weights, and laughing outright when she looked at the naked pudenda, remembering what a water show the slut had made for them all. She reached for the younger girl's chin with her elegantly manicured hand, her nails grazing the tender flesh.

"That'll teach you!" she said, and, still laughing, gestured for Joe to lead the whore away.

Toy's cheeks burnt with shame. She knew exactly what Rebecca meant. She meant, your breasts may be more beautiful than mine, you may be younger, your cunt may be tighter, but look at you now, look at what you are. You could have been a free girl, just playing submissive games with a kind and handsome boyfriend, but no, look at you now. See where your beauty and nature has brought you, see what you are. Owned property that we can do just what we want with.

And Toy knew it was true, and knew that she had brought her fate entirely upon herself.

Chapter 17

The brand healed quickly. Within a few days the skin was unbroken once more, decorated now with the insignia as clear as if it had been drawn in fine, red ink. Joe explained it'd gradually fade to a silky smooth white, but remain perfectly legible for the rest of her life. However long that might be. He chuckled, and told Toy she had many decades of service to look forward to. Sinclair slaves were so well trained to please that even when they had lost their beauty they were still used to please men and make money for their owners: strapped in place out of sight in peep show booths where men could watch young girls dancing whilst having their cocks sucked by a Sinclair whore, not seeing her face, seeing the lovely face and body of a pretty young dancer who got paid for her work, but still enjoying the results of the Sinclair training as they were fellated and deep throated by the expert lips and mouth of an owned slave.

Toy's time at the Manor was drawing to an end. Soon she'd be sold, and make a tidy profit for the Sinclair family, just another item from their production line of fine quality whores. But there remained the little matter of her modification. Up until now, branding had always marked the end of a slave's training, the final seal that showed the product was up to scratch. Toy was up to scratch alright: she was one of the classiest amusements they had produced. But they had further plans that would make her an even more appealing purchase.

One morning a private ambulance drove into the courtyard. Toy saw it as she was tethered outside in the summer sunshine, salivating as she watched the other slaves feeding at the trough. For some reason she was not allowed to join them today. She had had nothing to eat or drink since last night, and her mouth was dry, her stomach rumbling.

As the paramedics stepped out Joe walked over to greet them, and gestured towards Toy. They were both big, black men, and Toy felt herself blushing as they inspected her. They did not seem used to seeing slave girls, they were asking all sorts of questions: was she really willing, could anyone have sex with her, was it really just a game?

Yes, Joe was explaining, she had signed away all her rights.

Yes: anyone could use her until she was sold, then it'd be up to the discretion of her owner.

No: it was in no way a game, she was a slave and the correct way to treat her was as one would any other work animal, except that her work was sex.

The men were getting excited now. Toy could tell by the way they were grinning and adjusting their trousers. By way of encouragement Joe reached forward and tugged at her nipple rings, nodding his head towards her as if to suggest the visitors should also feel free to enjoy the whore.

Tentatively, the taller of the men- he must have been at least 6'4"- reached for her full breasts, and cupped them easily in his big hands. His colleague stepped round behind her and, pressing up close, slid his hands lightly over her taut belly and silky thighs. The slut moaned softly is response to their touch, then gasped as the roving hands slipped between her bare lips and found her slippery clit. The big man handled her with an expert touch; soon she was moaning so loudly that the other sluts stopped feeding to watch.

The man fondling her breasts put his hands on her shoulders and firmly pressed her down, whilst the other held her hips so that she stood, bent at the waist, her mouth presented to one man, her pudenda to the other. He fumbled with his zip inches from her face as she waited patiently for the cock. It sprang out, long and lovely, and she needed no bidding to bend her head and perform as she had been trained. As she sucked on her Master's beautiful organ she felt the heat of another cock pressing at her pussy lips. The next second she had two men up to their hilts in her mouth and cunt, enjoying themselves immensely.

Any reservations they might have had as to their right to enjoy her thus had, of course, now quite gone, and they thrust into her with all the roughness typical of men who have not had the pleasure of using owned flesh before. Men who have always had to hold back, as girls have asked them to be gentle and expected their own pleasure to be relevant to the act of sex. Now they had the liberating experience of using a girl who was no more than property. Her enjoyment or otherwise was, as Joe had carefully explained to them, utterly irrelevant. She existed to serve, and serve she would. They hammered into her mercilessly. She didn't even know herself if her moans were from pleasure or pain.

The man in her throat was so deep inside her that she thought she might pass out, his shafting was quite unremitting. It was with relief she felt the great organ shudder and shoot its seed deep into her belly. Moments later his fellow emptied his sac into her bruised pussy.

Toy had been only seconds away from orgasm, and she moaned in frustration as the cock slipped out of her. Joe laughed at her cross little face, and decided to take pity on her. At any rate it'd make a pretty show for the visitors. He called over to where a stable boy was untethering the feeding sluts and gestured for him to bring a girl over. A sweet little thing, blonde and tiny. Not yet branded, quite a new acquisition in fact.

Her pretty face showed shock and disgust as he ordered her to clean up the whore, but she knew better than to protest when the man who'd used Toy's pussy presented it to her, resting Toy's little ass on the mounting block. Joe held one of Toy's legs, the man who'd enjoyed her mouth the other. Joe grabbed a handful of the blonde's soft locks and forced her face down onto Toy's open pussy, where she obediently licked the semen that dripped from the owned cunt and, at

Joe's bidding, flicked her pink tongue over the swollen clit. Soon Toy was screaming with climax, her slim hips bucking as wild as any animal.

Of course, both men were ready for further pleasure by now. The two girls were bent over double, side by side, and found out just how big those big cocks felt when forced up sweet young assholes. It really was such a treat for the two big guys to be able to thrust away with full force with no regard for the girls' feelings, less so for the girls, who were sore and tearstained both by the time the men had finished enjoying them.

It was with regret that the paramedics told Joe they had better be getting along. Without further ado they swabbed Toy's round buttock with alcohol, jabbed a needle into her, and carried her to the ambulance. By the time they got her there she was already deeply asleep.

She awoke gradually. Her head was aching, and her pussy hot and burning. She had no way of knowing, but the two paramedics had stopped en route for a little more entertainment. They might as well make the most of the opportunity, they reasoned, it wasn't every day they had a beautiful girl to use exactly as they liked. Still, after they'd each had her one more time they still had some time to kill, and not enough energy to use her further. So they hit upon the bright idea of taking some photos of her lithe body being fist fucked by each of them in turn. A suitable souvenir of a pleasant morning, but more to the point, they could post the picturess on the net and make some money out of her.

Toy knew nothing of this. She tried to move a hand to touch her sore body, but found it was tied above her head. A voice was droning on a little way above her, she was still too groggy to understand what was being said. She wanted to go back to sleep.

Then there were hands on her breasts, prodding them, tugging them this way and that. A voice said, "We'll make the incisions here… …and here…"

She opened her eyes.

She was in a white-tiled room with no windows. A bright fluorescent light hummed softly above her. She was completely naked, on her back on a hospital bed. Her arms were tied somewhere above her head. Her legs were spread wide, her knees bent, her feet strapped into high stirrups at the foot of the bed. Four men were standing round her, each wearing a white coat. One of the men was elderly; she guessed about sixty, maybe more. The others were all young. Medical students, Toy thought to herself.

It was the older man who was talking. He'd moved away from her breasts now, and was standing at her hip, facing the students who were gathered between her legs, looking at her most private parts. The older man reached over her and she felt, rather than saw, his two latex sheathed hands parting her labia. The students shuffled forwards for a better view. He was saying something to them, again about an incision.

"We'll insert the device just here." Poor Toy moaned helplessly as the gloved fingers prodded her clit. The young men tittered.

"Yes she's a hot one alright, but just think of the pleasures she'll provide after she's been fitted with these devices. Now, are there any more questions? No? Don't you want to know if you can use her now? I'm sure you do. The answer is, of course, yes: that's what she's there for. However, I want her scrubbed and ready for the pre-op by three o'clock," he looked at his watch, "which gives you two hours to enjoy her. Have fun."

With that he gathered his clipboard up and swept from the room, shutting the door behind him.

"Well, what are we waiting for? It's playtime!"

It was the biggest of the three who'd spoken, a broad young man with an ugly bent nose and the build of a rugby player. He put one fat finger into Toy's open pussy and they all laughed as she moaned, instantly aroused.

One of the others was fiddling with the stands that supported her stirruped feet. He loosened her ankle.

"What're you doing, Mark? I like seeing her strapped open!"

"I want her really open, as far as she'll go."

He was refastening her, so that her feet were higher and her legs more spread. She groaned as her thighs were pulled so wide they were quite taut.

"Oh nice one! Who'd have thought she'd open that much. What a most excellent view of her cunt!"

The finger had been withdrawn, and they peered at her pussy, which was slick with her own love juices. Now the cocks were coming out, and without further comment the big man was inside her. She felt her pussy gripping tight round his big shaft. He came within a few thrusts. Perhaps he hadn't had sex for a while she thought. His friends followed suit, and came just as quickly. She felt sorry for these men who needed so little from her to reach climax.

Mark looked at his watch.

"I've had an idea."

The others looked at him, questioningly.

"Year one anatomy finishes in five minutes. That's almost a hundred lads many of whom haven't had a shag for weeks. We've got use of a whore for another hour and a half...
...what do you say we make a bit of pocket money out of her?"

"Excellent!"

"A tenner a go?"

"Seems reasonable to me"

"Ok. Dave: you go and wait outside for them, bring them over here. Andy: remember the raffle at the prom? Well, the leftover ticket roll is in my locker. You go get it, we'll give em all tickets so they don't have to queue, we'll be in deep shit if we make it too obvious what's going on."

"How many do you think she can take in that time?"

"Dunno. Not all of them for sure. Hey, let's tell em there's a three quid refund if they finish in under two minutes. That'll speed it up. After all the more she takes the more dosh for us, right?"

And so it was that Toy spent the next hour and a half of her life taking cock after cock after cock. No sooner had one man shot his load inside her than another took his place. Her pussy was dripping with semen. Her three young pimps were gathering in the money with increasingly gleeful faces.

Someone asked how much it was for a blow job. Of course, they would make more money if she was getting used by more than one cock at once. So pretty soon she was unstrapped and on all fours, a man in her pussy and a man in her mouth. Then a man up her asshole and a man in her mouth. Then she was pulled to her feet, lifted onto a cock, and felt the familiar pressure against her asshole as another cock pushed into her tight hole.

It was totally unremitting, her pussy and ass were burning sore from so much hard use. But by the time the bell rang for three o'clock lectures she had been taken by half the class; and Mark, Dave and Andy had made enough money for their planned flights to Florida.

Toy felt utterly humiliated. But the men had all had a lovely time.

The three lads strapped her back into place, then cleaned her up, chatting happily about what they planned to do on their holiday, as they rinsed her cunt and anus out with antiseptic and swabbed her with alcohol, wiping saturated cotton wool pads over her breasts and nipples and outer labia. She gasped as the liquid dribbled between her pussy lips and onto her clit, stinging the already sore tissue. Then they took a final swab, and wiped her clitoris and her pussy, paying no attention to her cries as the harsh fluid tormented her most delicate flesh.

When the elderly surgeon returned she was clean and ready for the operation, though it had to be said that her pussy hole did seem rather red. He poked at it inquisitively, but contented himself with remarking, dryly:

"You seem to have made good use of your time."

With that he jabbed a needle into her arm. Within minutes she felt curiously float and dreamy, the drug coursing through her veins, lulling her into an ever deeper chemical passivity.

They didn't bother to cover her spread legs as they wheeled her through to the operating theatre. Nurses and auxiliaries and cleaning staff all gawped at the beautiful, naked, bound girl, half unconscious and with her thighs apart so everyone could see her reddened pussy, and it was more than one girl who fantasized about being a helpless sex slave that night as her boyfriend pumped between her legs

A mask came down over her face. "Breathe deeply," said a voice. So Toy breathed, and immediately fell into a deep sleep, dreaming as she fell that she was in the soft arms of someone who loved her dearly, someone who was flying away with her. Far, far away, to a place she had never been before.

Chapter 18

When she came round she was once again in the small, white-tiled room. Somewhere outside she could hear a bird singing, but she could not see the window. She tried to move, and found that she was again bound in place, her arms high above her head, her legs spread. Her pussy was burning. She had been sore before, her cunt bruised by being made to take so many cocks, but now the worst pain came from her clit. A deep, ugly throbbing that made her feel quite sick.

Her nipples too were sore. She looked down at them and saw a few tiny, neat stitches at the edge of the areolae, closing an incision no longer than a few millimetres. And then she realised her breasts were different. They had always been full, she had richly deserved all the derisory comments about her udders. Now they were huge. With breasts like these, even if she was dressed perfectly demurely, no man could look at her without thinking about what it'd be like to enjoy her. Naked, as she would doubtless usually be, they identified her absolutely as a sex toy, a designer plaything concocted for male amusement.

She drifted in and out of an uneasy sleep, tormented by her throbbing clit.

When she finally awoke properly there were men in the room again. The elderly surgeon and two other men of similar age. They were inspecting her perineum. The surgeon touched her clitoris with his gloved finger. The pain was so intense she bucked like a wounded animal. But they seemed to think things had gone well.

"A little redness and swelling, but she should be back in use in less than a week."

"Excellent. And how long before we can give her a 'test drive'?" The man sniggered.

"Oh, around the same time I'd say. Once she's healed externally I can see no reason not to put her back to full use, it's what she's there for, afterall. She'll quite likely be sore for some time to come- maybe months- but that isn't really of any consequence. It won't affect her response significantly, and it certainly won't affect how enjoyable she is to ride."

At that all three of them laughed.

They turned their attention to her breasts, agreeing the implants already looked excellent.

"And you say they won't sag now?"

"Correct. The artificial tissue is a little firmer than natural breast tissue and keeps that texture, doesn't degenerate at all. As we've fitted it in below her mammaries it'll work to support them from the inside, almost like an invisible brassiere. In the past we've noticed that if a whore with large natural udders is subjected to a lot of breast torture premature sagging can be a problem, but these implants make sure that doesn't happen. However much time this beauty spends with weights dragging down on her nipples they'll be as perky as ever once you take them off."

He reached forward, and trailed a finger lightly over her swollen breasts.

"And the nipples?"

"They've taken the implants well, should work perfectly. They'll heal at least as quickly as the clitoris, so you won't have long to wait. Six days I'd say before you can use her properly. In the meantime…" his latex sheathed fingers lifted to her face. She could smell her own juices above the odour of rubber, "…content yourselves with use of her rather lovely…" he pushed all four fingers between her lips, "…mouth."

The two other men came up to the head end of the bed. A simple adjustment made the uppermost portion fold down, so her head dangled back, unsupported. They continued to discuss medical matters as a large, thick cock was pressed into her mouth. The man was impatient and perhaps really wanting to enjoy her pussy; at any rate it was not the soft attention of her lips and tongue he was after but the tight depths of her throat. She did her best to relax as the cock pounded deep into her with callous roughness, his balls flopping against her face with each thrust.

Whilst he used her he talked dispassionately about udder size and control mechanisms. She didn't understand much of what he was saying, but was shamed by the clear casualness of his enjoyment of her; there was no pause in the dialogue as he plunged his cock up to the hilt in her accepting mouth. As he came he held her head very tightly, tendrils of her hair wound around his fingers, and shot his load deep into her, pressing so hard against her that she was almost overwhelmed by his harsh, male odour as his soft balls enveloped her little face.

She gulped at the fresher air as he pulled away, but there was only the briefest of pauses before the other man took his place. He fucked her face very slowly, plunging just as deep as his colleague but pulling slowly out then pausing before shafting her once more. At least that meant she could breathe without the panicky feeling that she would never get another chance to. The thick, dark curls of his pubic hair scratched against her delicate skin. The men's conversation had turned philosophical:

"Do you think a slave is still human, then? Or are they more like animals?"

"Hmmm. We live in a society which has artificially constructed an equality between male and female. This is unnatural, and no more than a sham. Women are naturally the weaker sex; it is very easy to physically overpower them. Evolution has worked to make women so much weaker than men......... men have been taking their pleasure of women for millennia, and no modern rules that say women are equal can change that. And even with current protocol it is still the men who are in charge; just look at the lists of who are the richest: women rarely appear in those tables except as the pampered chattel of their husbands or fathers. So no woman is actually equal to any man; they are all subject. Unfortunately at the present time it is not expedient to articulate this inarguable truth."

The cock was deep in her gullet once more, and paused there, so that her face was covered with the cool touch of the man's testicles. She could not breathe and felt panic rise as her throat began to gag in involuntary response to the invasion.

"Because so many women now live under the illusion of equality those who are still visibly subject must bear the brunt of their natural inequality; they must suffer not only for themselves, but accept the punishment due to their disobedient sisters."

"So the answer to both your questions is yes. They are human, but they are not the equal of any man. No woman is. They are also animals. There is no clear line between humans and animals after all. A girl is closer to being an animal than she is to being a man...... this is true of any female, free or enslaved"

"But what about free women? Do they have greater status than slavegirls?"

"Why yes. But their status comes only from the man who owns them. It is not something they carry within themselves. Take Rebecca for example. Rebecca has far more status than this slut, but that is because she is the chattel of a powerful man, whereas this slut is a mere plaything. Rebecca has no status of her own. If she should displease her in-laws it is more than likely that she'll find herself as lowly as this one here, just a toy, nothing more.

"Men allow their women to assume status because it amuses them to do so, but in the end all women are slaves. Some are just subject to a rather more explicit slavery than others, that is all."

As he said this he pulled partly out of Toy's mouth, coming as he did so. Her mouth was suddenly too full with a bitter mass of thick semen, and final hot spurts splattered over her lips and face, dribbling down her inverted cheeks to end stingingly in her eyes. She swallowed his load, but could not lose the sour taste of him. She felt herself saturated in maleness, permeated in it, like white fabric that has been plunged into hot dye and is forever stained scarlet.

The days passed slowly after that. She was kept in her bonds, unable to touch herself in any way. The students returned to enjoy her mouth, once again charging their fellows to use her. She swallowed load after load of semen, but no hands strayed to her breasts or clit, no cock pressed at her pussy or anus. The pain of the operation quickly lessened as the days went by, and she ached to be touched by the many hands that held her head steady as they plunged into her throat. At night she lay sleepless, burning with desire, but she could not reach her clit, which swelled of its own accord in response to her thoughts and dreams, black desire dancing through her mind through the long empty hours. Her pussy was perpetually moist, waiting to be stuffed full but always ignored by the men who used her.

They would gather between her legs and discuss her clit as though she was a specimen in their laboratories, and when their gloved fingers lightly touched her she writhed in frustrated desire to be fucked.

On the sixth day the surgeon returned, surrounded by his consort of fawning students. Ordering two of them to spread her legs more widely in the stirrups, thereby increasing her accessibility to hand and eye, he inspected her. He poked and prodded her clitoris, ignoring her moans, then slipped his gloved forefinger into her cunt, which hugged it tight in pure lust.

"Yes, the stitches can come out today." He frigged her gently with his single finger, smiling slightly at her helpless passion. But dispassionately he slipped out of her and ignoring her mew of frustration took the scissors the nurse was holding out. He seemed about to remove the stitches, but instead handed the scissors to one of the older students before slipping his lubricated finger into her asshole. She moaned more loudly as he repeatedly pressed into her, his knuckles hard against her ring as his finger slid entirely inside her hole. Meanwhile the student snipped carefully at the sutures. Toy whimpered at the stinging pain as he pulled the threads from her clit. Next it was the turn of her breasts. Again the sting as he tugged away at the fine cords. But it was only a few minutes before he was done. All the while the fat finger pressed into her anus. It was so long since any man had used her thus that the finger felt hugely fat, as though it was the first that had demanded entry to her most secret space. Ripples of desire quivered through her trussed body.

He gestured that her wrists and ankles should be unbound, then pulled her to her feet. Almost gently he led her to the mirror that hung at the other side of the room.

Toy looked at her reflection and blushed in shame. Of course, there was no visible difference in her nipples or clit. But she had underestimated the change to the size of her breasts. Huge udders jutted from her slender frame. No man would ever notice her lovely brown doe-eyes first now, nor yet the pretty curve of her full lips. No man would think of stroking her long lustrous hair before he thought of handling her huge breasts. She was designed for sex, fitted to her purpose as though custom made, which indeed she was. As manufactured as a blow-up sex doll, which was what she resembled now, more than ever, more than anything else, just a delightful combination of succulent holes, each one ready to satisfy cock, carried in a chassis that had no other function than to optimise male satisfaction.

She was, in fact, the perfect woman.

The elderly surgeon was holding her with her arms behind her back, standing just behind her and a little to one side. Now he reached round with his free hand, digging his bony fingers tight into her soft flesh to maintain a firm grip with the other. He softly caressed her weighty breasts, circling the nipples with the lightest of touches. She moaned and leant heavily against him. It was so long since she had been touched, her whole body was aching with longing. He let his hand slip down over the firm, slight swell of her belly, down to her naked lips, from which the thick gold clit-ring peeked so enticingly. His fingers brushed over her plump labia but did not venture inside, so she moaned louder in frustration, wanting so much to have her pussy stroked. The men, gathered around in a hot tight circle, pointed and laughed; and looking with even deeper shame at her reflected image she saw what had prompted their amusement: her sex juices were so copious that they were already spilling from her hidden crack onto her silky mons, glistening an open invitation to all men that she was ready to be fucked. The surgeon slipped two fingers between her nether lips and spread them wide, so all the young men surrounding her could see her swollen clit and moist hole, a hole available now for use of each and every one of them.

A tousle-haired student pushed to the front of the throng and went down on his knees in front of her. Pausing to breathe in the rich scent of her juices he then reached between her parted legs and cupped her taut buttocks, thus lifting her slightly off the floor, spreading her legs wider and raising pussy to his dipped face as though she were a cup from which he might drink.

His strong, hard tongue plunged between her lips, the sensation so overwhelming that she cried aloud with desire and shock. He battered her clitoris with swift, rough strokes then dipped his tongue hard into her little cunt, thrusting like a cock. The beauty moaned and pushed towards him, on her tip-toes, her muscles straining with the effort as she pressed her cunt to his face with all the decorum of a bitch in heat.

He pulled away from her, a sardonic smile twisting his

pleasant features. The slut moaned in disappointment. "I want to hear you beg us all to fuck you," he said.

"Please fuck me, Masters." She didn't even hesitate.

"Beg. Beg us to use you three at a time."

"Please Masters, take me. I want you…" she paused because the words were so crude.

"Say that you want three cocks rogering you at once. Say it! Say you want a cock up your asshole and a cock in your cunt and a cock in your mouth. Say it!"

"I want… …three cocks… …rogering me at once, Masters. I want cock in my cunt and cock in my mouth and cock in my asshole. Please, Masters."

"Say that you're a dirty slut who wants come dripping from every hole. Say that you want your face covered in come. Now!"

Toy was trembling. She was overwhelmed with lust, but never before had the men who owned her demanded such explicit submission. They had always taken what they wanted from her whilst she had merely acquiesced. This man was demanding her total compliance in her degradation.

"I'm a… …dirty slut. I want come dripping from every hole. I want… …I want my face… …I want my face covered in come."

As she spoke these last words she blushed, a dainty English rose now whorish scarlet. The men were all laughing at her. Hands reached and squeezed her tits and thighs in happy anticipation of the pleasure to follow.

"Good slut. One more thing before we grant you the beneficence of our cocks. Beg to be beaten. Beg us to beat you so hard that you are crying for mercy. Beg us to keep on beating you despite your pleas that we stop. Beg us to beat you with our belts until we tire".

The girl spoke now almost as though drugged, repeating the words as a child might repeat an unintelligible poem.

"Please beat me, Masters. Beat me so hard I beg for mercy. Keep on beating me when I plead for you to stop. Beat me

204

with your belts until you tire. Please Masters."

There was much merriment in the small room now. Someone tied her arms tightly behind her back, laughing at the way her breasts stuck forward like two round melons. Someone got hold of her nipple rings and tugged and jiggled them up and down, making her tits wobble as she whimpered in pain. Other hands fastened a lead to her collar. Then she was led out of the little room, past the nurses who turned away their faces, to hide embarrassment or jealousy, who could say? Past the orderlies who gawped in open mouthed desire. Past junior doctors who had seen it all before, and smilingly remembered the perks of their own student days. Into the lift, where she was crowded in, her naked body squashed between so many clothed male ones that she had no idea whose hands were squeezing her breasts, whose fingers were spreading her pussy lips, which fat digit was being forced into her resisting anus.

Then out into the sunshine of the hospital grounds, and over the grass to the wood.

They tied her there, flat on her back against the rough bark of a felled tree trunk, nailing a strip of leather into the wood to trap her wrists high above her head, splaying her white thighs so that they must fall either side of the trunk, her knees very bent. Then they nailed leather bindings over her ankles to hold them securely in place, low against the harsh wood and just lightly kissed by the long, soft, green grass. She looked very lovely lying there, like an illustration maybe, for an ancient myth of a Sylvan raped and her forest glade despoiled. The defenceless flesh of her swollen breasts added to her look of total vulnerability. The cocks were coming out now, a dozen or so. All big, thick organs, all looking forward to taking a girl without having to consider her feelings at all. Delicious that she had actually begged them to treat her thus, really rather a good joke.

The old surgeon took first turn, the younger men automatically according him the respect his years and expertise deserved. His penis was fat and curved, thicker in the middle than at the root. He clambered on top of her and in one quick movement thrust into her moist flesh. Then he rode her like a possessing demon, digging those hard fingers into her sweet udders so that she cried as she came. But come she did, in a tumultuous orgasm that gripped the cock inside her as tight as if she was holding it in a strong young fist. He shot his load deep into her belly.

The next man took his place without pause, and hammered into her with a similarly rough manner. His cock was longer however, and each deep thrust had her gasping with pain. But she loved it too, and would likely have moaned little cries of encouragement if another of the men had not chosen that moment to straddle her face and push his fat organ into her little mouth. This cock was not particularly long but it was hugely wide, stretching her lips, then pressing on to find the tightness of her throat. She could not take it and started to gag, but he didn't pause, he just pushed deeper into her so that for a moment she thought she was lost. But he knew what he was doing, they all did; his semen spurted deep inside her and he pulled out, smiling his approval of the hole he had used. He rubbed his testicles over her mouth, then decorated her sweet face with the gobbets of spunk that still dripped from his spent cock. All the while the man using her cunt hammered into her as though trying to nail her to the wood with his long rod, the rough bark under her scratching at her fine skin. She was so ashamed now that she tried not to come, but of course, this resistance was in vain. She could not help but love cock; it was what she had been born for, this role of sex toy. He felt the tightness of her hole as she orgasmed for him, and filled her with another load of semen.

So it went on, until all the men had had her thus, some using her cunt hole, some her mouth hole. Her mouth and face were messy with semen and trickles ran down her thighs from her well-fucked puss. She shivered when she saw that several men were now unbuckling their belts. They were going to give her the beating she had begged for. She had expected to be untied, that the blows would rain down upon her firm buttocks and strong, slender back, but no; they were going to beat her as she lay helplessly strapped open. Beat her breasts and belly and soft inner thighs, her sweetest, most womanly parts. Despite her fear she felt her clit swell urgently at the thought of the heartlessly cruel treatment she would receive, and ruefully wished she could have had a nature different from the whorish one that had led her to such a sorry state of willing subjugation.

A big man, solid as an ox and with heavy features and small, mean eyes now straddled the log, towering over the tiny girl who was pinioned beneath him as defenceless as a butterfly. In his right hand he grasped a wide belt of thick leather. Leering at her with an unpleasant grin he trailed the tip of the stiff leather over her breasts, letting it catch and tug slightly against her erect nipples, before progressing down to her naked mons, where it glanced against the sensitive labia, then caught at the top of her pussy crack. He let it drag against her clit so that she moaned, swinging it against her swollen nub again and again, but touching her so lightly that she tried to lift her hips to increase the contact. Then, in a movement so swift she had no time to steel herself to take the blow, he raised the belt high, and brought it down over her breasts in a slicing, 'thwack!'

She screamed as the fire of pain leapt through her right breast and engorged nipple, and tried to pull away. But that was, of course, impossible. Her urgent tugs against the strap that held her wrists did not loosen it one jot, all she contrived to accomplish was an enticing jiggling of her huge udders, making them an even more delectable target. The next stroke hit her left tit, and she screamed again, and did not stop, for the third blow bit before she had recovered from the second. The man above her was grinning broadly now, the others gathered round in a tight group, fingering their cocks and pressing forward to get the best view they could. But she could not see any of this, her eyes were blinded by tears. Before long she was begging them to stop, but they took not notice, for hadn't she asked them to do just this, hadn't she begged to be beaten till they tired? The cruel leather now licked her belly and thighs, precise blows that grew ever closer to the centre of her. Then she took a stroke full on her clit. The pain was overwhelming. Her wrists and ankles were red raw from pulling away, trying to evade the blows, but her struggles were utterly pointless and she had no choice but accept that for which she had begged. Oh treacherous body! Why was pain so tempting and seductive when it was a dream, even when she knew the reality was so terrible? The pain was now such that she was drifting into a tormented delirium, then suddenly it stopped. She felt the weight of a man upon her, and a cock pushing into her pussy. She could only lie, wooden, whilst he took his pleasure of her, quickly followed by another and then another. And still she lay almost as though dead, insensible to arousal so thoroughly had she been beaten.

They freed her then, slicing through the leather strapping with the ease which comes from power and a sharp blade, in one moment accomplishing that which all her struggling had been unable to. They pulled her to her feet.

She could not stand alone, but that was no problem. A man held her by the hips and bent her over, pressing his cock against her tight anus until it had to soften and grant him entry. She whimpered a little at the unfamiliar bulk inside her. She had not taken a man *in culo* for over a week, and her slight body struggled in vain against the invasion.

Once he was fully in her he pushed her down so that she was on her knees. Another man slipped between her thighs on his back and quickly she was impaled on his fat cock. She felt too full, and squirmed and wriggled, trying to get away from the two hard cocks, but the men pressed her between their strong muscular bodies so that she was as trapped as a songbird snared in a cat's paws. They started to fuck her in rhythm, the man behind her squeezing her ravaged breasts, the man she straddled holding her hips to slide her pussy up and down his thick shaft with deep, hard movements. Before she could adjust to the amount of cock pumping inside her cunt and ass a third man stepped forward. She knew, of course, what he wanted from her. He stood astride the man who was lying back on the grass, using her cunt. His big, hairy balls pressed gently against her soft lips, and she licked them, tentatively, the pounding of the cocks already inside her pushing her face deep into the pungent balls rhythmically and repeatedly as though she were washed by waves. She licked and suckled on them. They smelt so sweetly male, so much the smell of the dominant creature that she lapped as though at worship. The proud cock rose out of them, rigid and hot. She mouthed the great shaft then licked it delicately along its length, flicking her tongue with delicate precision over the dripping glans. But it was not her expert mouth that he was seeking to enjoy, rather, like so many before him, he wanted the depths of her throat, and drove himself deep into her. As her body struggled to accept the swollen organs that penetrated every part of her, one small section of Toy's mind was able to step outside of the discomfort and degradation that could have overwhelmed her, and see herself as an outsider might, see her little body so totally the focus of male lust and pleasure-seeking. She knew now what she was, what she had become, and whilst she was deeply ashamed to be such a lowly slut, nevertheless, the thought of her total subjugation was intoxicating to her. She arched her back towards the possessing rod, like a she-cat will arch her back to be stroked. It made a pretty picture to the men stood around: the beautiful tiny girl offering herself so freely for male plunder, the heavy thick limbs surrounding and grasping her dainty ones, the red welts that marked her out as owned property.

CHAPTER 19

By the time they had finished enjoying her she was too exhausted to walk. She was half carried, half dragged to the waiting ambulance and driven back to the Manor. Joe whistled then chuckled when he saw how cruelly she'd been used but it was no more than he had expected. Free use of the slave was part payment to the hospital and surgeon for their work.

He weighed her enormous udders in his coarse hands, appreciating the effect of the implants, then closely examined her nipples, giving a satisfied grunt as he noted there was no visible scarring from the incisions. Hooking his hands behind her knees so that she fell back on a straw bale, he pulled her legs apart and inspected her clit, prodding and poking at it to see where the surgeon's blade had cut. Again he seemed well-satisfied. He tied her hanging belly-up from a thick waist-belt of leather, her arms pulled down behind her to rings set in the ground, her head dangling. Her feet were likewise tethered to the ground with her legs well spread, for he knew the masters would want to inspect her pussy and tits without having to bend to get a good view. He was looking forward to seeing the clit and nipple implants operated for the first time, a delight that would be reserved for the man to whom she was being sold.

He hadn't intended to tarry, but the sight of the delightful flesh so appropriately displayed and the huge, accessible breasts made his cock stiffen. Of course, she was suspended at an ideal height and he slipped his thick manhood into her easily. She whimpered; she was still sore from her ordeal at the hands of the doctors, so he drove hard into her, deliberately rough lest she think any gentleness was for her benefit. A whore had to be reminded, time and time and time again, that her own pleasure was irrelevant and she existed only to further the enjoyment of men. He squeezed her udders, hard, so that the tender, red, striped flesh bulged in soft mounds between his strong fingers, noting with satisfaction her little, resigned gasps of pain as his coarse skin grated against her abused flesh. Joe wasn't a sadistic man; he mainly used pain to teach his mares their place, but like most men he had a latent taste for cruelty that was occasionally roused. He had a sudden urge to tug the slut's nipples high, stretch them as far as they would go. At the Sinclair Manor such urges were not suppressed, as they would be in most marital beds the world over. No, here they were applauded. The whore yelped in pain as he pulled on her nipples, elongating them and lifting the round udders into sharply pointed cones. He pulled harder still, so she screamed. Then he let go so her tits fell into gentle mounds once more. The nipples, however, still nearly an inch-long. He reached a fat finger between her pussy lips: yes, she was wetter than ever. What a slut! He hammered into her, at the same time casually rubbing her plump clit. They came together, and she screamed again with the force of the climax.

He wiped his cock clean on the soft fall of her hair, and strode off with a satisfied swagger. He would report her return to the gentlemen.

Toy could only wait, dangling helpless and exposed. The thought of what she must look like, hung and spread, as passive as a delectable and expensive ham, ready to be devoured by some rich man, made her pussy wetter still. She had yelped with pain under Joe's cruel hands, but it was a pain she loved. She was intoxicated.

It was almost dark. The rich scent of the roses wafted over from the garden. They were in full bloom still, and the perfume was so wild and sweet that Toy wriggled and moaned, wanting to be quite part of the darkened beauty that surrounded her.

Footsteps rang out on the cobbles of the courtyard. Men's voices, low but laughing. She shivered in acute anticipation. She knew what they were coming to see.

An oil lamp was raised above her, throwing the shadow of a thick arm on the rough wall behind her. She could not see the men but could sense their presence; three or four of them, gathered together looking at her pink, displayed meat.

Something smooth and cold against her fat clitoris. She moans, and they can see the trickle of her fuck juices issuing from the hot, dark cunt hole. With the tempered glass instrument they prod her clit this way and that, inspecting the fine scar line, grunting approval. A rubber gloved finger reaches inside her and searches the width and depth of her cunt, as dispassionate as a medical examination. Then the whole handful of fingers presses into her, bruising her already tender flesh, but again, there is no desire in the act, the fingers are simply reaching to survey her cervix. She is nothing but a product, receiving its final inspection. The fingers switch to her asshole. Just two of them now, forced up inside her and probing her flesh, assessing. But whore that she is, she cannot help but moan in pleasure as she is examined. Her clit is throbbing with desire. The men are talking, but always to each other, never to her. She recognises Sir Jonathan's voice. He is saying something about her first test drive being the prerogative of her new owner. The others are chuckling.

The fingers are withdrawn, the soiled gloves thrown down upon the straw. The men all move to her head end. Joe holds the lamp close by her face so that she squints and screws her eyes tight shut. Again the latex-clad fingers come probing her, this time opening her mouth, rolling back her lips to inspect her teeth and gums. Again the dry grunts of approval. Then a bunch of fingers press towards the back of her throat. She feels it tighten, but manages not to gag. Now they press deeper and she must swallow as though it were cock. Someone laughs softly. She is deep-throating a man's fingers.

Satisfied, the hand pulls away. Now they turn their

attention to her swollen breasts, saving them for last as one might save the strawberry from the top of the cream cake. The fingers prod and tug her nipples. A voice remarks how well the tissue has healed. The sound is muffled because they are crowded round by her head, someone's trousers are pressing up against her face, she can feel his flaccid cock through the material. Her cheeks burn with shame.

Satisfied that the nipple surgery is fine work they inspect her breasts. Ribald comments about how she'd be a good milker, as they pat her breasts back and forth to see the weight of them move. They are laughing at her, they think enormous udders like these are ridiculous, but she's to be sold to a man who enjoys owning plentiful breast tissue to torment. She hears a remark about, 'bristling with pegs,' and the others laugh in a way that makes her shiver. Someone comments that the implants can stand just as rough treatment as natural tissue, and without further warning he grabs a handful of each tit and squeezes as hard as he can. The whore yelps in startled pain. The cock against her face finally grows hard. Casual hands find her pussy is wetter still, but they have other pleasures in mind tonight. She's thoroughly broken in, ready to be sold as soon as her welts have healed. They are all trainers, and like any trainer love the challenge of a wild mare. This one has been so utterly enslaved she holds little appeal for them.

The fingers that have been probing her cunt are wiped clean on her arching belly. She feels a sudden panic when she realises they are going, leaving her dangling and open to the night. She wants to ask them to stay, but she knows her place.

Their footsteps clatter back across the cobbles, the voices die away and she's left alone, hanging like an unworn dress in somebody's wardrobe. The night is long and it's impossible to sleep suspended and spread as she is, but she realises she must have dozed off nevertheless when she wakes in the grey light of dawn to the rough pounding of a cock in her vagina. She cannot see who is using her, and he is efficient and single-minded, humping hard until he shoots his load deep into her belly, then leaving her without a word.

Later Joe arrives and stables her properly. For the next two weeks she remains tethered in the stables apart from brief exercise sessions round the yard. She is fed, watered, hosed and otherwise ignored. Nobody beats her, nobody fucks her. She has been sold, sight unseen, to a man on the other side of the planet. Now the merchandise awaits collection.

Several thousand miles away, in the necessary comfort of his air conditioned office, Prince Rajik settles back comfortably in his leather upholstered chair. Idly he rubs his cock. He has enjoyed watching the portfolio of video clips, enjoyed seeing a virgin degraded by her own rampant sexuality and deservedly reduced to a sex toy. He is extremely rich and wants to be the first to own one of the new, modified sluts. He weighs the sleek, elegant remote control in his hands. It could be designed to operate an extremely expensive television or video. But no, this device controls an altogether more amusing toy. He smiles to himself. His plane leaves for Heathrow tomorrow morning.

Chapter 20

Toy woke around dawn. The chill breeze that pushed through the open window carried a rich smell of decay: roses spoilt by rain, fly agaric growing on the sodden ground. Autumn was close now. She shivered, and snuggled deeper under the horseblanket that Joe had thrown over her after her evening grooming.

She heard his steady footfalls across the yard: he was early. That meant something was going to happen. Although when 'something happened' at the Manor it inevitably meant pain and suffering for Toy: tit torture, meek acceptance of penetration by strangers and beatings that left their mark for weeks; still, she felt a surge of excitement. It'd been dull of late, and she was burning with frustration, not having had an orgasm for a fortnight. In desperation she had tried to pleasure herself, squatting astride her feeding trough so that she could rub her clit against its hard rim, but Joe had caught her in the act. She had expected to be fucked and beaten as punishment, but even that release had been denied her. He had simply fitted her with a sort of metal chastity belt that cupped her clit like a cold, hollow, hand, so that when she pressed her mons against the trough after he had gone it was only the thick outer labia that felt the pressure. Her clit was isolated and unreachable.

Joe unchained her, and removed the chastity belt. He led her out to the yard, and she stood still, trembling with cold as he hosed her down. The icy water blasted everywhere: he washed out her mouth and ears, shot the freezing spray over her heavy udders so that the nipples jutted out like fat pencil stubs, then made her stand with legs spread so he could force the hose first into her vagina, then her asshole. He took particular care with her anus, making her take the long, slick nozzle to its fullest extent, repeating the process again and again to ensure a good eight inches of her rectum was clean and ready for use.

215

By now her teeth were chattering and she was shaking. He sprayed the hose again over her whole body, standing back and directing the jet with full force onto her tits so that they jiggled amusingly as they were buffeted by the water. Then he led her back to the stable, and rubbed her dry with a rough towel so her skin glowed pink.

He gestured that she should bend over the whipping stool that had stood unused this past fortnight. But once she was in place, he did not strap her. He merely parted her labia, and gave her perineum a thorough inspection, pulling back the hood of her clit so she gasped, rotating the ring that penetrated, and thus labelled as owned, her most intimate flesh. She was slippery with desire now, and arched her back, hoping his fingers would glide into her cunt and reward her with a frigging. But when he'd finished he pulled her upright, and out of the door, and hosed her pussy and cunt back to cleanliness. She almost cried in disappointment.

Back inside he reached in the bag he'd brought with him, and pulled out something of black and shiny fabric, that snaked over his hands almost as though alive. Seating himself on a straw bale he sat her on his lap and began to pull the garment onto her little body.

It was a catsuit, of thin rubber that was very fine and silky. It was all in one piece, and as he gradually worked it over her legs and body and arms she discovered that it was to encase her from head to toe, but with the familiar cutaways to expose her sexual parts. At the top of the thigh there were cutaways to mimic the effect of stockings, leaving a four inch strip of pale flesh, with just a strap reaching from the bodice to the stocking top. Her genitals were completely bare, as were her buttocks and her udders, for again there were holes, small and thus uncomfortably tight when he tugged her tits through them. It felt as though two cruel hands were squeezing her breasts by their stems. The effect was most pleasing to the viewer however, and Joe rubbed his cock, regretting for a moment that this whore's cunt was now outside his jurisdiction.

Folds of rubber hung at her neck, and as Toy wondered what they were for, Joe pulled the fabric through her metal collar then up, over her face, pulling the mask totally tight with straps that cut across the back of her head and were hidden by layers of hair. She panicked and tried to pull away, but of course he was far too strong for her. The smooth rubber mask covered her eyes. But it did have a mouth hole, so as to facilitate male access of that orifice, and nasal holes so that the slut could still breathe whilst her mouth was in use.

Finally, Joe eased her small feet into ludicrously tall stiletto shoes. With five inch heels they were very precarious, and Toy found she could only take tiny, mincing steps, somewhat reminiscent of a hobbled animal.

He strapped her arms behind her in the accustomed fashion, tighter than ever so that her breasts jutted forward, offered and available.

She stood there: blind, hobbled, painfully strapped, swaying slightly on her heels and trying not to fall. There was no movement from Joe, or none that she could hear; the rubber mask covered her ears, deadening sound.

After what seemed an age, during which time Joe had used her displayed but unknowing body as porn, resting back comfortably and pulling on his engorged cock before shooting his load onto the straw, she felt a tugging at her collar, then at her nose, nipples and clit. Now there were chains, one to each of the four rings that went through her flesh, another to the collar that was so immovably welded round her soft neck.

He took a moment to brush out her long, silky tresses that hung like a pretty mane right down to her buttocks, then led her slowly across the courtyard. Toy minced her way over the uneven cobbles, all her efforts concentrated on not stumbling. At last they reached the doorway, and he led her inside, onto the smooth stone tiles of the manor kitchens. Her heels clicked repeatedly as she took small, irregular steps in her solitary darkness.

She followed him to the back stairway, up two floors and along a corridor, silent now on thick carpets. She had never been this way before, she did not know what rooms lay around her. She felt a slight draught as a door was opened in front of her. Joe tugged sharply at her chains, the rings pulled against her pierced flesh and she whimpered a little. Blindly she followed him into the room.

As soon as she was inside, someone shut the door. It fell to with an echoing bang that made her jump.

The room was warm. She sensed that there were people around her, that they were looking at her. But no one touched her, and she just stood there, swaying in her hobbled dark and trying not to fall.

Prince Rajik watches the whore. She is trembling slightly, he notices with satisfaction. She is dressed exactly as he specified, and his cock hardens as he lets his eyes trail slowly over her displayed body. She looks, and indeed is, an exquisite animal, groomed for pleasure. But no... ...the way she is covered apart from her three sex-holes, the way she is blinded by the mask, and unable to move freely in her bonds and on her silly shoes... ...she is less than animal, she is mere object. A sex object. A toy, to be played with. And here in his hand, smooth and sleek and apparently innocent, lies the control for the toy.

He smiles, and speaking softly, issues his commands to his translator. A word to the whore-handler and the toy's arms are released from behind her back. He sees her relief from the tension and his smile deepens at how very short-lived that relief is, as now her arms are raised high above her head, and hooked to the chain that dangles there. The breasts really are magnificent, and so very English. He will enjoy splattering his Moorish spunk all over the face of this lovely English rose. He knows she is very beautiful, even though her face is hidden. He has watched it on his computer screen, and more, watched it in his private cinema. Seen the lovely face crumple with tears as she is beaten, seen the doe-eyes open wide with shock when she's had to take man meat up her anus. But for now, he wants to see her just as a body, and for the whore to see him not at all.

Idly he toys with the remote control. Everyone is awaiting his pleasure. He knows the function of each button perfectly, having had the instrument for several weeks now. Without warning he presses the punishment button, having already set the rating at high. The whore screams in shock, literally. Implanted in her clitoris and nipples are tiny electrodes. The shock they deliver is miniscule, so much so that anyone enjoying her at the moment of electrification will experience only the slightest tingling sensation, but embedded as they are in her most sensitive tissue the pain is evidently more than satisfactory. He flicks an impatient finger at Joe, barks a command. He wants her gagged. A fat dildo gag is stuffed into the mouth, strapped tight round her head. Another barked command, he wants to see her cunt. The handlers thick fingers spread the soft nether-lips and the wet pussy glistens its betrayal. Just as he had expected. This female was made for cruel treatment.

He blasts her again with the punishment button. Only a muffled mew escapes the gag. Far more satisfactory. Another blast. The unfortunate girl is trembling from head to foot, and sweat is glistening on those huge breasts. She is slumping, her weight now partially taken by the chain that holds her in place. He presses again, but not the punishment button this time, the orgasm button. This device gives him utter, complete control and it is gratifying to see her body jerk in helpless climax. Another mew escapes the gag.

He plays with the device, modifying the intensity of the shocks, prolonging the orgasms, randomly awarding her pain or pleasure according to his whim of the moment. He notices that there is only the slightest of differences between the way her body bucks then slumps when he gives her pain, and the way it responds to pleasure. This prompts an amusing game, which soon has the whole audience of businessmen laughing uproariously, as he invites them to guess whether she is in orgasm or agony. They find it quite impossible, excepting only Sir Jonathan, certainly a wise slave dealer, who is alive to the subtleties in the toy's piteous moaning.

By now the whore is hanging exhausted, barely conscious, her full weight on the rope. He orders her taken away and rested whilst the gentlemen eat and finalise the purchase details. He has far more in store for his new property, but he is hungry.

Toy comes round as she is blasted with icy water from the hose. Her clit and nipples are still throbbing painfully. Again Joe hoses her, inside and out. She is lying naked on the cobbles, too weak to move. But move she must; already he is tugging at the chains that lead to her piercings, so wobbling and yelping she clambers to her feet. The expression on Joe's face is crueller than she has ever seen it. Perhaps seeing her body but being unable to use it is making him spiteful, at any rate he has thoroughly enjoyed seeing her so badly treated, he's looking forward to the resumption of the entertainment, his cock throbbing with need.

He dries her, brushes out her beautiful hair and calls in another slut to make up her face. Only a little adornment here and there. The fat Arab wants to see England's purest virgin beaten into whoredom, not some street-corner slut.

This time Toy is to be naked. The prospective owner wants a proper look at his purchase, every last little bit of her. Joe rubs rose oil over her slender limbs, then decorates her with some gold jewellery: a gold circlet that hangs below her slave collar, prettily trailing fine trickles of gold over her neck and breasts, a golden girdle that hangs low over her belly. Suddenly she looks very much like a harem slave, very beautiful and very meek.

Barefoot now, she follows Joe back into the old house. Back up the stairs, back along the corridor. He opens the door, and leads her through. And again it slams shut.

To one side sits Sir Jonathan, with Marcus and some other men, some of whom seem vaguely familiar. She can't remember when she's seen them before, but that's because a whore seldom pays much attention to a Master's face when she is trying not to gag from the depth of the deep-throating that she is performing. To the other side are Charles and the younger Jonathan Sinclair, and a few more businessmen. All eyes are on her, unashamedly enjoying the sight of her body. Some of the men have already got their cocks out and are stroking them. All of the faces look very intent, and none of them show any sign of friendliness.

In the centre, seated comfortably on a chair that is almost more a throne than a chair, is a fat, balding man of middle-eastern appearance. He is holding something in his hands; it looks like a remote control for a television. He is smiling at her, his mouth twisted up at one side, an eyebrow a little raised. Slowly, deliberately, he points the remote control at her, and presses a button.

Toy falls to her knees as the pain hits her once more. On all fours, through eyes blurry with tears she looks up at the smiling man and understands at last. This is her owner. All the events of the past months, the operations, the inspections... ...all fall into place, suddenly intelligible. She is no longer a free woman, she is no longer a woman voluntarily submitting to a life of servitude in praise of the greater sex, she is now only what her name says, a toy, that can be operated in the same manner as any other toy of sophistication by a simple, hand-held device.

Her eyes meet those of the man who controls her and she screams, in pleasure this time, as the orgasm buffets her.

Her Master is speaking again, but the words are in a

language that she cannot understand. Joe tugs at her chains, and she crawls towards him like a bitch, then watches as a large, high table is set in front of her Master. She is pulled back towards it, and obediently she climbs on top. There are straps set deep in the wood. Joe fastens her in place, again on all-fours, pulling each strap tight, then a little tighter still so that it is uncomfortable and very secure, then a little tighter again so that each biting strap around wrist and ankle reminds her of her servitude. He pushes her shoulders down so that her forearms rest against the wood. Her wrists are so widely spread that her breasts are now pressed hard against the table. And now there are more straps, just below the elbows, and again he fastens them so tightly that tears well up in her eyes. Her Master is seated so close that he only has to reach out a hand to lift her chin; he is gazing directly and deeply into her eyes. She feels now as though her very soul is owned by this man.

The position in which she is immobilised is ideal for mounting: her upper torso low, her face almost resting on the wood, her arse raised and offered to any man behind her.

The Arab speaks again and gestures. A man who has been standing behind the others steps forward from the shadows. He is tall and muscular, a black man, with gleaming ebony skin. He is wearing only a robe, and now he comes to stand next to his employer. His eyes are fixed on the face of the immobilised slut as he slips off the robe.

Under it he is entirely naked. His cock is hard, and it is huge. Toy gapes at it in desire and horror, and as she does so she feels a delicious sensation in her pussy and nipples as though a man's tongue were flicking her clit, skilled fingers brushing her nubs. Involuntarily arching and moaning she suddenly realises that there is no man behind her, playing with her. Instead she is being controlled again by the slim instrument in her Master's hands. She cannot fight against it, she is being operated as effectively as any new toy. She arches and moans and offers her taut rear to be fucked.

The black man goes round behind her, steps up to the table, and begins to press the head of his giant penis against her tight-closed anus. She gasps; this cock is a huge one to take into her pussy, she cannot believe they expect her to take such an organ anally. But as the great head presses against her muscles the wonderful sensations from the remote control ripple through and through and through her whole cunt and breasts and genital area, so that she softens and relaxes and slowly and steadily the man is able to enter her without resistance.

It takes him quite some time to be fully inside; after all, the last thing he intends is to cause damage to this valuable piece of merchandise. But eventually Toy sighs in satisfaction and amazement as she feels his pubes scratching up against her hole. He pauses for a moment, savouring the way her little body grips him so tight. Then he begins to fuck her, steadily increasing in speed as he quickly nears climax. The Arab watches intently. When he sees that his servant is close to orgasm he presses down sharply on one of the buttons. The toy yelps in anguish as the shock ripples through her sensitive engorged clit. All her pussy muscles contract in sudden spasm, her anus suddenly squeezing the invading cock so hard that it brings him off, and another load of spunk is shot deep inside her small body. Now he feels far too big for her, and she cries as he slowly slips out of her burning hole.

She looks up at her Master, humiliated and defeated by what feels like a betrayal, and finds he is laughing at her.

"What are you?" he says quietly to her, in heavily accented English.

"Your slave, Master," she answers at once.

Another bolt of pain. She is trembling all over, shaking like a leaf caught in a current of turbulent water, but she knows her pussy is wet as much from the suffering as from the pleasure.

"No, no, no, no, no. You are less than that, are you not?" His voice is quite soft, yet somehow chilling.

"Your toy, Master?"

"Good!"

The delicious sensation begins again in her pussy, waves of warm pleasure rushing through her clit. She looks up at him, gratefully.

He laughs, and this time it is with genuine amusement. How easy she is to command! The result of her many months of training, of course.

He undoes his flies, and pulls out his ample organ, darkly swollen.

"You may suck."

Toy bends her head and works on the cock with just her mouth, her arms still immobilised, her arse still raised and ready for the next fucking. As she sucks and licks at him he idly plays with the controls, so that the waves of pleasure that have been growing in her puss beat ever higher. It is easy to keep her on the brink of orgasm as she sucks at his fat penis. At the moment of his climax he pulls away, shooting most of his load into her mouth but splattering the rest over her face. As he does so he presses the button to reward her with an orgasm. She moans in delight, then slumps forward, grateful for his kindness.

"From now on, I think you will only come when my spunk is on your face. Do you understand?"

She doesn't really, but as she feels a man penetrate her cunt and begin to thrust hard into her it becomes clear. Although she is aroused, there is no feeling of the arousal building to orgasm. Instead her clit begins to throb unpleasantly. It is not exactly painful but all the same, she wishes it would stop.

"I am controlling the sensation. It does not please me that you should experience pleasure at this moment, so you do not. Now however," he wipes his cock over her face, her eyelids, her lips, "you will enjoy this." And so she does, for he has adjusted the controls so that the warm, delicious waves are once more wafting over and through her. Eagerly she opens her mouth to suck, and dedicates all her efforts to pleasing this most powerful of men. It takes her quite a while to give him an orgasm, it is not long since the last, and he is not a young man. But eventually she succeeds, and as her mouth and face receive the come she is granted another lovely climax of her own.

He chuckles again, as she slumps once more, panting with exhaustion.

"And now I will enjoy seeing you suffer again." He gestures to Joe and to the whore's arse.

"Enjoy her. Take her in whichever hole you wish. Be my guest."

Joe has been watching the girl he has had so often as her mouth and anus have been used. His cock is rock-hard, and he stands behind her and plunges it into her fiercely. The girl under him moans, her cunt tightens deliciously but not from the pleasure of the fucking, rather from the steady pain that her Master is directing through her clitoris. Again he watches the man using her intently, and again precipitates his orgasm with a bolt of pain to the Toy. She yelps and her pussy muscles grip harder than Joe would have thought possible, giving him a huge orgasm as he fills her with his spunk.

As Joe dismounts from the pleasure ride, the Arab gestures to the other men in the room.

"All, please. She will suffer to be had by you all." And so it is. Each man in turn has her, and she gets no pleasure from their thrusting, and each man, whether using her cunt or her anus is brought to orgasm by her muscles spasming in shock as the tiny, but oh so effective, dose of electricity bursts through her.

By the time they have all had her she is as limp as a rag, slumping helpless and unable to move. Her Master has a throbbing cock once more…… he really enjoys seeing girls suffer…… and again he permits her to suck him to orgasm, and again as he climaxes he gives her his blessing by orgasm.

Then she lies quivering and spent, almost unconscious once more.

Prince Rajik turns to Sir Jonathan.

"Yes. She is most satisfactory. I will take her. Kindly have her packaged for the flight. Many thanks for your hospitality, I hope some day you will partake of my hospitality in return. We have many young girls who would pleasure you well."

Joe carries Toy away, hoses her down for a final time, then hogties her so that she makes a small, neat package. The crate is waiting, and he fits her inside it, suspended from the corners by elastic webbing so that whichever way it is turned she doesn't graze herself against the wooden sides.

The crateful of merchandise is loaded into the delivery van, which departs to the little airport where Prince Rajik's plane is waiting. Toy's new life is about to begin.

THE SLAVE PATH

FRANCINE WHITTAKER

The Slave Path is the hard and tortuous route to self-knowledge which both the feisty Jo and the beautiful Kelly are about to set out along.

At its start is the treacherous Lovell Bains who is stealing from his employers. Kelly is onto him but is foolishly 'playing' at being his slave, unaware that events are about to take a sinister turn for the worse – both for her and Jo.

Hawks the slave trader is about to enter their lives and take them along the path that leads from suburban England to darkest Africa and finally to the plantation owned by Solomon Mwangi.

Along the way both girls must come to accept harsh discipline and obedience as part of everyday life for those who are on the Slave Path.

Francine Whittaker is one of Silver Moon's most popular authors and once again she gives her readers her uniquely feminine slant on erotic domination and submission.

SLAVE PATH II

(THE JOURNEY CONTINUES)

FRANCINE WHITTAKER

Jo and Kelly have now been enslaved on Solomon Mwangi's estate in Africa for several months. While Jo frets for the man she really wants to serve, Kelly is happily reconciled to serving the ferociously cruel Solomon. However, fate has far from finished with them and while Jo hatches plans for escape, Kelly is kidnapped.

The Slave Path still holds many twists, turns and cruelties for both girls…………

Amber in Chains

Francine Whittaker

Amber is a rich young woman who lives a double life. She believes she is in full control of it and uses it to indulge her passion for sex with a liberal helping of SM.

But then; as part of a shady deal, she is set up by her employer and finds herself in the hands of Josh Cordell. Suddenly Amber is no longer in control. Josh is experienced and dominant; and he has very special plans for her…

Dark Surrender

Kim Knight

Leigh Goldman, a young psychotherapist is disturbed and strangely fascinated by Mel; a beautiful girl who calmly relates to her, her experiences of harsh sexual dominance at the hands of her master. Leigh has never come across the world of SM and is soon out of her depth as she desperately tries to help Mel escape from her slavery.

First she must find out who the strange and sinister master is, then she must convince him that she is a dominant too. But most importantly she has to explore her won sexuality to the very limits and that leads her into darker and stranger places than she could ever have imagined.

A Slave's Desire

(An Unchained novel)

Kim Knight

Mel, recently freed from slavery, is determined to win her lover's freedom. But Natalie is still a slave and has been sold into slavery in Russia. Helped by the mysterious Claudia, Mel tracks her but is foiled at the last minute.

The vicious mistress called 'Faith' has had the beautiful Natalie taken to a training camp in Algeria. Here her torment seems never-ending and she sinks into complete submission.

Inventive, cruel and clever; Kim Knight's second volume in the 'Unchained' series is as absorbing as it is highly erotic.

BOUGHT AND SOLD

TESSA VALMUR

As soon as Zoe Farquerson steps off the plane in the tiny kingdom of Al-Saram, she walks straight into trouble with the secret police. But she is not the innocent tourist she claims to be, she is a field agent for British Intelligence; and she has been betrayed.

Soon she is a helpless pawn in an international intrigue, caught between ruthless and dominant players in a game where allegiances shift as fast as the desert sands. But as a beautiful European girl, she is highly prized and there are plenty of people willing to pay any price to get her in their power.

DARKER DREAMS

TESSA VALMUR

Lara Lustral is beautiful, wealthy and bored. The only place where she can find the action she craves is the Dreamscape Institute. The year is 2027 and at the institute you can actually live out your most secret fantasies.

But when your secret fantasies are as erotic as Lara's are and the enigmatic Dr Mackennan is watching everything......the Institute is not a safe place to be! Lara finds out that the reality of submission is a lot harder than she had ever dreamed.

Darkest Dreams

Tessa Valmur

Having lost her friend Lara, Serena decides that the sinister Dreamscape Institute is somehow involved in her disappearance. She meets Dr Mackennan who persuades her that she must first explore her own dreams before she can enter her friend's to see where they may have led her.

In 'Darker Dreams' Lara Lustral discovered her real sexual nature but so did the Doctor and he was ready to make full use of it. No0w he has the bonus of discovering that the beautiful Serena is intent on finding her friend. How long can it be before he makes quite sure that she finds out far more than she really wanted to know!

Controlling Catherine

Elana Gregory

A minor burglary leads Catherine into a meeting with a very dominant policeman and before she knows what's happening, she finds herself falling under his spell. But she doesn't slip easily into the role of submissive and some strange adventures lie in store for her before she finally comes to terms with being controlled.

Elena Gregory gives her readers a fascinating glimpse into the secret world of the submissive woman in this, her second Silver Moon novel.

Silver Moon have over a hundred titles of erotic domination in their catalogue. You can join the readers' club entirely free of charge and receive regular magazines with features, interviews and readers' letters plus a full list of available titles – many of which are only available by mail order.